Dark of the
Center Line

Dark of the Center Line

Schuy R. Weishaar

Winchester, UK
Washington, USA

First published by Roundfire Books, 2016
Roundfire Books is an imprint of John Hunt Publishing Ltd., Laurel House, Station Approach,
Alresford, Hants, SO24 9JH, UK
office1@jhpbooks.net
www.johnhuntpublishing.com
www.roundfire-books.com

For distributor details and how to order please visit the 'Ordering' section on our website.

Text copyright: Schuy R. Weishaar 2015

ISBN: 978 1 78535 269 0
Library of Congress Control Number: 2015949727

This is a work of fiction. Names, characters, businesses, places, events and incidents are either
the products of the author's imagination or used in a fictitious manner. Any resemblance to
actual persons, living or dead, or actual events is purely coincidental.

A CIP catalogue record for this book is available from the British Library.

Design: Stuart Davies

Printed in the USA by Edwards Brothers Malloy

We operate a distinctive and ethical publishing philosophy in all
areas of our business, from our global network of authors to
production and worldwide distribution.

For Kyle

What was scattered gathers.
What was gathered blows apart.

Acknowledgements

An early draft of a portion of the second chapter appeared as "The Dyslexic Jew" in *The Other Journal: An Intersection of Theology and Culture*, No. 18, in 2011.

The meditation of yesterday has filled my mind with so many doubts, that it is no longer in my power to forget them. Nor do I see, meanwhile, any principle on which they can be resolved; and, just as if I had fallen all of a sudden into very deep water, I am so greatly disconcerted as to be unable either to plant my feet firmly on the bottom or sustain myself by swimming on the surface. I will, nevertheless, make an effort, and try anew the same path on which I had entered yesterday, that is, proceed by casting aside all that admits of the slightest doubt, not less than if I had discovered it to be absolutely false; and I will continue always in this track until I shall know with certainty that there is nothing certain.

Rene Descartes, *Meditations on First Philosophy*

I went on my way, that way of which I knew nothing, qua way, which was nothing more than a surface, bright or dark, smooth or rough, and always dear to me, in spite of all, and the dear sound of that which goes and is gone, with a brief dust, when the weather is dry.

Samuel Beckett, *Molloy*

Blessed are the poor in spirit: for theirs is the kingdom of heaven. Blessed are they that mourn: for they shall be comforted. Blessed are the meek: for they shall inherit the earth.

The Gospel According to St. Matthew, 5:3-5

A Song

I headed west to see the mountains,
To feel the desert, baking dry,
All the way to the Pacific coast
To see the sun set on the other side.

When I was staring into a canyon,
The desert sands, or out to sea,
All I could see was something wasn't there,
Like something missing inside of me.

Can you tell me, even tell a lie?
It ain't written in no book that I can find.
Can you tell me, can you tell me true?
Does the dark of the center line lead somewhere too?

I was driving through Kentucky
On that old, familiar line
That marries Tennessee to Illinois
Like they were ribs on a concrete spine.

I was mirrored in the windows,
So I was smeared on every tree.
And across the sky and every billboard sign
There was a faint, blurry picture of me.

Can you tell me, even tell a lie?
It ain't written in no book that I can find.
Can you tell me, can you tell me true?
Does the dark of the center line lead somewhere too?

(Repeat refrain)

Chapter 1

"It's all darkness," Jacob said. He swept his upturned palm in a half-circle, his arm outstretched, as though he were gesturing at something obvious, the way the maestro draws applause for the orchestra he's just conducted, the orchestra which, more likely than not, would not have missed a note if the man had dropped dead after the first movement. Such a gesture is always an admission. Its meaning always the same: *Can't you see? For all my pains at controlling this, it is beyond me. It is out of my hands. It belongs to you, to them, to the world. It is the world.* It's the gesture of a fallen god.

The boy had asked him a childish question. "Why do the shadows get long when it's almost night?"

"Look around," Jacob said. "You're right, the shadows are getting longer, but, look at the light too. Look at what's happening to the light. Shadows are dark, always dark, even when they leak out across the grass into the street. But what's happened to the light?"

The boy paused and peered into the distance. He squinted his eyes. Such conversation had become commonplace between father and son, and the boy had learned when to feign reflection. Finally he answered, "At lunchtime the light is brighter. The light gets dirtier closer to night."

Jacob seemed pleased with this. "Yes, yes, the darkness slowly joins itself to the light, so slowly, so calmly, patiently. It winds itself around the center of light, sullies it, soaks it, until it's permeated the light completely. Until the light is gone. Until the light has become darkness." Jacob stood without moving or talking for a long time, gazing into the changing sky. The boy watched, too, as night overcame day, just as his father had said. As he looked up at the man, he saw the sunlight die in the distance on the tree-line behind him. Darkness washed over

Jacob's crumpled pork pie hat, his hairy face, his worn, denim work shirt, his wrinkled black trousers. He had become a silhouetted scarecrow or circus clown, a rigid strong-man, or a prophet. Darkness seemed to have overtaken his father, along with the rest of it, almost. There was a brightness in the eyes that was not extinguished with the sun, a brightness that was, for the moment, lost somewhere in the sky in some star-lit reverie. Jacob's eyes seemed to blink with the same faint sparkle of those stars. It occurred to the boy that he couldn't quite decide whether his father had merely been describing the dreary play of darkness and light or if he had cast the darkness into the sky with his words. Then the man's eyes shot down, and their light was trained on the boy.

Jacob spoke, his tongue a darting flame, almost unable to keep up with the rambling words he spit into the air. His wide eyes never left the boy's. "There was a time when everything was dark," he said. "No sun. No stars, nothing. Just dark. Light has always been the exception, a luxury, a fake. Light and heat are accidents. People talk about balance and harmony—of darkness and light—as if they were equivalent, as if they weren't out to devour one another. But darkness has its own harmony with cold, with stillness, with peace. Light is a mistake. Its very presence corrupts the dark and cold of space itself. Look up there. It's darkness that overcomes all. There's no balance. Our day is a delusion, a lie we tell ourselves, tell each other, because we fail to face the facts: that we are pathetic accidents of the light, that stupid life is part of what's wrong with the universe. And worse than that—"

Then he seemed to remember himself and broke his gaze from the boy's, shaking himself as one shakes off the cold. "Never mind," he said blankly. "Let's head home." Jacob took a few steps. The boy didn't follow. When he noticed what looked like a tear shimmer down the boy's nose, Jacob softened a little and gestured somewhat obscurely toward him, as if to say, *Come along* or *I don't know* or even *I'm sorry*. But, whatever it was intended to convey, it was also the maestro's gesture. The sun had gone down now. It was night.

* * *

It was hot as hell; so hot that by midmorning people had begun to do ridiculous things. The newscasters and weather people had warned of what they called a "heat wave" and tried to explain its origin and the threat it presented in terms that anyone and everyone could understand, but no one listened or cared. This was Central Illinois, and it was summer. Of course it would get hot, they reasoned, but what's the real danger of a few more degrees of red in the thermometer. It wasn't snow. It wasn't ice. It wasn't a tornado. It wouldn't prevent them from getting to work or wherever it was they wanted to go, and a heat wave didn't bring down power lines and tree limbs, nor would it demolish mobile homes or hurl livestock into people's living rooms. It didn't crash cars or freeze confused elderly or children. People here didn't really register a "heat wave." They carried on with their lives. Unconsciously, though, the heat worked its way into their heads quietly, through their bodies, as through a forgotten side entrance or a cracked window. There was no official drama yet to the heat wave. Nothing had gone wrong that had caught the attention of the news people in Champaign or Decatur, so there was no caution, no speculation, no worry. There was just stupid action.

Mrs. Segal had shed her clothing relatively early that morning, when the temperature started climbing, all the way down to her underpants, mostly just to prevent having to adjust the air conditioning. She was on what she referred to as "a fixed income" (a phrase she had borrowed from a story she'd heard on the TV), now since Carl had died two and a half years ago, and she felt the extra expenditure just for the sake of her own comfort amounted to vanity. She thought that since her widow's routine rarely took her from the house anyway, there was no shame in the exposure. By four o'clock in the afternoon, when the pastor came by to check in on her, she had become accustomed to her prelapsarian state. She answered the door when the bell rang as she would any other day, and then everything seemed to unravel.

She only remembered her nakedness after she had knelt to roll the prostrate man on her porch, as she sat on his thighs, straddling his slender hips between her knees, and removed his priestly collar in order to check his airway, and heard one of the neighbors gasp, while another said "What in the hell?" with both awe and confusion. Mrs. Segal looked around, like a confused parakeet, just in time to see the paper boy crash his bicycle into a parked pick-up truck with the words "Raw Power" painted across the tailgate.

Don Hadfield, apparently impelled by the uptick in temperature, set himself to transplanting a whole bed of "shade" flowers from their peaceful spot by the driveway to a specially cordoned-off bed behind the fence. He had finally sold the Chevelle to some moron out-of-towner who didn't know any better, which meant that the spot beside the driveway was now exclusively for "sun" plants. So things had become confused. His "shade" plants were in the new "sun" section, and the sun itself had gone batshit crazy. He thought he had better get them moved before their wilted brown petals and lazing stems blackened completely. Ever a man of thorough gardening practices, he had started early by tilling the bed behind the fence, the new "shade" bed, and then proceeded to relocate the "shade" plants one by one to their new home in the shadow of the fence. By just after lunchtime, Mr. Hadfield's blue, ribbed tank-top was soaked with sweat, as were his khaki cut-offs and his knee-high white sport socks, all the way up to their multi-color horizontal stripes around the calves. The fat old man finally slumped himself down on an overturned clay flowerpot like a circus elephant, leaned against the siding on the garage, and shook his great jowls with exhaustion. His face burned, and he heard a faint but clear and constant tone that sounded like someone was holding down the number seven on a push-button telephone dial-pad.

He thought he had the strength yet to clean up the tiller before he quit for the day. Heat wave or not, you don't leave a job half-done. He poured some diesel fuel into the little tumbler he had been sipping lemonade from earlier and started in scouring the caked dirt from the blades of the tiller with his gas-wet rag. The heat and fumes hit Mr. Hadfield wrong somehow, and he drifted off with his head pillowed on the fat flesh of his arm, which was propped on the engine casing. He awoke in a panic seconds later, spewed vomit all over the half-clean tiller blades, all at about the same time the clay pot he was sitting on gave up and crumbled. He ached all over, and he was thirsty as hell and delirious. He propped himself up and downed the diesel in a gulp before remembering that it was not, in fact, the lemonade he had finished hours before.

And not far from the Hadfields' on Main, just outside the limits of the same little township of Cisco, a swollen teenage girl had just collapsed into the bubbling tar of a country road, after finally making good on an overdue new year's resolution.

In Weldon, a young mother had baked her baby boy in a minivan, after returning home from dropping the other three monsters at a friend's and drifting off in an easy chair in the house, not ten feet from where the forgotten infant lay strapped into his car seat, his blood bubbling like scalded milk.

In La Place, the mayor's wife was emptying the contents of her purse onto the hood of her next door neighbor's pickup in pursuit of her nerve pill. She raked through the mound of used tissues, melted "fun-sized" candy bars, and pharmacy bottles with the barrel-tip of the small pistol with which she had just shot down a black pug that she was pretty sure was rabid.

In Monticello, a mechanic had nearly incinerated himself and his shop after attempting to weld the half-filled gas tank on a Suburban.

In Bement, an accountant sat in the grass in a bloodstained undershirt, counting and recounting the remaining fingers on the hand he had just reached under his lawnmower in an attempt to retrieve an injured plastic Batman.

And at the beach at Clinton Lake, in DeWitt County, a throng of boys had punched and dunked one another as they had swum out to the line of buoys where they had spied an enormous lopsided black beach ball or balloon with the rather terrifying face of a grinning clown on either side, and the smallest boy had not come up yet. And it was this story that led the ten o'clock news in the all of the larger cities in the area, for its strange tangles outstripped what even the Holy Ghost Pentecostals were capable of believing.

* * *

The kid had drowned. But by the time the news was airing, the poor little bastard was less than a footnote to the story. It was the resurrection of a crucified man that captured the popular imagination. Apparently, the boys, having noticed the absence of their comrade, had returned to the beach to see if he had turned back, perhaps soured on the "fun" of suffering some good-natured abuse, one of them grabbing the clown ball as an afterthought. When they reached the shore, they realized that they had dragged the corpse of the boy back with them, though twenty or so yards behind, in the knotted tethers tied to the knobbed base of the clown ball. They reeled him in and spread him out on the sand to try to bring him back. All eyes were then aimed at the attempts of the EMTs when they arrived a short time later. Nothing. And as an orange-skinned woman in an egregiously undersized moo moo looked away through her salty tears toward the water for some relief from the scene, she spotted a black blotch floating in the otherwise sun-drenched, vacant waters of the lake. Others began to take notice when the woman gasped an "Oh my God!" as she made out a head on the figure.

Two of the EMTs were soon wading into the shallows to snatch this second body from the lake. He was dead. There was no doubt about that. It looked as though he had been in the water for some time. Green and brown strips of vegetation matted to his clothes and flesh and beard as to some abortive gothic piñata. Curiously, he wasn't bloated as you might expect; quite to the contrary, the man was emaciated and bent, kind of rigidly curled in upon himself, as a fetus is within the womb. The face had been mangled somehow or other, beaten or nibbled at by critters, or a little of both, the lips swollen and upturned on one side so that, if you looked closely within the thicketed beard around them, they seemed frozen in what looked like a smirk. The skin was a pale blue-green with purple, black, and red blossoms of recent wounds here and there. One eye was swollen shut.

They discovered the holes in his hands after several moments of beholding the face. It was the same with the feet, though here the nails remained, having been driven into the toes of the black leather boots. One foot had only been half done, however, and this seemed to have been what first caught the tether of the clown ball, in which the man's legs were mummied up to the knees. He wore an unbuttoned black shirt under the tattered black sport coat, and they all suspended a breath when the EMTs finally uncurled the body and laid him with his back to the sand, and they saw, several few inches above an ill-stitched, jagged surgical wound across the stomach and a stab in the side, these words in a slanting scrawl across the chest, with all the art of a box-cutter prison tattoo: "King of Jews." Someone in the crowd said "Jesus!" in shock, which made for an awkward couple of seconds, given the circumstances. Another voice announced that the coroner had arrived. A young boy looked on, his mouth gaping. A flock of waterfowl landed noisily in the distance, and the clown on the ball dizzily blew in and nudged the dead man's head and then rested there, one of the clown faces staring crazily into the man's vacant countenance.

At first, his resurrection came on slowly: some movements in the abdomen. And so subtle were these that they were mistaken for a shift in light as a gull flew by. But moments later someone acknowledged them. "Did you see that?" a man said, almost whispering. "In the stomach, by the scar, do ya see it, look, there it is again." The coroner had just pronounced the man, but now all eyes were drawn to the corpse's abdomen and what looked like faint spasms of the muscles there. No one spoke as they waited for the movement to return. And it did, after a minute or two, and then again. The coroner searched in vain for a pulse. The muscles shuddered again. Again. Now, the whole abdomen sucked in, then rested. There was no respiration, none of the stifling air moving in or out, only what looked like the corpse's struggle to find it. This kept on for a matter of minutes, as the coroner studiously placed his hands here and there in a pointless search for life. With each failure, he would grunt and peer into the sand. Finally he stood and crossed his arms atop his belly, resolved, it seemed, to wait it out. "I wonder," he said, "if somethin's done crawled up inside him, some critter, and now that he's out of the water—"

The corpse was creaking now. The sound rose from deep in the throat and resembled, the coroner thought, his daughter's first attempts at drawing music from her cello, a low, resonant, scratching tone, somewhere between the moan of wet brake pads and the distant howl of a hunting dog. He squatted on one knee and tilted his head over the dead, smirking mouth, screwing his eyes up in concentration. No one breathed. They all listened and heard the creak again. A small, cotton-candy cloud blew across the sky and the clown ball followed its trajectory, finally breaking its gaze from the dead man, and came to a rest a few feet from the circle of onlookers. Everything was frozen.

There seemed to be no stopping the corn when it came. The corpse vomited a thick spray of whole-kernel raw corn, some small rocks with it, straight up into the coroner's hovering face. He jerked and fell to the sand as if he'd been shot. The geyser of grain and gravel spewed from the now yawning mouth into the air and pelted the onlookers as it returned to the earth. Then it stopped. Then the body heaved out more and more, its workings on the corpse-man violent. The crooked, wounded body bent again and fell to one side. The man seemed a man again, sort of, as more and more corn found its way out of his mouth, now with deep, garbled screams and wrenching, pumping convulsions. This continued for about a quarter hour, and then the body just quaked for a time, seizing dramatically for a few seconds, until the veins seemed about to burst through the still-greenish skin, and then releasing back into the shakes. At some point, two of the women looking on had begun bawling, the tallest man there had fainted, and the boy had become giddily drunk on the spectacle.

At length, the resurrected man worked himself up to his feet and stood, contortedly, the guiding lines of his hips and shoulders slung in confliction. His limbs shook still but now with the gentle persistence of the aged. He spat to one side and looked about him. The coroner started, "Sir?" but wasn't sure how to go on, so he didn't. The resurrected man's color settled in, still hinted with ashen green. And as he called out in a gravel-strangled roar for some water and a cigarette, his wounds began to bleed. The drops fell from his holey hands and streaked the scattered grain beneath them with red. The cut in the stomach oozed, while the stab in the side spurted like a child's water gun, before slowing to a trickle, and running into the waistband of the black trousers. A goose honked from a patch of trees in the parking lot. A crying woman whimpered in the sand.

Chapter 2

Saul stood mute as the doctor mouthed words at him, but none of it meant anything more than the foggy x-ray image on the backlighted board. He'd stopped listening. He only stared into this black and white picture that hazily hinted at the contents of his insides. Sure as shit, he thought. The cancer was back. The doctor's drone followed him as he turned and walked through the double doors and back into the waiting room. Its lilt peaked at certain intervals, as the white-coated bastard tried to turn the old man's attention back to treatment plans that could be tried, even as Saul continued on through the ruined bodies lingering there for permission to die and out into the adjacent waiting area for the ER. "Though at this stage, and with your history, I have to be honest—" the man said before Saul was out on the sidewalk, in front of the emergency entrance, with his foot wedged against the door to prevent the doctor from following. The doctor continued, as though he hadn't realized he'd been trapped inside his own hospital. But through the glass, it was just a murmur. Saul lit a cigarette, half intended to piss off Doctor Death, and half because he hadn't had one since just before he'd arrived for his appointment hours ago, and it was damn well time to burn some stress.

He dragged hard and exhaled the fog out into the daylight. He watched it rise slowly, a loose cumulus, to the roof, over the ambulance drive-in, where it spilled out across the breadth of the awning, like a drink poured out upside down, before it swept out and joined the ruined world beyond the confines of his tragedy. He chuckled at his pity for himself and dragged again as he moved away from the door. The white coat on the other side of it had disappeared with its recommendations and concerns, and a gurney was coming, pushed by two EMTs with bloodied uniforms, one of them with reddened rubber gloves still on. He looked on as they rolled it by, a man strapped to it with three bands, shoulders, thighs, and ankles, moaning curses, as the EMT with the gloves held a small clump of reddened rags over an oozing wound in the man's chest. Blood dripped from the gurney and left a trail that followed them all the way inside. Things could always be worse, Saul thought, as he stared into the drops nearest him. One looked like a sunburst, one like a bird, and one like a profiled face with a long beard. And he thought of Abraham.

He'd always thought of him as the kid he'd never had, and it was true, there was a kind of kinship between them, an understanding, maybe even a friendship. But even as a kid, Abraham had seemed hollow somehow. He spoke passionlessly, always, as if whatever he was talking about didn't really matter or might not be true, as if everything he said, even about himself, was quoted from somewhere else or bore some dry irony Saul wasn't in on. His gaze always fell flat, his eyes cold and staring, like the glass ones they stick in a ventriloquist's dummy. He was a cypher, like those military codes he'd heard about, the ones that are only there, only transmitted at all, so that they could throw off enemy intelligence. Underneath there was nothing. He was a ringer, a drone, a sad mud-monster like he'd heard about as a child, a golem. He was capable of anything, but he was a depthless doll. "What's sadder than that?" Saul asked himself, not realizing he said it aloud.

An ancient man not far from him, whose trembling right hand held a cigarette to a hole in his throat, as the left fiddled with the tubes that leashed his face to an oxygen tank strapped into some kind of wheeled apparatus responded, his voice demonic, "Not much. Some guys have all the luck." The man laughed, as though not to would have been beyond his control. He laughed in trembling sputters and rattling wheezes and then just broke into coughs and gasps. Then his eyes grew serious. They were wet and rimmed in red, and dark greasy bags hung under them like wads of filthy dough.

Saul locked eyes with the man, then flicked his smoked-out butt at him. "Fuck off," he said, holding his gaze for a few seconds more before walking off.

"Some guys have all the luck," the man croaked again after Saul when he'd finally caught his breath. Saul got to his car and put his head on the steering wheel. Another ambulance pulled in noiselessly. It stopped and Saul watched as two men in uniforms unloaded a dead man. Dusk was settling in and it began to rain.

* * *

A fetid yellow ice-cream truck crunched into the gravel and idled outside the fenced microwave tower, about a mile outside of Cisco, Illinois. Aside from the few glaring grain bins in the distance, and the winking cyclopean eye of the elevator at the Co-op in town, the buzzing tower was the only vertical sign of human progress in the broad labyrinth of grains, beans, and stands of trees, black roads cutting a skewed crosshatch into the countryside.

"Babel," Abraham Jacobsen said to himself as he killed the engine and climbed down from the driver-side. From within the truck, some ranting nonsense roared out the cracked window. Abraham opened the passenger-side, rolled up the window, grabbed a small wooden guitar, and slammed the door shut. The sound persisted. "No-no!" he barked, banging his fist on the side of the vehicle. The sound quit. Abraham lit a cigarette, sat on the crooked back bumper, tinkered the guitar into tune, and looked up. A large dark bird rode the wind down from the tower, its wings pumping and stretching out as it landed by the road.

Abraham caught himself thinking for a moment how different his life would be if he could fly, stopping only to perch briefly in the high places. But if such a fiction were truth, he thought, he would almost certainly be finding himself where he was now, stuck on top of the tower instead of at its foot. He was a flightless bird. This life was his life, and even if it were different, it would still be very much the same. He strummed the open chord. "Vanity, vanity," he said. "Vain-tee, vain-tee," a voice echoed from inside the ice-cream truck. Abraham peered out into the black, beyond the fading yellow that burned from the top of the lamppost above the truck and gave in to the darkness after a hundred feet or so, just past the bobbing shadow-dance of the black bird digging into something dead in the gravel. The roar of nonsense began again. He sighed a plume of smoke and closed his eyes.

* * *

Abraham was born early, feet first, five months after his mother had discovered she was pregnant, and by that time his father was already dead and, moments later, so was the spindly, twisted sibling with whom he'd shared his mother's womb. Abraham was early for everything. Spoke sentences by the seventh month, was walking by the ninth, and just after his first birthday, he'd begun to put on little plays for his mother. He was labeled a "child prodigy" after his mother discovered him sitting in bed with his crippled great-grandfather, the ancient man's head pillowed by Abraham's legs, the infant reading to him from the book of Job in a large-print King James Bible balanced atop the broad side of the old man's head.

His mother showed him off to friends in her parish in Oxford, and before long, at the suggestion of the Father Appleby, she found young Abraham a tutor, Randolph Stevens, PhD, a fellow parishioner who had quit his university job to make his mother's last few years easier on her. When the boy was seven, the tutor gave up. "I don't know what else to do with him," Dr. Stevens had said. And then, half-jokingly, "I suggest you find him an agent."

Abraham's mind was a warehouse of diverse gifts, but the one act that stuck was as easy for Abraham to carry off as it was for him to count backwards in multiples of seven or recite pi to a hundred digits beyond the decimal or rehearse the birth and death dates of every American president. His mother encouraged him to read the Bible, and he took to the practice of reading to his mother, grandmother, or, if no one else was to be found, his decrepit great-grandfather. He soon discovered that the text itself had become a superfluous prop. This became the root of Abraham's act; the plays he had performed as an infant transformed into off-the-cuff recitations of portions of Exodus, Leviticus, Chronicles, or whatever. The act only became popular when Saul, the agent Abraham's mother had secured, failing to catch Dr. Stevens' tone, suggested a certain dramatic flair and began testing show names in each of the boy's performances. As The Young Rabbi, Abraham dressed the part and took requests or challenges for entire chapters, sometimes entire books, of holy writ. He once performed a stirringly naive rendition of the Book of Revelation under the name The Little Revelator. This sort of thing proved to be impressive in the abstract but boring in the concrete; after an hour or so, even the pious were leaving for the restroom and not coming back.

Saul finally struck gold, after numerous such attempts, with The Dyslexic Jew. This was a novelty act that played well in the Bible Belt, but one with a "human element," as Saul put it: "They'll be amazed by you, but they'll also pity you and feel better than you, all at the same time!" He was banking on the undercurrent of anti-Semitism that he felt had always been stitched into the curious attraction in the run-of-the-mill evangelical imagination to the first children of Father Abraham.

And this was Saul's armchair definition of dyslexia: whatever Abraham said or recited, he had to do it backwards. Saul had a tailor friend make a Hasidic costume, and Saul himself manufactured a number of tattered scrolls, scrawled with gibberish, for

Abraham to carry around in a converted golf bag, a quiver of swollen, blunted arrows. Saul became convinced that the "dyslexic aspect" required everything Abraham said, did, and wore to be backwards. So, by the time of his performance on "The Tonight Show" when Abraham was seventeen, his clothes were on backwards; he walked backwards; and he shook hands using a trick that one of Saul's contortionist acts, Bob Bend, had taught him, wrenching his elbow around like a loose hinge. But after the biggest moment of both of their careers, Saul found himself still waiting for his protégé in the car hours after Mr. Carson himself had hailed a cab. Something sank and stuck in Saul's gut, reached up and gripped his throat, as he realized that he would have to pay the boy's mom a visit to explain how he had lost her son. He stabbed cigarette number ten into the cupholder.

* * *

Abraham had disappeared himself. But as much as he had tried to cut loose from his life, it bore the black shadow of his act, as though he had been typecast for the role he was playing in the real world. He settled. He married, had a kid, bought a house, and tried to live a normal life, built upon the scaffolding of carefully constructed fictions about his age, his past, his childhood, and his family. He worked as a file clerk in a nondescript, low-ceilinged ad agency under the alias Jacob Abrams.

Whatever troubles lay simmering under the surface came to a boil when his boy was seven or eight. One afternoon, the boy found a little manila envelope with a number of photographs inside hidden behind some books on a high shelf. Struck by an impulse thirsty for fire, the boy, after carefully looking through the contents, took them to the bathtub and carefully held them to matches, one by one, as his mother pinned laundry to the line strung in the backyard. He crouched next to the tub, watching the images shrink, crinkle, and curl. He gazed dumbly at the smooth cursive words from a black indelible marker, "Loved your bit, Johnny," on a picture of a man with a turban and an Alfred E. Neuman face, standing on a stage next to a tall boy with a false beard and a black hat and his clothes on backwards, and the boy's eyes fluttered when those words ignited and blazed across the rest of the photo, as though the note had been written in gasoline.

The boy stood mute as Abraham lectured him on right and wrong, on justice and mercy and vengeance, on darkness and light, and, though the mother protested and threatened, the boy stood silently crying as Abraham took up his son's treasured possession, a hamster, explained his purpose, and wrung the furry little thing like a dirty rag. As he dropped it on the floor between the mother and child, he muttered, "This is what you've done." The mother came at him, but he knocked her down with one blow. And he went off to pack a bag and catch a bus.

* * *

There are only rumors, echoes really, of what happened to him during his time in the ether. What the real contents were of the years between the murder of the hamster and his phone call to Saul is a mystery. Bob Bend thought he saw a gaunt version of him on the streets, begging change with a hat and a guitar in Vancouver, but he had disappeared into a train station before the contortionist could unwind himself and catch up. Harry the Great swore he saw him for a moment in the middle of a chalked outline at a crime scene he happened by in Baltimore. The cops had traced the oozed circle of dark blood around him, such that, when they bagged the body, about the time Harry got there, the sketch left behind looked like a pregnant gingerbread man. And someone saw him with a needle in his arm in a back booth in dark bar in Iowa, and another was just shy of certain that he was working fields in California. Others spied him as a clown in a firefighter gag at some state fair, or maybe in a bare-knuckles prizefight in a barn in Kentucky, and so forth, on down to the one who was pretty sure the dancing preacher, entwined in rattlers, in a tongue-speaking church in Georgia was "the Jew." Wherever he'd been, when he limped into Saul's office two weeks after the phone call, he looked like a bent, rumpled, graying original of the parody he had once played as a child performer: faded black shirt under a threadbare black sport coat, crumpled black fedora, a salt-and-pepper beard down past his shirt-pockets—the hollow look of a wounded prophet. Saul saw opportunity.

* * *

"Great Tales from the Bible!" would be the name of the new act, Saul said. "Wait here. I gotta make some calls and see what pans out."

Abraham fell asleep in the old man's office. When he awoke, three clown dwarves were staring at him, leaning in to inspect him more closely. One of them, who was rasping gruffly to the others in what sounded like Italian, had a bent, thumb-like index finger extended towards the scar on Abraham's throat and was about to poke him. The contorted little clown dropped his arm when Saul emerged from a back room, picked up a call he'd put on hold, and said to the party on the other end, "Three hundred is the offer. Who else are you going to sell it to?" He paused as a voice chirped from the earpiece. "I understand that, but that's as high as I can go. What're you gonna use it for now?" Saul clapped a hand over the phone, "Pederasts," he said, as though he'd been dealing with them all day. Pause. "Alrighty, then, it's a deal."

Saul hung up the phone triumphantly and asked Abraham if he wanted to go for a drive. The dwarves looked quizzically at Saul. Saul pointed to the clock on the wall. "We'll be back when the long hand goes one time around," he enunciated, jabbing his finger at the face of the clock.

"Go one time round," one of the dwarves repeated matter-of-factly.

"That's right," Saul said with a cigarette in his mouth. He lit it. "Now you boys be good."

Saul took Abraham to pick up his "touring bus." They arrived at a dusty trailer parked, forever, on top of a makeshift foundation of cinderblocks and two-by-fours. A paunchy man in a soiled white tank-top pleaded with Saul in twangy whispers that leaked out through a wispy brown mustache. The man wrung his hands at certain intervals when his whisper became emphatic, after which he would cross his arms as though to comfort himself, and then look back to where Abraham was smoking at the picnic table, in front of the trailer, to ensure that he couldn't hear the details of the conversation. Abraham watched as this sequence repeated three or four times: whisper, whimper, hand-wringing, self-hugging, nervous glance, as Saul kept saying, "A deal's a deal" and "That's not my problem" and "Damn it, we're already here!" The man's tangled grey poodle sat in the dirt driveway between them, inclining its snub-snouted Lenin-like face towards whoever was speaking. Finally, the man tearfully relented and took Saul's three hundred dollars, signed over the title, and gave him a set of keys.

"It's in the back," the man whined. He gestured with a thumb and stared off at a blank white billboard across the street. The Russian dog stood at his feet and barked at nothing.

Saul explained that the man had been an ice-cream man for twenty years and was having a hard time letting go of that life. He was some kind of pedophile, and the law had finally caught up to him and sent him away for a while. Now, the ice-cream man was out on parole, but to ply his trade in the ice-cream-man business would be a major parole violation, given that his clientele would be predominantly under the age of eighteen.

"All that to say," Saul summed up cheerfully, "son, I got you a touring bus for a steal!"

Saul pointed here and there in the back of the truck, impressed at the "roominess" of the ice-chests: "Space for costumes. Bolt a fold-up cot to the wall over here, a hot plate over there. This is it!"

Abraham started the ice-cream truck after pumping the pedal a couple of times, and after the thing coughed and chugged out rich white smoke for a few minutes, he followed his agent back past where the ice-cream man stood by the trailer, still whimpering into the void, little Lenin curled in the dirt, licking neuter scars. The entertainers drove back through town to the office where the dwarves were waiting for them.

When Saul ushered Abraham through the door, the dwarves stood, one of them barking complaints that Abraham could not understand, waving his pretzel hand at the clock. Another simply queried, "One time round?" Saul issued apologies, smoothed their feathers down. He was a professional.

"Abraham, these fine fellows will be your troupe," he said.

Abraham studied the dwarves. He had worked with dwarves some in the past and knew their versatility and history in the business. Saul had taken on these particular dwarves as clients when they had lost their jobs in mainstream circuses due to recent shifts in middle-class consciousness that had turned toward pitying their "handicap," robbing from them their livelihood and the opportunity to practice the arts to which they had dedicated their lives.

The dwarves could sense that Saul was going to make the necessary introductions, and, accordingly, for the sake of propriety, they began to remove their clown wigs and false noses and ears, leaving their makeup without the other accoutrements of their characters. The one with the sad-clown getup smiled within a painted frown, whereas another stood deadpan, though his makeup smiled against his will. The third, with somewhat maniacal painted-on features, a mouth smeared like an open wound and thick, angry black checkmarks for eyebrows, shrugged at Saul and said again, "One time round?"

Saul introduced them. Since the trio was Italian, Saul had given them names that seemed to him Italian-sounding names, but that also seemed to capture their essences, so he wouldn't mix them up. Eco, with the crazy clown paint, was an even-tempered man of an indeterminate age. He had attempted to learn English, though his method of scholarship had simply been to repeat the words he heard people say. He looked about like anyone else, just smaller, as if he had stopped growing at the age of four or five but continued aging. Grotto's appearance bore some of the more extreme signs of dwarfism, and he seemed altogether twisted up. He was older than the other two and quite slow but was never any trouble. Saul had named him according to his tendency to let his mouth gape when he wasn't speaking, and he almost never spoke. Even as Saul introduced him, Grotto's painted mouth hung open, a slack cave. The most irritable and vociferous of the three men was No-no. He babbled a gravelly rumble of Italian most of the time. No-no seemed to be the spokesperson of the group, which was, perhaps, unfortunate, because he spoke no English. Saul remarked that he was almost certain the man was capable of speaking and understanding the language perfectly well but refused to because he enjoyed the idiotic ways in which people attempted to communicate with him. No-no was an angry drunk and something of an alcoholic. He'd once crippled a side-show giant in a bar scuffle over a gypsy fortune-teller by dragging a hunting knife across his Achilles tendon and then stabbing the balled-up calf muscle where it had nested behind the giant's knee. "Loyal but merciless," Saul said of him.

Abraham gazed at these bonsai pretenders. He fingered his coat pocket for a cigarette, lit it as he glanced at the wall, and told them with vacant ceremoniousness that he would be honored to work with them. Each reciprocated with a nod or grunt.

Over the next couple of days, Saul helped his "prodigal son," as he called Abraham, and the troupe of dwarves, gather the necessary accommodations for their travels, trim out the ice-cream truck, and work through the generalities of what the productions would entail. Then, while Abraham wrote loose scripts at a typewriter in the back room, Saul spent a whole day making calls to churches, camps, private schools, Bible colleges, small-town theaters, community groups, and even a few church-affiliated universities, and by the end of the day, he had gigs for "Great Tales from the Bible!" for the next six months.

"I can make one more call if you like," Saul said to Abraham as they prepared the bus for embarking on an all-night drive south. "Your mom still lives around here. I'm sure by this time she thinks you're dead. She'd be glad for a resurrection."

"We're both better off. A prophet and his home, and all that." Abraham turned to load a garbage bag stuffed with wigs. "Time is a cure for distance," he said, but Saul had gone back to the office and had not heard.

* * *

"Great Tales from the Bible!" proved to be a success. Nothing to the degree of "The Dyslexic Jew," but it was steady work, enough to keep fresh oil in the ice-cream truck and enough that Abraham and the dwarves hadn't needed to stop anywhere more than two weeks in the past two-and-a-half years. They had done dramatic versions of any tale from the Bible that had drama to be squeezed from it. Audiences seemed especially sucked into the stories Abraham had tried as jokes and knew were shit. No-no had recently played leads in "Post-Tumble Sampson" and "Lazarus Wakes." As Sampson, he struggled, cried out, and died over a half-hour narration from Abraham's guard. As Lazarus, No-no simply lay in the grave, trying not to fall asleep, as Abraham and Eco (as "child") paced around weeping loudly and filling in the details. *These Christians really are artless suckers,* Abraham thought, but a shepherd to his flock is as a master to his slave, and the other way around. Each has his role to play. Each, in a way, needs the other, in order to become what he truly is. It's playground wisdom. Nobody plays follow the leader alone.

Cisco, Illinois, would be no different. As the sun rose, Abraham drank some coffee by the fence, smoked a couple cigarettes, strummed a little on the beat-up guitar, and watched as the dwarves emerged and stretched in the cool morning sunlight. "Good morning," he said, and each of his brothers responded in ways he'd become accustomed to: one with a nod, one with a grunt, and one with a kindly, "Morning." Abraham explained the day's performance, Babel, which they would play at the Methodist Church in town. Eco sat up front as they drove, which Abraham preferred, since the little man had a way of repeating what he said to him back in a broken-down form that made it seem like some vague prophecy.

The little man pointed to his wrist.

"We'll be on time. Don't worry," Abraham said. He thought for a moment and continued, "You know, maybe this life is God's crucifixion of time and place. Maybe that's what Jesus is supposed to be."

Eco silently stared out the half-opened window, at the mazing rows of corn on the plain, as the cool air whispered into the truck and eddied the long, thin, straw-colored hair atop his head into a little tongue of fire that leapt up and down.

* * *

The Babel-themed drama went just as planned. That is, right up until the end. After the close of the play, it was a matter of course to turn things back over to whoever was in charge: the head of the ladies' group, the lead camp counselor, the alpha male at the men's breakfast, or as in this case, the pastor. There was often a chance, particularly if pastors closed out, for an altar call, a "love offering," or an opportunity for parishioners to share their own stories of God's faithfulness, or other such bullshit. So, this time, as with all of the others, when the pastor took over, Abraham stood at the front of the sanctuary with his troupe. He smiled a practiced smile, one designed to come off as meek, without turning the corner to unctuous, hoping for the "love offering." He got an altar call.

As a few weary souls made their way down the worn strips of carpet that led to the altar, Abraham and the dwarves stood and tried, then, to look pleasant, though not so pleasant that someone would pull them into whatever pathetic crisis had urged them there. As the recommitted faithful trickled back to their pews, Abraham noticed one young woman remaining. She mumbled in an audible baritone, her hands clasped tightly, her neck bent, her face crushed into her double-fisted hands, as she rocked her body back and forth. Abraham looked out at the gathered townsfolk and discovered mostly patient gazes, the kinds of gazes people have formed over time, when they have become accustomed to something that might otherwise be out of place. Then his gaze met with a pair of cold, hard eyes.

"She's a retard," the boy with the eyes said. And then, as the boy contorted his face and mimed what physical abnormalities he thought accompanied "a retard," he added, "Duhh! Ugh, ugh."

An old man made his way over and scolded the boy in an angry whisper.

"She don't pray," the boy said. "She don't even talk!"

Then he was marched out.

Abraham looked around nervously, and, to wrench the tension a turn more, he realized that the girl was clumsily making her way toward the altar space, behind which he and the dwarves were standing. Someone stopped her on the way and gently recommended that she go sit down, but the girl mumbled and ran toward Abraham, sliding on her knees the last couple of feet, as she took her place at the altar in front of the performers. "Shit," Abraham sighed under his breath. The girl removed her thick, black-rimmed glasses and gestured with her hand at Abraham. He hesitated, but then bent to listen when she clutched his sleeve and thrust her hand into his. Eco leaned in to hear the conversation. The girl mumbled on interminably, it must have been a matter of minutes, while Abraham nodded and said, "Uh huh" and "Mm hmm." Then she released him.

The faces of all in the congregation were fixed on Abraham. He stared back. What did they want from him? He had not an inkling of what she thought she had conveyed through her grunts, mums, and buhs. Then, noticing Eco, she grabbed him and mumbled into his ear, laughed, and released him. The faces turned collectively to Eco, and there was silence while the girl mumbled and giggled at the altar.

Then Eco recited aloud in his pleasant, old-man-child voice, "Life is crucifixion of time and place. This Jesus is."

Eco smiled at the girl, cleared his throat, and led the other two dwarves backstage. A woman from the congregation stood and came forward, weeping, holding a tissue over her mouth to muffle her bleating sobs. Abraham watched a number of women gather around the altar, sniffles and horrible joyful moans rising from the lot. A few glassy-eyed men kept their vigils in pews. One of them honked loudly into a handkerchief. The pastor shook Abraham's hand, grabbing his arm just above the elbow, then just gave him a full hug, which Abraham confusedly recip-rocated with a pat on the man's back when, after a generous three-count, he thought the hug needed to be murdered.

"You just have to be one of us to understand," the pastor whispered, as he slipped a check into the prophet's hand and started whimpering to himself in a high whine.

Abraham rallied his men, quickly packed the ice-cream truck, and departed. He parked at the rest stop off of I72, a couple miles outside of the limits of the township. He dialed a number at the payphone, lighting a cigarette as he waited for an answer.

"Saul," he said as a swirl of smoke trailed from his lips. "Where to next?"

Chapter 3

There were rumors that Sgt. Moore had been a ballet dancer, sometime before going to the academy and learning how to be a cop. Abraham watched him through the curtain that hung at the window by the front door. The man was still elegant. Each movement seemed calculated. He didn't waste time sitting in the car like most of the cops Abraham had seen before, pulling up to someplace, and then lingering in the car, fiddling with the radio, or giving a traffic ticket, and then filling in forms on the steering wheel for forty-five minutes before finally putting the cruiser in gear and driving away. Sgt. Moore's key had hardly left the ignition before the door was open and he was on the pavement, tossing his cop hat into the passenger side, a gesture which Abraham assumed meant he was there to get down to the bottom of something, all formalities aside. The swift grace with which he kicked Mrs. Elbert's Rottweiler, Spunky, who was not fond of men in uniform, without interrupting the rhythm of his gait, sealed the deal. This man was a dancer. Abraham went to his room.

Before long his mother called him in to speak to Sgt. Moore. She led him into the living room and sat on the couch next to him and held his hand. Sgt. Moore sat opposite them in a straight wooden kitchen chair. Abraham watched Sgt. Moore as the man stared into the swirl of cream in his coffee. He was nearly bald on top like a monk from the Middle Ages, and his polyester uniform was a little too small. He sat with his spine erect, pressed to the back of the chair, his legs spread wide. His coffee sat on the front of the chair between his legs, his privates bulging beneath the polyester to one side. Abraham half-smiled at the proximity of the coffee to the organ by which it would later be eliminated.

"First off, Abraham, my name is Sgt. Moore," the man said locking eyes with the boy, as he leaned forward to shake his hand above the rug between them. "Second, why don't you tell me what you're smirking about? You think this is a joke?"

"He's just nervous, Mr. Moore. I don't think he's ever talked to a police officer before," the mother said. "Plus, he's been so anxious about the man in the red truck—"

Moore put his hand up. "Why don't you tell me what happened then? Why don't you tell me about the man in the red truck?"

Moore retrieved a little hardback notebook, an ink pen stuck in it, from the back pocket of his trousers. His eyes never left the boy. Abraham could tell he was trying to get a read on him.

"I was riding my bike home from Neal's house and the red truck was in the parking lot where the butcher shop burned down. The man was in it. I rode past on the street, and he backed out and started following me."

Abraham stopped and rubbed his eye. Moore had written nothing and had not stopped staring at Abraham. His mom squeezed his hand a little.

"I got kinda scared after a couple of blocks, so I went left on the side road by where the old antique shop was, where Mr. Dawson still keeps some stuff, you know, just over the railroad tracks? And I pedaled real hard into the alley in the back and rode in behind the bushes and watched him, 'cause he went on down the road. He came back around the block, then, and parked on the side by the tracks and got out. So I threw my bike down by the dumpster and went down in the cellar. There's a door back behind Mr. Dawson's place. I hid down there. I could hear him walking in the gravel. He opened up the cellar door and came down the steps. So I got out my pocket knife and stayed real still in the corner, but I could see him in the mirror that was on this dresser down there."

Abraham's voice broke, as if he were holding back a sob.

"Then the guy pulled out his dick and just walked around like that, like he was looking for me."

"Say penis, honey," his mom said, handing Abraham a Kleenex.

"Sorry, Mom," he sniffled. "Penis."

"Why don't you tell me what happened then?" Moore said.

"Nothing," Abraham sighed. "He pushed some furniture around, moved some stuff, with his di—penis out the whole time, and then he went back up the stairs and closed the door. I heard the truck drive away after a bit, but I waited awhile, just to make sure. Then I rode home."

"You get a look at him?"

"A little. He was thin, probably a little taller than Mom."

"So, like six feet?" Moore jotted in the book.

"I don't know."

"Well, I'm six feet." Moore stood up, motioning to the mother. They stood back to back. "Was he about as tall as me?" Moore held his pen in his mouth and his notebook as if it were a ruler between his head and the mother's.

"Yeah, I think."

"Hair color?"

"It was dark, but he was mostly bald on top."

"Hmm. Okay." Moore jotted. "I don't suppose you caught his license plates did you?"

"I think the first part was JTM, but I didn't get the rest."

Moore scribbled again, but stopped and then stared blankly at Abraham. "Mmhmm." His mouth puckered and shifted to one side. "You mind if I talk to Abraham alone for a minute?"

"Of course. Yes. I understand." The mother looked at Abraham. "I'm gonna be right out front pulling weeds, okay?"

Abraham nodded. His mom went outside. Abraham watched her ponytail bounce down the steps and then bob around in front of the wide window above the flowerbed from which he'd watched Moore just a little while ago.

Moore had not stopped staring at him.

"Why don't you let me ask you a couple more questions, and

28

then this'll all be over and done with?" He spoke more quietly now.

"Okay."

"Okay?" Moore repeated. "Did you see what kind of red truck this guy was driving?"

"I think it was a Ford."

"Older or newer?"

"Oh, it was pretty shiny, looked new, but I'm not for sure. But it did have a blue pin stripe down the side."

Then Moore spoke, almost in a whisper.

"Listen, kid, I don't know what the fuck you're tryin' to pull here, but you'd better lay off it and now. You think you're pretty fuckin' smart pullin' this shit on me don't ya. I don't know what you're after, but you need to cut it out."

The last three words he said emphatically, as if each one were its own sentence.

Abraham looked wordlessly at him, like he didn't understand. Moore tore out the little sheet of paper, crumpled it up, and stuck it in his mouth. He chewed it, hard, for a minute or so and swallowed.

"Fuck you." And then, as if for good measure, Moore said "Fuck you" again.

Abraham opened the door, and as he did, his mom rose from her weeding. She thanked Sgt. Moore, and he said he'd "keep them posted." Abraham put his hand out to shake Moore's, saying, "Thank you, sir." Moore took his hand and forced a laugh in the back of his throat. He looked at the mother and said she had quite a brave young man.

Moore walked off towards his car, as Abraham said something to his mom.

"Wait! Sgt. Moore?" She hollered across the yard. He stopped by the driver's side door. "Is it true that you use to be a ballet dancer? Abraham loves ballet."

"No!" he shouted across the yard.

Moore had stopped just long enough to attract Spunky's attention, and just as he answered her, Abraham's mom yelled for him to look out. But Spunky had dug into the meat of Moore's thigh. His mom ushered Abraham inside to keep him from hearing any more curses. About a minute later, Abraham heard a sharp crack from Moore's pistol, followed by the squeal of his tires.

That night at dinner Abraham's mom told him that she was so proud of him for being so brave. She said she could not have asked for a sweeter boy. She said, as she was like to do, whenever overwhelmed with sentimental emotion, "My cup runneth over."

This cup wants to be empty again, Abraham thought. He smiled as he thought of Sgt. John Thomas Moore, driving himself home from the police station in his new red Ford pickup, with its custom pin stripes, to peroxide and bandage his dog-torn flesh, though he was saddened a little at having wasted the finest performance of his meagre twelve years on a cop, who, as it turned out, was not even an artist.

* * *

Abraham woke up dizzy in the high summer grass along the roadside near the warped telephone pole which he'd tumbled into from the tar-and-gravel country road where he'd been riding a borrowed bike. At first he wasn't sure where he was or how he had ended up in the ditch between the road and the cornfield. The sun, alone in the blue above, beat heat into his face. But the confusion cleared a little as he heard two voices in the distance woohooing as though something significant had happened at a rodeo. He raised his head from its sky-borne gaze to see, above the beans on the far side of the road, a beat-up red Chevy pickup bearing left at the crossroads a half-mile down. Two oversized boys in overalls were standing in the bed waving bean-hooks above their heads like savages. They were laughing and knee-slapping like black-and-white cartoons. Abraham thought their high-five was going a little too far, so he raised both middle fingers on his clinched fists.

"Fuck you!" he roared.

They didn't seem to notice.

He raised himself and inspected the bicycle. It was a large purple ladies' cruiser with a basket and mirrors, on loan to him from the corpulent sunburned woman who helped her husband run the campground that Abraham and the dwarves had been staying at a few miles outside of Cisco. The bike had escaped the wreck with only a cracked mirror on the left side, which now cast a riven portrait of Abraham back to him. He pulled his hair back to find the protuberance on his hairline, where his head had hit the pole. He pulled a couple of splinters from it and pressed the mashed purple skin around it with his index finger. He walked to his hat a couple hundred feet away as he rubbed blood and gravel off of his elbows. He muttered "Bastards" a couple of times as he got himself together and mounted the bike, soon realizing that the bumpy rhythm of the ride from a warped rim was working against the mild concussion he'd probably sustained when the boys in the truck ran him off the road. Abraham stashed the bike in a little stand of trees, near what looked like a wide stretch of woodland, probably, he thought, not far from where the river went through. He decided to walk a bit in the relative cool of the woods, maybe find the water, until his vertigo cleared. He tied his handkerchief onto a tree branch, near where he'd hidden the bike, and set off along the tree line. Before long, he found a dirt trail into the woods and took it.

He thought that it must have been the red truck which sent him to the dream of his run-in with Sgt. Moore. He had mistreated the man, but Moore had a reputation for being a hardass; one who was known to pimp crack-addled twenty-somethings around to other cops, a hot point for talk among the boys of Oxford. The hypocrisy of it irritated Abraham. *If you're going to be something, then be it; there's no sense in bullshitting yourself by thinking you're bullshitting everyone else.* Besides, Abraham had been a little late getting home, and he didn't have good excuse.

At the same time, though, Abraham felt uneasy. It was almost as if the red truck had driven out of the past to brutalize him, then had hitched his mind to its bumper and towed it back into that past, cut it loose in that memory, where events played over and over, where the past went on without him. Or maybe the other way around. He continued his trudge through the woods without much thought as to where it was he was going and what it was that he left behind. He felt the sameness of the woods and the blank brown of the trail, and he found it restful. It seemed to share the principle by which he had learned forgetfulness. For one for whom the past never fades or withers away, forgetfulness is crucial. Since being marooned in these plains, Abraham had come to feel attuned to this country, like it worked within him somehow. It had a just-there-ness. There is no beginning or end to a sheer expanse of land or trees or a field. When you stumble through the corn, where you start is not its beginning, and it is not gone or over when you have left it behind. Prairies do not dissolve into nothing after you've passed through them. In this countryside there are no beginnings or endings; everything is already nothing. And it is free.

Abraham had become forgetful in just this way. His life had become, in time, what this country was in space: an expansive nothing, stretching out like a trail to eternity, to oblivion, in both directions, only blankly there, only *just* there. It was not that he "lived in the now" like some filthy hippie or a New Age guru, but that time had split apart for him. It was time itself that had passed, fogged off in the distance, withered, and all that was left was living forgetfulness, somewhere on this rubber band that widened and narrowed according to the elasticity of his life, or the moment in which he found it. He lived with the rhythm of a wave in a formless sea, of a wind that happened through the grasses, of a warped circle without terminus, with inertia that felt like stillness. No past or present or future crept in because time was dead. He lived out of blind obligation to continue, to be, to become, or to unravel, to diminish, to disintegrate, and return to the earth, beginnings left aside. He was not sure which, and it made no difference. Assurance is a lie. What troubled Abraham now was that this *justness* seemed to be decaying, drying out in the light, burning and shriveling up, like poor Saul's cancerous lungs. Now, it seemed, a stake had been driven down, a band of time anchored to it, everything winding around that rupture in the earth, like a drain back into a world of meaning.

* * *

"Where to next?"

Saul had not answered the question. He began with a sigh. The old man did not need to go on. Abraham heard, in that breath, everything that Saul had to say. But he listened and spoke and said things he thought Saul would like to hear.

"Abraham, you know I've always been fond of you, and I like those boys that travel with you real good. They're fine boys. Gentlemen even. Well, maybe not that No-no. That sonofabitch ain't quite right, but he's good at heart, and that's important."

He coughed.

"Well, hell, Abraham, I'm gonna come out and say it. You know I'm not much of a small-talker. Spent too long in the business."

There was a pause.

"I'm dying, son. Cancer's come back. Doctor Death says my time is pretty short. Surgeries and chemo again. I'm too old for that shit, you know. Lord knows I don't want to, but I've gotta tie up my dealings. I've gotta cut you loose. I've got some wrongs to right before I go. That kind of shit. I'm gonna use my last days that way. Seems right."

"Saul. I'm sorry. I'm damn sorry to hear that."

"I know I'm putting you out, Abraham, but it's what I gotta do. Time's short, doctor says."

"No, no, we'll manage. Don't you worry about us. I'm just, you know, I—"

"Now, Abraham. I never figured you for a sentimentalist. I love you too." He said it like it was a joke, but Abraham could tell he was making it easy for him. "Now, I figured you're probably not coming back?"

"No."

Saul had joked about Abraham having to mail the dwarves back to Italy, but, for the moment, they wanted to stay with him. Saul sent his "settle-up package" a couple days later to the post office in Cisco. The dwarves he had paid out in cash, stuck in little manila envelopes. For Abraham, there was a separate box within the big box. Inside were some old photographs; a notecard with his mother's phone number; a pocket watch; a small vial containing a human finger, floating in clear liquid, with the name "Sergius" written across a piece of masking tape on the side; a short letter in Saul's rough scrawl; and a little over thirty-thousand dollars in cash. Saul was making it easy for him.

* * *

Abraham looked up the trail. Some large rocks had been built into a makeshift bridge across a little creek bed. He stopped when he reached it, pitched his hat onto the stones, and knelt to rub the cool water on his face and neck. He had forgotten his wounds until they stung with the water. Then he rinsed his battered elbows too and blotted the knot on his forehead with the tail of his over-shirt. He slurped a little water from his hands, noticing a crude pocket-knife etching of a phallus on the flat side of the stone which held his hat. He stood, shielding the late-afternoon sun, looking further up the trail. In the distance, it seemed to widen out and slope gently upwards. He drew his eyebrows together and pursed his lips. He walked on across the water and started up the hill.

A breeze shook the high branches, and they danced and shivered against the blank blue sky. The sun was just dipping behind the thick hickories ahead, and shadows seemed to creep out all at once with the dull roar of the evening wind. Abraham heard someone say "Jacob" against the wind-noise. When he looked behind, though, he saw no one. He continued his march up the hill, until a green-grey figure appeared in a clearing, still a ways ahead. He stopped. The wind had died, and he listened. The crickets had started in, and he heard something moving through the underbrush, beneath the trees, off the trail. When he looked, he saw three wild turkeys, the tom, fanning its tail, seemed to be resting his beak back on his scarlet throat as he chortled a warning. Abraham started a little, and then snickered at himself. The big tom raised his wings and fluttered them. The hens' red and blue heads shot up, spotted Abraham, and stared.

"Okay, okay, I'm going," Abraham whispered.

He continued towards the stationary figure in the distance, which still hadn't taken shape for him. He watched the trail at his feet and the dust clouds that rose with each step in the dry dirt. Abraham glanced back at where he had seen the turkeys, on the edge of where the trees hit the trail. They were gone. A black figure far behind caught his eye though. Even in the coming twilight, the deep black of it rent a slit in the green of the landscape. Abraham stopped and studied it for a moment as it moved towards him. It was a man in a long black cloak, which seemed to cover his body, from his neck nearly to his feet, like something a monk would wear. Abraham fumbled in his shirt-pocket for his cigarettes. He selected one that had been broken in the fall. He bit the filter off the rest of the way and lit the short stub in his mouth. As his gaze found the man again, he watched him take a seat on the little stone bridge and light a cigarette too. Abraham heard a woodpecker add his noise to the crickets' scream. The wind came back up, and Abraham turned and soon found his pace again.

As he moved up the slope, Abraham's gaze volleyed between the greyish figure ahead and the black one behind. He finally made out the first as a statue, though he still could not tell of what, and he was utterly confused as to why such a hulking figure would appear in the middle of the woods. The black-clad man behind also began to take on firmer dimensions as he moved in closer behind Abraham. He seemed about Abraham's age; he wore a sharp black Tartar beard and a black skullcap, and Abraham could see a chain necklace hanging slack, with what he assumed was probably a crucifix stuck in the breast pocket on the left side. A priest. Abraham sighed as he came to this interpretation. He kept moving.

Even from several yards out, the statue was indecipherable. There was obviously a horse involved, but another figure seemed awkwardly bent over the front of it, and there was what appeared to be a human arm reaching out towards the rear of the horse, a smaller object holding its wrist atop the flanks. It was staged upon a wide, low slab of concrete which pedestalled the now blue statue; its green had faded as the light dissipated. And the closer he got to it, the larger and grander the statue appeared. Still ten paces out, Abraham finally recognized it as a centaur and whispered as much to himself as he did, shocked by the incongruence of such a creature among these prairieland rednecks, for whom only Jesus marked the union between men and gods. Abraham stood still, not yet close enough to study the centaur. He wanted to drink in its fullness first, the art of its staging, its friction with the wild woods it hid in. He glanced behind him, and the priest too had stopped and was fiddling with his pocket watch. He had closed the distance between Abraham and himself, and now the three figures, the centaur, Abraham, and the priest, were frozen, equidistant from one another, Abraham's head slowly turning from the centaur to the priest and back before anyone spoke.

The moment was broken when someone said, "I'm gonna fuck it in the ass." Two adolescents on bikes appeared, riding around from the far side of the centaur. One of them dismounted and poised himself on the back of the centaur. He clasped one hand around the lyre that the half-man held beneath his wrist, and with the other he gripped the centaur's closed fist, which extended on above the tail. The priest ambled up next to Abraham. Abraham glanced at the olive-skinned man in profile. Dark curls flowed out from his skullcap and into his bushy black beard. The man glanced back. The two men watched for a moment wearing the same stony, stoic expression, their beards hiding the smirks they wore underneath. As the boy simulated coitus with the centaur and moaned in rhythm with his grotesque gyrations, the priest silently offered a cigarette to Abraham, took one himself, and they lit up. About this time, the other kid, who had been watching from the other side, noticed the men by the scent of the smoke and had come around.

"Holy fuck, Randy! It's a priest."

"It's a centaur, dumbass."

"No, there," he yelled, pointing. "A priest. And some weird motherfucker. Let's go!"

The boy lowered himself, impeded by his own gasping laughter, and the two of them hopped on their bikes and started down the long stretch of concrete stairs that led away from the statue, down to the pine-lined lowland trail beyond.

"Lusty little bastard, no?" the priest said after a long drag. His voice was deep and his speech was ambiguously accented by whatever foreign tongue had been his first.

At once, both men started in for a closer inspection of the centaur. They silently moved around it in opposite directions.

Abraham looked in the direction of the boys. They were nearing the bottom of the stairs. Both glanced back, and all at once, they ran into each other and were flung into the grass. This was punctuated at certain intervals with grunts and curses. Abraham smiled.

"That is a troubling age, no?" the priest said. "It is like they are all on leave from the asylum."

"I can't disagree with that," Abraham said, stamping out his cigarette. "What is this place?"

"It is a park. Now, anyway. Allerton Park. I do not know the whole story. I only a couple of weeks ago got into the area. But I have been here a few times and asked around. Glorious, no? This is my favorite piece so far, the Death of the Last Centaur, it is called. The sculptor was Emile-Antoine Bourdelle. I picked up a little guide in the gift shop, I must admit it, but I have got a memory for facts. Details, you see."

"Chiron."

"Yes. Yes. So you know the pagans too, no? Robert Allerton, he was apparently something of a monster in these parts himself, you see. Part gentleman-farmer, part collector, part aesthete. A Thomas Jefferson, but with a little Charles Foster Kane and Oscar Wilde mixed in."

The priest stopped and slowly shook his head as if he were denying something.

"Well, he seems to have been a homosexual, rumors," the priest went on, "so Wilde came to mind, as the consummate aesthete homosexual. It is not on a par with the Jefferson-Kane association. Those were pretty accurate, no?"

Abraham reached out and touched the centaur. He rubbed the muscled bronze oblique where the bodies of man and horse joined in a line of fur. The priest seemed to be waiting for a response.

"I suppose," Abraham said after a moment, "but, then again, I can't really say. I'm learning all of this from you for the first time."

"Yes. Yes. Of course. There are things you do not know. You really should come back to explore though. This Allerton had a real imagination. He was an artist with the layout of the place. It is a perfect modernist pastiche of the past, of east and west. He has manicured oriental labyrinths made from shrubs, guarded by a statue of Cro-Magnon man. Then these romantic wild forests with Chiron here, and there is an enormous Apollo somewhere called the Sun Singer. Classic English gardens full of tiny Chinese players chiseled out of limestone. Something called a Fu Dog. They are from Korea. He has dozens. A great Georgian mansion with a Persian reflecting pool, flanked by sphinxes. I am not kidding, Abraham, sphinxes!"

Abraham stared at the priest. At length, the priest noticed his error.

"Have you something else to say, father?" Abraham said blankly, his eyes still wide.

The priest raised his palms up close to his ears, as though someone were holding a pistol on him. Then he smiled.

"You have got me, Abraham. I have talked too much." Then he shrugged, turning his palms up. He laughed a little, noiselessly. "I am a monk. I am fresh out of ten years of silence, a vow I was encouraged to make. That is mother church, my friend. Most of the discipline they dole out they make you inflict on yourself. Brutal, no?"

Abraham turned his head back to the centaur and cocked it to one side, as though he were emulating the fallen posture of the centaur's head.

"What is it you're after?" Abraham turned his gaze back to the priest.

"Listen, I know you, Abraham. There it is." He sighed. "It is my job to know you, learn about you, watch you, find out where you have been, *who* you have been, what you are up to. They flew me back from France for you, from the Alps. The Alps! Beautiful.

Quiet. Silent. Silent and cold as Dante's Cocytus. But I have got some connections here. They know my talents in reconnaissance, and the job was you. So I am going to be around. Hell, I have been around. I thought it would be simpler this way. Direct. Honest. We can be friends even, no?"

The priest fumbled for his cigarettes. He offered the box to Abraham. They smoked. The faint grey wisps trailed from their lips and into the evening grey around them. Both men were silent. The wood, though, was alive with the noise that had quieted with the priest's boisterous monologue. Abraham listened to the waves of cacophony with his eyes closed, the cigarette between his lips. He smiled a little when the voices blended for an instant and then fell apart again just as suddenly.

"Did you hear it?" he said to the priest.

"Hear what?"

Abraham said nothing for a moment. The sun was a mere haze of orange around the dark ruffles of tree tops to the west. Its light blended pink into the darkening grey, and the moon was up already, a yellow blot in the almost-dark.

"Yes," Abraham said, the smirk still on his lips, his eyes still closed. "We can be friends. I'll tell you whatever it is you want to know. But not tonight. Tonight, I just need a ride back to the campsite. It's getting dark."

"We have a deal," the priest said. "I'll get the car and meet you where you tied your handkerchief." Then he laughed a little. "I'll give you a moment alone with your god."

Abraham again studied the centaur. These moments suited Chiron's morte vivant, the fading day beaten back by the bleak black of night coming on, both depicting a change to the known unknowable, to the inevitable, to that eerie rest that is always waiting. The sculptor had captured Chiron's change, the final shudder of his failing flanks, his hind legs buckling underneath. His right arm leans on the lyre, plucks out the last notes of his immortality, the first sounds of death, the music that closes him off to suffering, that locks him in the stars. The left slopes limply behind. His neck strains as he turns his head down and away from the grim music. Or is he fading away, his head already fallen, hooves alone in holding out the frozen tableau? His doubled cages of ribs, one a beast's, one a man's, strain and rattle out a final breath, the breath of a god sacrificed for a man. An old, familiar story. Beastly man and holy god, a sacrifice locked in among the contradictions.

Abraham turned away and disappeared back into the dark woods which had brought him there.

Chapter 4

"Get your ass in there and swing, god damn it! Or all these fuckers are gonna eat you alive for we're done with," Bert was screaming.

The fighter nodded.

"You look like roadkill, Jake. God damn. Can you see at all?"

He nodded again.

"Put your hands out."

The fighter moved his hands from where they rested on his hips and held them out in front, between them, so they almost touched the other man's chest. The hands were clean, for the most part. A little spattered with the fighter's own blood, but, otherwise, clean.

"Now that's a god damn shame. You're just takin' it. You call yourself a fighter?" Bert popped him on the side of the head.

The fighter said nothing. Some men behind them hollered something unintelligible that ended with "fucker." Someone threw an empty beer can that hit the fighter's shoulder. He didn't move. Bert took the cigarette from his own lips and stuck it in the gashed mouth of the fighter, who dragged it a couple of times. As he did, the other man took the hands and rubbed them on his shirt, slipping a big D Duracell into his closed hand. The fighter seemed not to notice. Neither did anyone else.

"Now hit him, god damn it," Bert said, blotting the fighter's swollen eyes with a damp rag.

The fighter nodded again, the blood welling back into his eyes already. He headed back to the circle chalked inside of where the stacked hay bales bordered the chalked boxing ring in the broad metal pole barn. Someone slapped him as he found his way through the opening on his side. He seemed not to notice. He gazed out towards the man he'd suffered six rounds with already, not really looking at the man, but at the whole picture he was featured in. The man's hands were wrapped in wet towels, washed with pink streaks of diluted blood. He was shirtless, almost hairless, his head and face shorn, tattoos covering his arms, a rolling American flag across his chest with a swastika in the middle of a circle of thirteen stars in the patch of blue. He was framed against the back of the barn. A steer skull hung above the door. A blue tractor was parked to one side, behind where the hay bales rounded out the other man's side. His corner-man sat, chewing a cigar, his arms crossed. The loft and open space outside of the ring was filled in with denim-clad yokels in worn baseball caps and t-shirts. Their voices combined in a mocking static with the constant bark and growl of the caged dogs that would fight next.

The air felt tight and heavy with the earthy odors of men and shit, of sweat, blood, smoke, beer, and dogs. Jake breathed it deeply anyway. There was no alternative. He cocked his head as far towards each shoulder as he could, and it popped in both directions. He shook a little, wiped blood from his eyes with the back of an index finger, and spat more blood on the earthen floor. He stepped into the chalk circle and rung still more blood out of his beard with one hand. A jeering cheer went up with the fists that the onlookers rose and shook at no one in particular. He had promised Bert a win in the seventh round. It was time.

The other man shook the towels off his hands and stepped into the circle, as he blew his nose into the air, one nostril at a time. He wiped his hands on his bloodied denim cutoffs. The fat man seated on a bale on the perimeter of the circle, halfway between the fighters' sides, hit a large metal skillet with a wooden spoon, and both men put their hands up and moved in.

The tattooed man hit Jake with a wide-slung right. Jake spun with it, and the man added a few shots to his ribs, and then kicked him down in the dirt. Jake got up, spit, and put his hands up again. The tattooed man worked the same combination once more, but this time the kick in the ass didn't knock Jake down.

He spun again but then righted himself and got his hands up. The other man, for a third time, reared back with his right, but it was already too late. Jake had come alive. He caught him hard, square, across the bridge of his nose with his battery hand. The nose cracked, burst open, and blood spurted. The tattooed man's hands went to his face. Jake threw a hook that landed with a smack on the side of the bald head, kneed the man in the abdomen, and struck his throat with a winged-out elbow, before the man doubled over, hands still covering his face, blood flowing out between his bent fingers. The man gasped and roared out as Jake's fists came down on him again and again: back of the neck, high ribs, kidneys. He was still standing somehow. The strange noises he made had silenced most of the crowd, who now looked on with hungry faces. Jake lifted the man's head a little with one fist and knocked it down again with the other. He beat the man patiently, brutally, but without passion or anger, steadying him when he swayed. By the final shot, the tattooed man's wounded hands hung limply at his sides, his head turned towards the ceiling and a little to one side, his face a massacre. He gurgled incoherently from somewhere deep down. Jake struck him again in the throat, kicked him in the balls, and the man just crumpled down and spilled out across the dirt like a slinky from the last stair. No one cheered. Someone retched near the tractor. The fat man hit the skillet with the spoon, and Jake's breathing slowed to almost nothing.

* * *

Abraham awoke with one deep gasp. He looked out the window and then jerked his head around to the driver.

"Bad dreams?" the priest said.

"I wish."

They rode a black tar and gravel road that sloped down from the center. It seemed mostly tar now. The tires across it at forty-five miles per hour made a sound like tape being pulled off of an endless surface. Abraham figured he had only just dozed off a few minutes before. They were about to make their last turn before the campground, but they could already see the red and blue flashes that strobed against the dark. The priest made the right turn without signaling and, after a mile or so, another right into the campground entrance.

The gate was closed and a young sheriff's deputy stood by his cruiser on the inside. The priest lowered the window as the deputy rounded the gate in the grass and approached.

"Sorry, folks," the deputy said. "Park's closed. Won't be opened 'fore morning."

"What is going on?" the priest asked.

"I'm not at liberty to say. Park's closed. Come back tomorrow."

The priest looked at Abraham, whose deadpanned gaze conveyed nothing. The priest shifted a little in his seat, pulling the seatbelt away from his neck. The deputy leaned down, placing his elbows on the open window, looking in.

"Oh, shit. I'm sorry, father. Nobody told me you's coming. You gentlemen go on through. They're all the way around the circle. It's the ice-cream truck."

"Thanks, my son. I will just head for the flashing lights," the priest said with a wink.

"Yes, sir, father."

The young man struggled with the lock for a moment, finally giving up and kicking it a few times, and then pulled the gate free. He motioned officiously with one hand as he walked it open. The priest and Abraham watched his figure move through the headlights, red and blue pulsing out from the dark gravel circle beyond, where sudden images of men, cars, and campers flashed. The deputy disappeared for a moment when he tripped on the center-point where the gate anchored into a pipe cemented into the drive. They watched him resurrect himself, still motioning for them to move forward, and they finally did.

"Bad news if they are expecting a priest, no?"

"I'm afraid so," Abraham said. He looked out the window on his side of the car and saw two pairs of animal eyes glowing back from the black woods beyond the picnic pavilion. "Turn left at the circle. It's a one-way to the right, but no one cares."

The priest did as Abraham said, and they pulled into the empty campsite that shared an electricity pole with the one the ice-cream truck was parked at. Abraham sighed and got out. The priest followed.

"No," another cop said as he briskly made his way to them through the grass. He repeated the word a few times as he came, but he said it as if it were a question. "Who's the driver?"

"That is me," the priest said, raising his hand.

"I know it's you." The young cop stood with his hands on his hips. His right hand rested on the handle of his pistol.

"Why did you ask then?" the priest queried.

"You know that's a one way. You saw the sign. It ain't hard to read. It's a big fuckin' arrow."

The priest looked at Abraham. "It looked clear. I did not think anyone would mind."

The cop stepped in closer. "You queers? 'Cause there's a lot of queers out here. Too many, if you ask me." The cop stood working his mouth. He spit into the grass and stood dumb against the night.

Then Abraham touched the man's shoulder, almost affectionately, and spoke, his voice husked in irritation, but only just so. "We didn't ask. Not about your opinions on sexual mores, or about making a turn the wrong way on a drive, which sees about as much traffic as the strip of carpet that leads to your bedroom. Now that's my truck, and there's what looks like a bleeding bag hanging from that big oak next to it, and I don't see my friends anywhere. So I want you to shut your fucking mouth and get me whoever's in charge."

The priest smirked. The cop's shoulders fell. "Listen," he started, "I'm real sorry—"

"Fuck you. Go tell the sheriff you're fucking sorry. I'm certain it won't come as a surprise."

The cop stocked off silently, spoke to the sheriff, who was standing near the truck, pointed back to the two bearded men who stood smoking near the picnic table, then joined a small group of young cops who gazed up at the sack that was tethered to the tree, trying to guess what they would find inside.

"Good evenin', gentlemen," the sheriff said. "I'm Slocum." Then to Abraham, "Richie says you're the ice-cream man and maybe you've been in his house." Slocum stood waiting for a reply, his thin frame folded in beneath his arms, his lips tight beneath a broad brown mustache.

Abraham said nothing.

"A misunderstanding," the priest said.

Abraham dragged on his cigarette before he spoke. "That's my truck. This is my campsite. And I still haven't seen the men who are staying with me." Abraham blew what smoke remained within him out to one side.

"So that makes you Mr. Abraham. Camperman told us about you. Says you're real good people. Oddballs, now that's his word, but Friends Creek has always welcomed all kinds. And who does that make you?" He took a small notepad out of his back pocket.

"I am Father Valentin Zamir Alejandro Rabinovich Mayakovsky."

Slocum started writing but gave up. "You a priest then?"

"A monk-priest, yes."

"Black...monk...priest..." he mumbled as he wrote.

"Okay, listen, you're both involved." Slocum paused and put his notepad away. "You're both implicated in this someways. Now, that doesn't mean you're guilty of nothin' or that you're even suspects, 'cause you're not. Not based on what's been reported. What I mean is you're part of whatever the hell is going on here. Like it or not, you're a part of it. So am I. We been pulled in. Implicated. So I'm gonna speak freely with you 'cause we's in the same boat, far as I see it. Now, Sheriff Smalley's from Macon County, and he don't deal the same way I do, but we're working this together, so we don't fuck it up. Cause if we do, we're gonna end up with a bunch of big-city folks in here runnin' things, and that ain't gonna be good for nobody. Okay? So, Mr. Abraham, Mr. Priest: I'll keep you informed as much as I can, but don't blab it to no one. We's all working together to sort this shit out."

The men nodded.

"Now we ain't seen a murder in Piatt since Sawlaw's sheriff, before me some ways back, and none in Macon County since before that. And now we got what's soon gonna be three in the same day. A girl in Piatt not too far from here, out at Hog Chute, on the other side of Cisco, 'tween there and Monticello, and two of your midget friends. We've got one bagged in the ambulance, stabbed and beat up, and we're figurin' on how to get what we think is the other one down from that tree. But given what's been reported and that blood there, we can safely say three."

"Christ!" the priest said.

Abraham was looking into the grass. "Who is still alive?"

"Little feller with a big head. He don't talk none, but he's pretty torn up by it. Grow-toe or Grim-toe, somethin' like that, Camperman said."

"Grotto."

"That's the one. He's in your truck. Seems he got hisself hid in that stretch of prairie goes out to the road. We tried talkin' to him but couldn't get nowhere, so we let him go in there. We'll have to take a look at the vehicle eventually, of course, but I thought it'd be better than stickin' him in a cruiser or something. Thought that might make him nervous, and he already had hisself a fucked-up day."

"Can I see him?"

"Yes, course. Plus, I need you to take a look around anyways and see if you're missin' anything. See if you can help us with a motive. Now it's my thought that these murders gotta be related. I's out the other scene 'fore comin' here. Looks like same MO. Smalley's there now, and he says coincidence. How the hell he figures that I do not know. A donkey and a horse make a mule, and this here's a fuckin' mule, if I ever seen one. My investigation's assumin' there's some connection. We'll have to get your statement, formally, at some point, so don't take off or nothin'. Take a look, and see what you find. I'll be around. Right now, I gotta fetch a dead midget from that oak tree." He tipped his hat and walked off.

"I'm going to look in on Grotto," Abraham said to the priest. "Why don't you pick me up tomorrow, early. We'll talk then. I can't make any sense of this."

"Can I help?"

"No. We'll talk tomorrow. "

* * *

Camperman was driving the campground's mini-cherry-picker into Abraham's campsite. The cops scattered slowly like grazing buffalo as he maneuvered it into position under the thigh-thick branch to which the sack was tied. Abraham watched, leaning against the front of the ice-cream truck.

"It only holds one," Camperman said. Then he looked down at the basket, turning his head to one side, apparently considering the matter for a moment. "Or two. But only if they're real skinny." After a little more consideration, during which he sized up the job, looking up into the tree and back down at the ground and then back up again, he concluded, "I can operate her and bring him down." Camperman's voice was deep and warm, his words clipped and staccato, as if he had been a Northeasterner, but one whose words had been rounded by years in the country.

"Now, I don't know if that's a good idea," Slocum said. "We're not sure what shape he's in. Could be pretty grisly."

"I was a state trooper for twenty years, Slocum. It was the service before that. 'Nam. I've seen some things." He looked down at Slocum over his glasses, raising his upper lip a little, pulling back the corners of his mouth, as if he'd smelled something rotten. "I'll keep the bag closed if it makes you feel better."

"That'd be good, Camperman. Just get him down for Christ's sakes."

They trained the floods on the branch, some forty feet up from the grass, where the bag was tied with thick brown rope. The bag swayed in the wind, and Camperman ascended slowly and steadily towards it. Abraham watched him edge up and in, his hands on the controls. The man unsheathed his hunting knife and sawed at the rope, delicately holding his tongue between his teeth as he did. The bag lumped into the floor of the basket. He cautiously lowered himself and the oozing bag back down and turned the key to kill the engine.

"I still don't know how they got him up there," Camperman said.

"We'll work on it. Can you hand him down?"

Camperman lifted the bag by a corner up and over the railing to Slocum.

"Poor little feller can't be no bigger than a Jack Russell," Slocum said as he took the bag. He put it gently on the ground. "Now, you young fellers get away if you can't act like men. Miss Jolly says they done this boy real bad with a pipe and their hands 'fore that, so go on if you need to. I can't hold your hand. This ain't about you. Alright?"

One or two removed themselves to the shadows beyond, but most looked on. Slocum lifted the opening of the bag and stuck his arm in and cut the rough brown fabric back up to where the rope had tied it shut. He peeled the now-loose sides of the bag back like a surgeon clamping back skin around a wound.

"Ah..." he moaned. His eyes flared, and he looked around, like he'd lost something in the sky. His face was screwed up on one side. He suddenly seemed like a much older man, senile or stroking out. "Ah, hell." His mustache rounded as his lips contracted and he fought back a sob. He looked into the grass and then, after a moment, back again into the torn sack. "Hell." And this time he gave up and a couple sobs came. He looked around, but all of his men had gone. There was only Abraham, a few paces off. He held Abraham's gaze, tears puddled in his eyes, and said, in a high whisper, careful that his voice didn't break, "What'd they leave?" It seemed like he was really asking. Slocum removed his hat as Abraham stepped forward. He squatted next the sheriff, taking his black hat from his head and placing it on his knee, and gazed at what remained.

Whatever it was they left behind in the bag, it wasn't Eco. They left only meat and hair and blood and bones. They left only a testament to their brutality. They left only the texture of their violence.

Abraham felt something warm run down his face into his mustache. He thought it might be a tear. He wiped it with his palm. It was blood. The knot on his forehead had opened.

* * *

The cops were still milling about. Abraham had helped Slocum zip Eco into an oversized black plastic bag and set him next to No-no in the ambulance before returning to the truck to look in on Grotto. He opened the back door of the ice-cream truck and found the man sitting shirtless on his cot. His eyes were closed, though his mouth hung slack as usual. Abraham switched on a dim light that was velcroed to the ceiling. Grotto slitted an eye that seemed to recognize Abraham. In the dirty yellow of the camper light, the small man's twists and creases made him seem ancient, a relic from another world, lost in time. It occurred to Abraham that Grotto was quite old, and he marveled that he had never noticed it before. They stayed like that for a moment. Abraham did not know what to say, so he said nothing. The one eye squinted on. Abraham's dead gaze looked back.

"La luce," Grotto rasped after another moment.

"Alright," Abraham sighed. He realized that that was the first time in their years together that he had heard the man speak. He switched off the light and stood in the silence staring in. Grotto sat still, only hints of his face left in the dark, his deep-set eyes and open mouth black against the faint light coming through the windshield. Washed in that light, what remained of his face looked like a skull.

"Sono cresciuto stanco," a voice whispered from the truck.

Abraham was not sure what it meant. He nodded formally and closed the door.

Later, when he took a cursory scan of the contents of the ice-cream truck, Grotto was sleeping, hugging his misfit legs together, like a fetus locked safely away in the dark of the womb. He breathed in deep, even measures. Nothing had been disturbed.

* * *

"Mr. Abraham?"

Abraham came awake slowly, pushed his hat back from his eyes, and leaned forward. His fire had gone out, but some coals still smoldered and glowed against the eerie haze of dawn coming on. He rubbed his eyes.

"Mr. Abraham?"

He saw a mug of coffee held out to him by a woman's hand. He took it. Miss Jolly pulled a lawn chair close and worked for a few seconds to stuff herself into it and then leaned against the back, resting her own mug on the mound of her that stuck up past her breasts. Slocum was the only cop who remained. Abraham watched him snap shut his little notebook with some degree of finality and head toward the fire.

"Mr. Abraham?" Miss Jolly said again.

"Yes?"

"Who's Fagin? Little bit ago you said something about scissors and Mr. Fagin. I guess you wasn't woke up all the way."

"What's that, Miss Jolly?" Slocum said as he teepeed a couple small logs over the coals.

"Mr. Abraham. I's waking him up, and he said, 'I've got no scissors to sharpen, Mr. Fagin.' I think it was them words exactly." She sipped loudly at her coffee. "Must've been dreaming."

"I suppose so," Abraham answered.

Slocum poked at the fire with a stick that Abraham had set aside for that purpose. He let it rest in the coals while he found himself a cigarette. When the stick caught fire, he lit up then offered it to Abraham. He did the same. Slocum blew his smoke into the plume that rose from the burgeoning fire and watched it rise together.

"Now that's a curiosity," Slocum said finally. "Used to be a feller named Fagin, Declan Fagin, Irishman. They say in the days my grandfather was young, Declan Fagin. Most people called him Pat for some reason or other, probably 'cause he's Irish. Pat Fagin, the tinker, they called him. He would come through when it warmed up in the spring and then again in the fall, 'fore it got too cold. My Pawpaw use to talk about him some. Said he told the boys dirty jokes and taught 'em limericks. He'd tease their moms and such, sharpen knives and shears, do up their pots and pans. And then he'd disappear. One year he just didn't come back. Some said got too friendly with the wrong woman. Others said it was the boys. Never know, I guess."

"That is curious," Miss Jolly said as she wiggled with interest in the chair she wore.

They looked at Abraham, as if waiting for the details of his dream. Abraham smoked and sipped his coffee. They were all silent for a few moments, until it seemed clear that Abraham had nothing more to say.

"So, the other little feller, Abraham. How'd he fare last night?" Slocum said.

"Alright, I suppose. Considering."

"Yes, yes. I guess he lost about all the friends he had in the world, huh? Besides you anyways. You all been travelling together long?"

"Almost three years." Then after a moment, "What do we know at this point, Sheriff?"

"Well, Miss Jolly's the only one who saw anything. She's the one called us, but they scared her off. Camperman was out mowing on the far side of the trails, across the way there, out by the old school house. She can tell it better'n I can."

As he looked at her, Abraham pondered for an instant whether "Jolly" was a first name, a last name, or something else altogether.

"I can only say what I seen at first, before they fired that big shotgun at me. You can see the holes in our camper where they hit."

She stretched her arm and pointed to her campsite without looking at it. Abraham looked while she spoke and saw the dots that covered the side of the camper.

"They wasn't fooling around. I heard a shot whizzing by, so I got in fast as I could, but the lady on the phone said to try and watch from someplace safe, so I got up in the bed and watched them through the crack in the curtain there. They was all in black. Had t-shirts tied on their heads, you know, like ninja masks or something. They must of come out from through the woods, 'cause that's the way they went when they was done."

"Three of 'em," Slocum added.

"Yes. It was three big men in all black with t-shirt karate

masks. And they come in daylight."

"Little before six. That's when she called."

"Yes. I was getting ready to make Dale some dinner."

"Dale is Camperman. Only she calls him Dale."

"Yes. Dale was mowing, and in the summer he works till seven sometimes. You come and borrowed my bike a bit after lunchtime, and that ornery midget come a couple hours later wanting to borrow some spices for some chicken or something. I think they might have stole one of the Hendrix's chickens down the road. I give him some garlic and Italian seasoning, and that sweet little one waved to me. Then I went and laid down. Next thing I know I hear that ornery one raising a ruckus. I figured he'd just been drinking again, but I heard him say English, and I ain't heard English from him yet. He was yelling all manner of curses and saying he's gonna cut throats out and balls off. And that's when I come out and saw. This one here—"

"Grow-toe," Slocum said.

"Yes. He was nowhere to be seen. And one of them had stuck the sweet one in a burlap sack or a grain sack or something, and the other midget had a butcher knife on the other two. I yelled out for them to cut it out. That's when they shot at me. Near scared me to death. By the time I could see from the bed, they'd tied that sweet one to the tree, only he was lower then, and they was taking turns at him like he's a punching bag. Then they started in with pipes, and beat the poor thing 'til that sack was good and red and dripping out everywhere. The other one, No-no, that's it: he was splayed out on the picnic table, knife still in him."

"Then they went off into the woods," Slocum prompted.

"Just like it was nothing to them. It was still light out for a bit when they was gone. I waited for a bit, just to make sure, then when the Richie got here, I finally come out. By then that Grotto was sitting in the grass, facing that stretch of prairie, rocking back and forth, like this."

She rocked back and forth, though the lawn chair protested. "And he was talking his Italian about his wife or something." "What?" Slocum asked.

"He kept talking about Maria something. Last name with a G. I thought he'd gone crazy."

"Ave Maria gratia plena," Abraham said quietly.

"Yes. That's it!"

"It's Latin. He was praying."

Abraham saw the priest pull into the gravel drive. He waved out the window, and Miss Jolly and Slocum waved back. Abraham watched the black car turn right and make the long circle around the campground.

"So you know nothing else, Sheriff? Who or why?"

"Mr. Abraham, we're working on it. We've got people strung out on that meth shit wanderin' around. We've got some kids thinkin' they's doin' Devil worship in graveyards at night, crucifyin' cats. Had some boys burn down that black feller's barn that moved in out there on Monticello Road. Could be somethin' like that. Could be what they call freak-hunters—had a case of some fellers last year beat the shit out of some clown juggler that come through for Sage City Day. I ask 'em why they done it, and they say freak-huntin'. There's just no tellin'."

Abraham nodded as he walked to the truck to look in on Grotto.

"Grotto? You want breakfast? I'm going into town," he said from the driver-side door.

"La luce," rasped the voice within.

"I'll be back in a bit." Then to Slocum, "So should I clear out?"

"I don't think they're comin' back."

Abraham made his way to the priest's car.

"Hey! Mr. Abraham." It was Slocum. "You got a gun?" he hollered from the fire.

Abraham paused by the open door and shook his head no.

"Might not hurt if you did."

Abraham gave him a little wave and got in.

"Let's go," he said to the priest.

Miss Jolly waved back casually with her fingers. As they drove past the empty playground on the way out of the campground, Abraham realized he was still holding the coffee Miss Jolly had given him and shuddered at the realization that he would have to talk to her again. He set the mug on his knee and dug out a cigarette. He cupped his hands to light it just as the priest braked the car as they approached the shotgunned stop sign on their way out of Friends Creek, and the cup rolled off his leg, hitting the dash. The priest said something about being sorry for his loss. Abraham stared down at the jagged pieces in the floorboard between his big black boots as he blew smoke out the open window.

"It is no problem," the priest said with a dismissive wave of a hand. "You fill them all you like, but cups want to be empty again."

Abraham saw half his face in the passenger-side mirror, smoke trailing from his nostrils, his eyes half-shut, carrying crescent-shaped shadow-bags beneath. He thought he looked like a demon, but he recognized himself.

Chapter 5

"You want to start at the beginning?"

Abraham's voice was harsh and gravelly as it spoke from the priest's miniature tape-recorder next to him, through the wires, and into the headphones he wore as he lay on top of the covers on the thin mattress in Foster's Motel in Monticello. His eyes were closed, and his fingers were laced together on his chest across his cassock, holding the silver crucifix he wore. He had returned from his breakfast with Abraham exhausted. The lost prophet, that was how the priest had begun to think of him, had agreed to the recording without even asking so much as why: why the priest was making such inquiries? why had he been following him? or who had sent him? Maybe, somehow, he knew already. The priest had discovered that, with this man, the rules that govern human dealings did not necessarily bind. Did he know, or did Abraham simply not care? He did not seem to care about anything. He had been gracious with his time, though he had not been friendly. He spoke freely, candidly even, and even agreed to meet again, but he had not been eager to speak. The priest had asked, and he had complied. Nothing more, really, but nothing less.

"Yes," his own voice said.

"The beginning of what?"

"Just answer as you see fit. I have no dog in the fight, yes?" He wanted to see what Abraham would do with the question, to see where his mind would wander, to see how it worked.

"The beginning. Okay. So, when did it all start? Hell. Was there ever a time when things weren't this way? Skewed, bent, divided, discordant, busted? The world or life-force or spirit or energy, whatever you want to call it, is and always has been cutting against itself. You theologians have your own ways of naming it, I'm sure. It's an always already broken egg. And there's a half-formed, mal-formed chick right there in the middle of the mess of ooze and shell. Beginnings are tricky. It probably began in the beginning, however you want to mark that, but it begins again all of the time. Every birth, every rebirth, every recollection, every repetition. It's all implicated. The whole damned world is an abortion in the making, a refusal from the dark of a void or from the womb or from whatever. Things have been heading toward hell since 'Let there be light'. And now who's to blame for that? For breaking the water of the womb, the void, shining a light in there like some overly inquisitive gynecologist, and hollering things into existence, forever ruining that formless whatever-it-was, that pure potential, that ex nihilo, that quiet, that peace. So where did it all start? How do you start there, at the beginning? Of this, this slow annihilation of something real, some real peace? I'm not sure, but our recognition of it, that's another story. One you know too well. It's at least as old as our most ancient and most convincing lies."

The priest could hear, in Abraham's pause, the high hum of his plate being pushed away, the flick of his lighter, the creak of the booth, the sound of his exhalation.

"But I guess you begin to see this rupture, this evil at the heart of things, for yourself at some point too, you know, writ small, within some simple moment in your own life where it begins. But for you. And the perennial question is what the fuck do you do with it? This knowledge or whatever it is? I don't know that I have much of an answer for you there. But I did have such a moment."

He grumbled on: "I knew a kid when I was young, an older boy, maybe he was fifteen when I was ten or twelve, I'm not sure. Leon Pennock. He was always kind of a wild kid. He jumped from the high rocks at the falls. I saw him pay ten dollars to wrestle a muzzled bear at the county fair. He lost his virginity on the school bus. That kind of boy. He happened in to a little sideshow once when the carnival came through our town."

"More coffee?" It was the waitress. The priest could see Abraham's single nod fill the silence. He pictured the swirls of cream Abraham stirred in with the tinkling sound of the spoon on the tape as he continued.

"A kid we called Little Eddie went with him to see the freaks. Little Eddie said the only act they got to see was Sally the Salamander-Lady. She was an armless girl in a glass tank, half-filled with cloudy brown water. Said the whole scene was bleached out under bright floodlights. Her legs were all bent out and around her torso, not a rag to hide her sex. Her head and stump shoulders stood out of the soup, like a felled tree in a low river. Her hair had all been shorn away, and her eyes gaped, and she never blinked. Or maybe she couldn't, I don't know. She breathed through this lit cigar wedged into the topmost corner of her cloven mouth. And she just sat like that in that murky tank, vacant, dead, in her own piss and shit. Only the pulsing light of the cherry on the cigar and its correlating wafts of smoke indicated that the girl was even conscious. It blinked for her, slowly, rhythmically, like a light on an electrical appliance."

The voice paused with another flick of a lighter and the sound of a deep drag.

"Little Eddie said Leon turned into a pillar of salt. He was frozen, staring into the eyes of this misfortunate, amphibious gorgon. Trapped in her gaze. And then he vomited all over himself and the poor bastard in front of him. The Salamander-Lady laughed so hard she lost her cigar in the tank and set into a coughing fit. Leon ran home and shot himself in the temple with a BB gun."

The priest was a little ashamed at hearing the sound of his own laugh. Abraham had not even smiled. He held up his right hand, casually extending a finger, as if to say, "Wait, let me finish," but the priest, recollecting the gesture, recognized it as almost identical to the sign of blessing.

"No one found him for two days. That little pellet had lodged itself in Leon's brain and left him simple. That's what my grand-mother called it. Simple. But it's not that simple. Anything but. The only thing he could talk about now was Sally the Salamander-Lady. He spent his days with crayons drawing pictures of her or singing songs about her, like a toddler sings about the rain. And I'm sure he dreamed of her at night.

"He had to live inside that rupture he'd tried to erase with his BB gun. It pulled him in too. It's like some faint glow of this dismal evil that we only notice on the fringes opened up within him, some BB-sized black hole. And now it's sucking him in inside out. Because now it's his core, his essence. At the time, when I was a kid, this story, that knowledge, was a shock. But now, after so long, it's just tragic poetry. It's myth. But it's Leon's real life. There's no getting around that.

"I had this teacher who used to repeat this cliché: Knowledge is power, knowledge is power, Abraham. Maybe it is and maybe it's not. Me? I've always been drawn to the freaks and the what-have-yous, but for Leon, that run-in with the Salamander-Lady struck him hard with the rupture. It was his beginning. He saw afresh that fractured offness, the skew of the world against itself, what you priests and theologians call its fallenness.

"Leon, more than most even, was attuned to the world with his body, you might put it. I said before that he was wild, and maybe this is what I meant: his navigation of himself in the world was unreflective. Such a travesty as the Salamander-Lady never occurred to him. And until it got the better of him, his repulsion had been contradicted by its opposite. That's the genius of the freak. He could only remain frozen. In this fraught stasis. And in those instants before his insides erupted, he saw the world anew. Like I said, he had a new beginning. He was born again. He saw himself for the first time: who he had been, what he'd taken for granted, what he'd fucked up, what he'd done right, who he thought he was. His identity, or whatever you want to call it. And through the Salamander-Lady, he saw all of that negated, just like in logic or linguistics. He thought he was Leon, but now he must forever see himself as not-Leon, as Leon-crossed-out, as an abortion of the self he thought he was. Now that, as they say, is a hard pill to swallow."

There was silence. Just the noise of the breakfast hour in the diner. The sound of coffee being poured, of Abraham lighting his cigarette, and of the priest lighting his own.

"And you," his own voice said. "What about you? You have swallowed such a pill, yes?"

"Me? For me it's always seemed that way. My first memories are despairing ones. Most of the earliest ones are like fuzzy photographs. You know, moments hazed with vague yearnings that I can't otherwise name or place. Like images from a long-gone dream. My mother's face, washed in blues and purples, like it was bruised in watercolors. There are tears, or maybe they're not tears. Maybe she'd been out in the rain or in the shower. Her eyes are swollen. Her face misshapen. The whole day is washed-out grays, blues, reds, violets. And then there's panic, and everything is fast, and I'm crying, and then she's crying. She's really crying this time, hard. I hear her sobbing. Like a wounded animal. And then it's dark. I can't get out of it. I try but I can't. I lay down in the dark and think about my mother's wounded face. And I guess I fall asleep."

"That's your first memory?"

"That's one of two. Two sequences. They're braided together. I don't know which is first. But that's my beginning."

"My God..." And he heard himself say something else, but it was undecipherable and he couldn't remember what it was. And then, "And the other?"

"My mother's in the other one too. In infancy it all runs together, you know? But just a year later I can conjure like a shaman, anything, everything. But in the other one she's holding me up before a mirror, standing me on a counter-top. I can feel its cold on my feet. I look at her, then at her mimicked image, and back, and again, and again. And I see me there too. Out there. She looks the same in the glass and in the flesh. She's smiling. Her hair kind of bobs around and tickles my skin. She's pretty and funny. She's all of this when I see the her on the wall and when I turn to see the her behind me. They seem identical, doubles.

"But the mirror-me is all turned around. Now, I know, of course, that the mother in the mirror had to have been the normally inverted mirror image of her, but in my memory it's the other me that's different. That's what I notice anyway. He's like me, but he's not me because I am. He smiles and I don't feel I'm doing it. He waves his arms and laughs, but I'm only giggling a little. The other me is making my mother laugh and coo, and she hugs me close. But she's doing it because of the mirror-me, because of him, because she loves him. She's talking to him. And I feel whatever the infantile equivalent to resentment is. Hell, it's probably just resentment, but, you know, to call it precisely that would be anachronistic, since I didn't have that word for it yet. But you see what I'm getting at. She tells him, 'My heart beats for you.' I remember those words. Those are the first words for me. Then, 'My cup runneth over.'

"I saw him in the mirror. He wasn't the same as me. He was freer, happier. He made my mother laugh and smile. His movements were smooth. Everything I had been striving to do, simple things, he was already doing. I fucking hated him. But now I began to see him all of the time. Anywhere I was I could find him. When I could finally hoist myself up onto a chair, I began sneaking up on him with my grandpa's big black army flashlight."

Again, he heard his own little chuckle interrupt. But within they grey of his beard, Abraham had not laughed or smiled. He only waited until the priest was done.

"Within only fifteen or twenty minutes I had shattered every glass where I saw him smiling back. I would look each time at the mosaic of shards left on the floor. Here a light fixture. There the dark of my ear. Over there my right eye. Over here my knee. All a little specked with blood from my hand. Plenty of blank, dull grey glass, the mirrored side to the floor. Reflecting nothing. Reflecting blanks. Like the X's, you see? Abraham-crossed-out, this is not-Abraham. 'This is where Abraham is not,' it seemed to say. And that comforted me in a way."

The priest quickly moved his hand to the recorder and clicked it off. He pulled off the headphones and laid them on the bedside table. He turned off the lamp, sighed, and wiped the tears from his eyes. He could take no more.

* * *

The priest dined alone that evening at a little café on the Monticello square. It was busy, and he felt that it did him some good to be around normal people going about their lives. He was seated by a tall window that looked out on the sidewalk, and past that, the street, and the courthouse beyond. Teenagers cruised in pointless circles or sat in the grass, some smoking, some kissing, some laughing, some with ice-cream cones from the Dairy Queen on the adjacent street. Cops cruised about as frequently. They stopped and chatted up the kids. He even noticed the cop Abraham had cursed at the night before, radar-gunning a kid on his bike. They both seemed impressed by the boy's speed. It all seemed very quaint. It was a pleasant evening, the sun still warm through the glass of the window, as it slowly bid goodbye to the cloudless blue sky and kissed the flat of the countryside, far out, beyond the outskirts of the town. He sipped his coffee as the dusky grey set in and the street lights came on outside.

The waitress brought his half-chicken, rice pilaf, green beans, and baked apples. She spoke to him in a high, breathy, flirty voice. She was probably still in high school.

"So, my friend and me have a bet. I say you're a priest. She says not. You wanna settle it for us?"

"You win, my dear."

"I knew it. But you're not from here are you? Cause I go to Saint Philomena's, and Father Patrick's the only priest I ever seen there."

"Right again."

"You know Father Patrick? He's a real good priest. He's real sweet? I bet you're his boss or something. You ain't from the bishop's office are you?"

"I am afraid your luck is at an end. I am just passing through. On a vacation of sorts."

"Do you have to wear them clothes on vacation too? Father Patrick's usually in a polo when I seen him outside of church."

"It is easier this way. Less risk of falling out of fashion, yes?"

"I never thought of it that way. Well, you enjoy your meal. I didn't mean to keep you."

"Not at all. The pleasure is mine."

The girl disappeared around the corner of the high back of the opposite side of the booth, and he started in on the apples. He forked in a couple of bites as he watched the silent scene play on the street. The girl's head reappeared above him from behind his side of the booth and startled him a little. He smiled sheepishly with a mouthful of apples.

"You're European, aren't you?"

He chewed for a minute. "You have got me." It wasn't a lie; he had lived in Europe, but he did not want this to drag out unnecessarily.

"Well, you've got a real pretty accent. Real exotic-sounding."

He placed his hand on his chest. "You are too kind."

She smiled at him and disappeared again. He picked at the rice a little. It was overcooked and dry; the beans were fair; the chicken was under-seasoned and also quite dry. He ate it all anyway, with several cups of coffee. The girl kept appearing unexpectedly and disappearing, only to reappear again with more coffee or a question about France or about the church. He was sipping coffee, smoking a cigarette, when he felt her hovering just over his shoulder again.

"I think I will have a piece of pie," he said, mostly before turning, and just as the word "pie" left his mouth, he realized he was not speaking to the girl.

"I think I will have a piece of pie, too." It was Slocum. "Mind if I join you, priest?"

"Not at all."

"Hey, Jenny," Slocum hollered out. She appeared suddenly from behind the priest.

"Well, hello there, Sheriff. You want a special?"

"No ma'am. Trudy cooked some god-awful meatloaf tonight, sweetie. I may become a vegetarian." She laughed a little too hard. "But the priest and I would like a slice of pie. You got cherry?"

"Sure do, Sheriff."

"Well, I'll have a cherry, and, the priest here will have, what kinda pie you want?"

"Cherry sounds good to me."

"And another cherry for the padre. And I want a cup of coffee too, sweetheart."

"You got it, Sheriff." And she was gone.

"Jenny!" Slocum bellowed.

She reappeared, smiling, with her mouth open a little.

"I'd like mine a la mode." He looked at the priest and raised his eyebrows in wordless question. Jenny looked at him, though without actually asking anything or changing her expression.

"Yes, of course. A la mode," the priest said with a chuckle. And Jenny disappeared again.

"Well, I tell you, my friend, it has been a crazy day, what, with all the killin' and whatnot." Slocum sighed, peering out the window. His eyes were bloodshot and puffy.

"Do they know? Your townspeople?"

"Oh, yes. They know. Just don't change 'em none. Gives 'em somethin' to get excited about. I guaran-damn-tee you that's what them kids are goin' on about right now."

"Talking about the dwarves?"

"Well, probably not. I don't know that that news has travelled too far, 'cept by my own men, and I told them to keep it quiet as possible. But even if it has, they was outsiders, and midgets to boot. Freaks to these folks. If that story's out, it's bound to be a punchline or some such shit. These folks seem real nice, but most of 'em are assholes, like anywhere else. There's a treasured few, but most of 'em ain't worth much, morally speakin'."

Jenny brought the pie and coffee and left. Slocum worked with his fork to get equal parts pie and ice cream and took a bite.

"Ooo. Now that's a damn good piece of cherry pie." He savored it before sipping at the coffee. He waited while the priest tried his.

"Yes. A fine pie indeed." The pie wasn't bad, but he wanted to be polite.

"Nah, what they're talkin' about is the girl." The kids across the street laughed. "Ever notice that folks take pleasure in watchin' good people suffer?"

"The girl?"

"Yes, the one killed same night as those poor midget boys."

"Yes, of course. Did you know her?"

"Oh yes, everyone did. She's a real sweet girl. She's from one of the finest families round here. The Meadows. They've been round here since the county come up, 'bout as long as the Piatts. Nice folks. Bill, everybody calls him Bull—he's in farmin' and few other things. Audra, his wife, now, she passed away few years back 'cause some accident. Yes, and then there's Barbara Meadows. Everybody called her Barbie. She's a sweet little girl. Now, she was simple, mentally retarded, slow or whatever the hell is the proper word. I can't keep up. But there wasn't a sweeter soul. She's just like a little child."

"And how old was she?"

"Oh, she's eighteen or so, I think. It's a real curious case. That's what I wanted to talk to you about, priest."

"I am not sure I understand."

Slocum paused, knotting up his browline, frowning a little, his mustache, drizzled with ice cream and pie filling, and turned down around the corners of his mouth. He wiped his mustache with the cloth napkin from his lap, and pushed his plate to the middle of the table so he could rest his elbows on the edge.

"I told you I thought them murders was related, you remember? And I been turnin' the whole mess over most of the mornin', and I think I found a link. And I think it explains some things I been perplexin' about. Thought you might be able to help me."

"I will do what I can."

"You see, it's your friend, Abraham. Somethin' ain't quite right with him, that's clear as day, and he didn't act too mournful 'bout them dead midgets neither. Not even that poor mess in the bag. I'm sure he told you 'bout that."

"Well, no. You mean the bag that was hanging from the tree?"

"You see. That strikes me as mighty peculiar. I won't never get over the sight of that poor boy, left a mess of flesh in a bag, like he's a sack full of cats in the fast lane on the interstate. That's a human life in that bag. Hard to believe. I ain't cried since my first wife passed to cancer, twenty years now. And I ain't ashamed to tell you, I wept at that sight, priest. I wept 'cause I'm human."

"Yes, yes. Of course. My God."

"But your friend Abraham, who's a friend to that boy. Nothin'. Not a tear. Not a word. Stone face under that beard. Now, I looked close for somethin', somethin' small even. Hell, I wanted to find even some whisper of anguish, and I ain't seen nothin'. Now that concerns me."

"Yes. I see your point, Mr. Slocum."

"I guess, since you're his friend, I'm lookin' for an explanation.

'Cause he's the only connection I've got, and I've got the suspicion, it's gut level granted, that that means somethin'."

"Look, I feel I must explain myself first. I know Abraham well, quite well actually, but from the outside, yes?"

"I'm not sure I'm readin' you."

"This may sound strange, but I am only permitted by those on whose behalf I am here to say so much. So what I tell you, I tell you in confidence, yes?

"Okay, priest, but I've got a pretty damn serious investigation under way."

"Of course, and I will help any way I can, but there are limits imposed upon me by my superiors."

"Alright, for now. Shoot." Slocum leaned forward and rested his chin on his folded hands.

"It has been my job for some months now to, well, keep track of Abraham's movements, to look into his past, to figure out the extent of his ministry." The priest put the last word in quotation marks in the space in front of him with the first two fingers on his hands. "But until yesterday, my research has been under cover, yes?" He made the same gesture as he said "under cover."

"But isn't he just a Bible-story actor or somethin'?"

"Well, yes and no."

"Has he caused some kind of trouble?"

"Again, yes and no."

"Well, damn it. You're not helpin' me much."

"I will say more. To your first question. Abraham is not *just* anything. He has been a Bible-story actor, as you say, but you must not let the banality of his occupation detract from what he is."

"You lost me."

"Abraham is peculiar, as you say. But he is also special. He seems to have certain gifts which are difficult to understand. I do not fully understand them yet. That is the goal of my investigation."

"So, you're sayin' this is maybe why he ain't normal actin'."

"Precisely."

"Fair enough. Now what kind of trouble he been in?"

"I do not think I am overstepping my commitments to tell you that Abraham tends to leave in his wake confusion. Things become unsettled in the places he has been. His Bible stories seem silly but they change people, and this is not always welcome."

"You mean like some damn evangelist?"

"Not exactly." He paused. "I don't think I can say more."

"Well, that ain't much, priest." He shook his head slowly and squinted out the window. "That ain't much at'all."

"Now you said Abraham was your connection between the scene at the campground and the murder of the Meadows girl?"

"I've spent the day findin' out where all she been, tryin' to get a timeline down. I've got witnesses put 'em together at the Methodist church. Say she come down and spoke to him after his play was through."

"That was the girl who was murdered?"

"You was there?"

"Yes. I saw that moment. But, and I am no policeman, Mr. Slocum, that seems rather scanty evidence for anything like a motive, yes?"

"No, you're right, on that count. But that's a connection, and that's what's got my gut workin'."

"Yes, but Mr. Slocum, that was a public performance. The exchange between them was no more than a moment or two."

"That's true enough. But I don't understand two things." Slocum righted himself against the hard back of the booth. "What'd he talk about to a retarded girl that don't talk none? And why'd Camperman tell me he seen Barbie Meadows comin' out of that ice-cream truck some time later and sittin' by the campfire with Abraham and them midgets?"

The priest lowered his eyebrows and brought them together, making creases between his sharp, blue eyes. He rubbed his beard.

Slocum spoke again after a moment. His words were quiet, bitter, and hard. "So what am I to think, priest? Am I supposed to ignore it? 'Cause you say he's real special someways?" He stared on at the priest.

"Look," the priest began, gently, "I have no answer to this, but I will try to help. He has willingly agreed to help me with my investigation. To talk with me. I will find out what I can." They were quiet then, both looking at the kids who were left across the street, smoking under the lamppost. "I would just ask that you not make your mind up yet."

"That's a hard sell, priest," Slocum said, "'cause damn near every time a case of somethin' like that gets reported, you know what I find?" The priest knew where this was going. He said nothing, but he didn't look away either. "Some fuckin' pervert," Slocum said, a little too loudly. He looked around, and this time he spoke quietly, leaning in over the table. "And you know who it was the last time?"

"I do not," the priest said, matching his volume.

"The fuckin' priest at Saint Philomena's. And before that?"

The priest shook his head no.

"Pastor at the Church of the Nazarene. And before that a school teacher in the middle school. So can you tell me who's more *special* than a child? You think your friend Abraham is?"

"No," the priest said. "No."

The priest peered blankly out the window again, at the teenagers gathered on the square. One of them said something he couldn't hear, and they all shook with laughter.

* * *

Abraham had spent the afternoon attempting to repair the wobble in Miss Jolly's bicycle with some tools borrowed from Camperman. When he thought that he had made some headway, he took the cruiser out for a test drive along the tar roads that led away from Friends Creek. As he pedaled along, he thought about the breakfast with the priest that morning. He thought about beginnings, how this sojourn, this interruption, in the middle of Illinois, had begun to seem like the beginning of something, the end of something, but also a repetition of something past, and a premonition of what was coming, all rolled together. He had spoken openly of the past to the priest. He had decided that if the past was going to infiltrate his present, he would welcome it. He would court it. He would provoke it, and dive headlong into whatever came to him. He would chase his whims and memories through the priest's cloaked inquiries and dig down into the heart of whatever designs the past had on him. He would crucify time itself, pin it down in the intersection of past and future, and get to the bottom of whatever the hell the world had in store for him.

Abraham rode past the fields, and a gentle breeze came over the corn and tousled his hair and beard. Sunset was still an hour or so off, but the sky had darkened some to a blue-grey, touched here and there, on the horizon, with pink and orange, and a few cumulus tufts hung in the sky, merging, then pulling apart, like lumps in a lava lamp. He rode past the only farmhouse on that stretch of road between the campground and the stop sign. He saw some livestock grazing behind the fence and a man working near the faded red barn in the pasture, back behind the house. The man stuck his shovel in the ground and waved vigorously. Abraham waved back as he continued riding on up to the cross-roads where the stop sign was. Then he turned the bike in a gentle half-circle and headed back the direction he had come.

When he approached the farmhouse this time, though, he noticed the man with the shovel standing on the roadside, one hand on the shovel, the other waving a pair of leather gloves. Abraham looked behind him. There was no one.

"Whoa there, young fella," the man bleated. He wasn't much older than Abraham. He wore soiled denim overalls without a shirt, and the aroma of fresh manure wafted in the breeze from his boots. "Whoa there," he said again.

Abraham brought the bike to a stop and put a leg down but didn't dismount.

"Hello," Abraham said.

"Good evening. It surely is a fine evening for a bicycle ride, wouldn't you say?"

It was a reasonable observation. "It certainly is."

"But, alas, sunset approaches, my good man, and there is work yet unfinished."

"Okay," Abraham replied. And he lifted his foot to the upturned pedal.

"No, sir! Please! I have yet one task I must complete 'afore dark, and I fear I haven't the strength to do it alone. I am asking for your help, my good man. I can pay you for your time and your precious toil. But the task needs be done, else the corpse draw coyotes at nightfall."

"I see. So you need some help digging a hole then?"

"Yes, indeed. And moving the beast down within. Now, I can spread the lye and cover her over, but I am an old man, and my days as a digger of holes are behind me, and my sons have gone thither to live in the city. Would you be so kind?"

The man grimaced weakly and puffed out his cheeks as he frowned. Abraham thought he might cry.

"I can pay you. I have not the wealth of a rich man, but I done alright."

"Okay. I'm set for cash, but I'll help. You got another shovel?"

"Yes, of course!"

The man smiled and bounded back through the pasture, stomping piles of shit left and right, to the barn. Abraham followed, though making his own path, and found the man, the extra shovel, and the dead beast near the hole the man had started close to the barn.

Abraham peered over at the beast. It buzzed with a flurry of insects. It rested among the piles of animal shit. "What the hell is that?"

"Why that's Petunia." The man said it as though Abraham should already have known.

They worked at the hole for a time. Abraham would catch glimpses of the beast now and then, as he shoveled the dirt into a pile outside the hole. It looked like a small horse or maybe a discolored donkey or a mule, but it wasn't so thickly built as either of these. It also resembled a goat or maybe a llama, but it seemed far too tall.

He tried again, "So what species of creature is Petunia there?"

"Oh, well she is quite dead. You can smell her." And the man took a few deep sniffs, inclining his head in the beast's direction. He shook himself. "Dreadful. She bore the affliction of a defection of birth."

Once he got down inside the hole to dig deeper, Abraham could no longer see the creature. He had given up trying to get more out of the man. After all, the old man was right. Whatever else she was, Petunia was dead. He had smelled it too. So what difference did it make?

The old man turned on the floodlights that hung on the side of the barn when it got darker and busied himself moving the black earth Abraham dug out from the pit into a single pile.

"Alright, my good sir," he said finally, "I think that will suffice."

Abraham looked up at him from the small, dark cave he had dug out beside the barn and nodded. He climbed out of the grave.

"You, sir, are stronger than a bull." He looked at Abraham as though he were proud of him. "And a fine digger."

Abraham did not say anything.

"I suppose the time is ripe to drag her in," the old man said.

He grabbed a wooden chair from inside the barn, near a tool bench, and dragged it outside. He stood on the seat of it and adjusted one of the floods with a gloved hand so that it shone on the corpse. Abraham approached it and inspected it carefully. It was unlike any creature he had ever seen.

Its fur was matted, filthy white, though it had a darker silver stripe that ran the length of each side, down to the haunches, at least of the side that was upturned. Its snout was shaped like a donkey's, with a snub nose, but the upper regions and lusterless open eyes had the wild look of a goat. The beast was the size of a small pony, but its body was built like a goat, thin and wiry, except for its ample belly, which, in its prostrate position on the ground, bulged in the air like the broad side of a sack of feed. Its head rested in some horse shit. Abraham pulled the neck of his undershirt up over his mouth and nose and leaned in over the head. Mostly hidden in the creature's own shadow from the lights behind, between its body and the side of the barn, he saw a single horn, filthy white, like its coat, that twisted once and protruded crookedly out from the center of its head, just above the eyes.

"You ready?" the man asked.

Abraham nodded.

"Would you be so kind as to drag the head around this way? Then we shall roll her in with greater ease."

Abraham squatted behind where the corpse's mane flowed out into the grass and considered where he should grab.

"Now, she is in a place beyond pain. She's dead," the man said encouragingly. "So if you hear something crack or pop out, you just go on pulling. Gentleness is a virtue, but one wasted on a corpse."

Abraham grabbed the front of the neck with his gloved hands but failed to find a grip that worked. The rot stench was getting strong. He pulled off the gloves and tossed them against the side of the barn, where they fell near the wooden chair.

"Okay, Petunia," he said. "Be a good girl."

He stroked her head between the ears, and then it happened.

The corpse became a cataclysm. The beast shook violently, kicking its legs, rearing its head, writhing finally to its hooves. The top of its skull butted Abraham's forehead, knocking his hat off and into the open grave, where Abraham also fell after stumbling back a few of drunken steps.

He woke an instant later. He held his palm to his head. The knock from the unicorn had opened his old wound, and he was bleeding again. The old man stood frozen next to the grave, his hand still gripping the shovel. He shrieked in a high animal squeal over and over and over. Abraham climbed out of the grave and beheld the unicorn in the bright of the floods in all its twisted, bulging majesty. She shook herself and bellowed out some near-equine moan and then started grazing. The old man shrieked on.

"Hey," Abraham said after a few minutes.

The shrieking continued.

"Hey!"

Its rhythm slowed, but the shrieking went on.

"Shut up!" Abraham roared.

Petunia looked up. The man shrieked once more and came around.

"What in all fuck?" the man said. "What in the world?" And then he shrieked four or five more times.

Abraham waited.

He shut up finally, and there was a moment of calm.

"I've got to be going. Okay?" Abraham said.

"What in all fuck?" was the reply. The old man's eyes were as wide as silver dollars.

Abraham handed him the shovel, and the old man took it, still staring at Abraham.

He got Miss Jolly's cruiser, walked it through the tall grass, back out to the street, and rode off into the night.

After a few minutes, he heard an arrhythmic, knocking clomp building from behind him. He pulled to the side of the road and stopped in the gravel there. The unicorn galloped clumsily, then trotted, and stopped near him, making its horrible sound. He patted it on the head.

"No, no. Come on."

He led Petunia back home. The old man still had not moved. Abraham led the unicorn back into the pasture. He waved a goodbye to the old man, who did not reciprocate.

This sequence repeated itself two more times.

Finally, Abraham said to the old man, "Look, you want to tie her up or something?"

"Take her. Just take her away," he whispered.

Abraham rode off again, Petunia at his side, the old man bawling tears of confusion somewhere in the distance from the pasture.

Chapter 6

There was a woman down by the pond, and the stench from her rose in the heat from the sun. It was late in the morning but already hot. She was dressed in skins, and flowers, feathers, and rough-hewn jewelry were tucked into her clothes and were scattered around. Most of the flowers had wilted. There were trees all around, sycamore, walnut, and a big white oak stood right down near the water, its thick roots reaching down beneath the surface. A dark man approached, his details obscured by the bright sun, from the far side of the pond. He was little more than a shadow. The shadow-man kneeled beside her and said something that never ended. Was it a song? Some kind of chant? He placed a child in the space between her arm and her breast. It seemed to sleep. The shadow-man dug a wide, shallow hole. Whatever words he intoned didn't stop, but they rose and fell with the strains of his labor. The sun moved slowly through the blank blue sky. Sounds of insects hummed along, birdsong intermittent. Time passed with the sounds of his work, his song, the world around. Then the child woke, and the shadow-man sat it on the ground near the hole, pulled the woman into the earthen womb, and mounded moist, dark dirt over her brown skin. Flower petals scattered, and some blew off with a hot wind. The song went on.

Things changed. The insects hummed, birdsong intermittent. The water grew and now it moved. The moving brown water rolled wide between thick forest on either side, high weeds and shrubs tucked beneath them. The song was gone. The sun returned to morning. A lone broad walnut tree grew from an island in the center. The water cut around it and puddled in the green grasses there beneath the tree. Two white men waded out, then swam a little, a long saw binding them. They emerged on the green island

and spoke in voices muffled by distance, by sounds of the water. They moved with the rhythm of the saw. Tree flesh came away like flakes of snow and fell softly in the summer air which carried the perfume of the wound. The sun moved slowly through the blank blue sky. A cracking came like thunder. The tree fell across the water. Its high branches splintered against the hard earth on the banks where the undergrowth gave. The bug hum stopped. The birds flew away. Horses screamed. Then all was quiet for a while, except the water. The men's distant voices chirped. They made their way across the trunk, the saw shouldered between them. They jumped down. One man said something, his voice rough, his words lost still. The other man spat. "Coffin tree," he said. And then they went back to work. A lone cricket tested the air with its legs. Then they all started to sing with the sound of the saw. The sawdust scattered, and some blew off with a hot wind. The song went on.

Things changed. There was no water, but a sea of prairie waved for miles and rolled its golden tides in wind, islands of trees here and there, their leaves shivering silently under the high sun in a blank blue sky. A handful of bodies stood in cut grass that lay long in brown clumps on the turf. A long box stood above it in their midst. A man stood near it. He wasn't young. His hand rested on it, and sometimes he rubbed the box with its grain. The only sound was the wind. The only smell was the wind. Men held their hats, their hair blowing around, their foreheads and necks reddening in the sun. Women's long dark dresses billowed. They hid their hair in black bonnets. A black-cassocked man went near the box, a black book tucked beneath his wing. He patted the shoulder of the man near the box and spoke into his ear. Then he strode on and faced the small stand of mourners. He spoke, but his words were lost in the wind, nulled, as blank as the sky. Though his mouth worked at words, there was only wind. The sun moved slowly in the blank blue above. Two children wandered near a deep hole and played in the mound of dark earth beside. A gray stone had been planted to mark the spot. "Mrs. Ezra Meadows" was chiseled in block letters near the top. Two lines followed: one said, "Wife, mother," and the other was a spread of thirty-five years. One child lay down on the pile near the stone. A woman scolded, her correction lost in the wind. Four men moved to the corners of the box, where there were ropes, after the man in the cassock mimed out a cross. They all followed the box a few yards to the grave. The men bent, their arms working in rhythm, and the box disappeared into the earth. They threw in the ropes. Then they all sang together as each one passed by and scattered earth into the grave. Even the children. The dirt scattered, and some blew off in the hot wind. The song went on.

The pond again, at night, in autumn, trees half-naked. The shadow-man is gone and his song. The child is gone. The wind is dead. The earth cries out, the bones beneath it. The water is still. Two figures lay their rifles by and dig into the mound. They find her, her bones. They take the jewelry. They take what they want.
Can these bones live?
One brings the butt of his rifle down, hard, on her spine.
Prophesy upon these bones.
He takes her skull away. Wolves call out, long.
Coyotes scrap and play. A bullfrog moans.
Prophesy upon these bones.
The dark shapes speak in children's voices.
Can these bones live?
They disappear back into the black trees.
The earth cries out. The bones cry out.
The wind blusters through.
Leaves fall, dead, upon the bones.
There is nothing. There is the dead.
The moon shines like the back of a skull.

Prophesy upon these bones.
There is nothing. The wind is dead, and there is nothing.
And there is no breath in them.

Abraham pulled away, within himself. It had become too much. He strained within to back away from whatever door had cracked open between himself and the world, to grasp the dark, to hoist himself away from the grave, and, finally, he again felt the wind. Everything was silence in its void-sound. It did not drown it out with roaring; it cancelled it, with nothing. He coiled himself within it. He drank it in.

* * *

"Abraham!" It was the priest. He had parked near the pavilion and walked into the campsite in the grass alongside the gravel drive. There was no fire this night. He heard Grotto cooing to some large beast on the other side of the ice-cream truck. He was stroking its snout from a stool in the grass. In the faint haze cast by the moon, they looked like one tangled creature.

Abraham came down, stepping lightly, near where his hat lay, onto the seat of the picnic table by the fire pit. The knot on his head had returned and was bleeding a little.

"My God! I thought you had hanged yourself."

"Why would I do that?" Abraham said.

The priest started, "Up there. My God! And the tree behind, and these shadows." He didn't know what else to say.

"Keep your voice down," Abraham said calmly. "You don't want to wake Miss Jolly. We'd never get rid of her."

"What is that thing over there with Grotto? Did you get a horse?" He closed the distance between them so he could speak more quietly.

Abraham rubbed his beard for a couple of seconds. "No. She followed me home a couple of times. She's not a horse. That's

Petunia. She and Grotto have become friends."

"I wanted to see about doing another interview." This was true, but he had not come for this reason. He was unsure why he had come. But the shock of the scene he had found had not left him, and he felt he needed to say something mundane, if for no other purpose than to calm himself.

"Sure. Tomorrow morning?"

"Of course. The diner again, by my motel, yes?" He was still panting.

"Yes."

The priest huffed a little more. "May I sit for a moment? I just. . ." he said, but he did not go on.

Abraham gestured towards the picnic table with one hand while the other found a cigarette in his shirt pocket. He offered the pack to the priest. Abraham lit up with long wooden kitchen match, holding the fire out behind his cupped hand to the priest after. They sat and smoked and listened to the sounds of the woods and the gentle noises between Grotto and the beast. The quiet and the cigarette had done the priest some good. He breathed more easily, and finally, relaxed with a faint tremulous sigh.

"Do you know Italian?" Abraham asked after a moment.

"Well enough. I am better with Spanish and French, but I am conversant in Italian."

"Do you know if there's a monastery in Monte Casino?"

"There certainly is, yes."

"Listen, Grotto understands English but doesn't speak it, and I'm no good with Italian, but I think that's what he's been talking about."

"I can talk to him."

"Grotto," Abraham called gently.

"Eh?"

"Come here a minute, will you?"

They heard him baby-talk to Petunia reassuringly in his native tongue before he limped around the front of the ice-cream truck.

"Mmm?" he grunted.

"The priest understands Italian. Will you tell him about Monte Casino? He'll tell me, and we'll see if we can help you."

Grotto sat down in a child's canvas lawn chair. He crossed the back of one knee over the top of the other and stared in their direction. His mouth hung open, his tongue lolling to one side.

"You want to go to Italy, yes?" the priest asked him.

"Monastero di Monte Casino."

"Ah, to the monastery. It is a nice place. I have been there. But why Monte Casino?"

"Mio fratello c'è."

"His brother is at the monastery."

Abraham nodded.

"Is he a monk?" the priest asked.

"Si. Giardiniere," Grotto rasped.

The priest explained to Abraham, "His brother is a monk and he works in the gardens."

"You want to leave because of what happened to No-no and Eco?" Abraham said.

Grotto's gaze seemed to focus on neither of them any longer, "Si. Sono cresciuto stanco."

Abraham looked at the priest.

"He says he has become tired," the priest said.

"Si," Grotto said again.

"It appears he wants to leave you and go back home, Abraham."

Abraham gazed at Grotto for a moment. He gave him a small smile. "Okay, Grotto. Okay."

Grotto looked at Abraham now. His face was serious. "Si non sono male." He paused. "Un po' di un asino." Grotto uncrossed his legs and rose from the chair. He went back to where Petunia had gone to graze on the edge of the prairie. He fetched his stool along the way.

"He says you're not a bad man, Abraham." The priest

chuckled a little. "You're just kind of an ass."

"That's kind of him to say," Abraham said. The priest chuckled again.

"Oh, I've been meaning to offer to do a funeral mass for your other two friends. Mr. Slocum says the coroner's office is planning on burying them as wards of the state, which means cremation, a mass grave, and a name on a plaque. He doesn't know what else to do. He says they can be released to you for burial, though, for a casket fee. I took the liberty of opting for the latter. I hope that was okay."

"Yeah. That's good of you."

"There's a little hill on the other side of Cisco. Croninger Cemetery it is called. I can make some inquiries, yes?"

"Okay. We'll talk tomorrow."

Abraham headed to the truck. As he gripped the handle, the priest spoke again.

"Abraham?"

Abraham opened the door and reached in to lower his cot. "Yeah?"

"Your hat?" the priest said after a brief silence.

"It'll be alright there."

He stepped up into the truck.

The priest spoke again. "Before. . . ? When I first arrived. . . ?"

"Yeah?"

"I am sorry. When I arrived. Before?" He was unsure of how to go on. "Never-mind. No, never-mind. . . Goodnight."

Abraham waved a hand, disappeared, and pulled the door to.

The priest made his way through the dark back to his car. He wasn't sure what to think or where his thoughts should even begin. How do you tell a man, especially a man like Abraham, how do you tell him that you saw him suspended in the moonlight, like Barlach's Floating Angel, raised up in the mist, hovering above the ground, below the mid-branches?

How do you ask such a man if what you saw was real?

Chapter 7

"Long ago and far from here an old king died. His only son, the prince, was crowned soon thereafter, and he became ruler of the land. His first act as the new king was to tour his country, to survey what his father had done, and his father before him, and so on. For the new king deeply desired to be a great ruler, one who was loved by his people. He wished to be remembered as a good king. So, his men prepared the horses and the royal coaches, gathered the necessary provisions, and they set out to make their tour.

"What he found dismayed him. The people did not love his father, and they did not love him. They worked doggedly for what little they had. They struggled to pay their taxes to the king. They kept the laws, but not because they thought them just. They kept them only out of fear for their lives and liberty. 'No,' the king said to himself, 'they do not love me.' He thought, in his innermost heart, that, had they the chance, his people would surely murder him and live like animals. 'This is not good,' the king said to himself, but he did not know where to begin his reforms. He returned to the castle in great despair.

"One night after a great feast, the jester entered the dining hall. The bells shook on the ass's ears he wore, as he tramped in and made a ridiculous genuflection before the king. 'I have no use for laughter today,' the king said, 'for I am in great despair.' 'I have come not to annoy,' the jester said, 'but turn your great despair to joy.' The jester shook and danced with excitement. 'What game is this? Do go away,' the king said. ''Tis no game, sire,' the jester said, 'No, 'tis most grave. For I have found a magic cave, a cave where deepest dreams come true, for everyone, not just for you. But your dreams must first be pure, for whims and fancies can't endure, else others suffer your manure.' The jester laughed and danced again. His bells echoed throughout the hall.

"So with the jester's help, the king found the greatest men of the land. He wished to find among them one who, with his pure desire, could enter the magic cave and bring true happiness to all in the kingdom. So, his men prepared the horses and the royal coaches, gathered the necessary provisions, and they set out, the Rich Man, the Holy Man, the Philosopher, the Judge, and a Dead Man among them, to find the magic cave. The jester mounted his ass and led the way with the sound of bells.

"The king was happy, for with the magic cave he would bring true happiness to his people, and he would forever be remembered as a great king.

"They arrived at the hill where the jester had found the magic cave and made their way to the small passage that led within. The cave was filled with darkness. Each man received instructions, and then they drew straws to see who would enter first. The king's first knight was given the task of riding to the nearest village after each great man had entered the cave, and then of riding back again to report the change in the kingdom.

"The Rich Man entered first and, after a time, came out. The knight reported no change. 'Rich Man,' the king said, 'you were chosen that you might bring great prosperity to my people. Of what did you dream?' 'Sire,' said the Rich Man, 'I could only dream of luxury.' And the jester danced and shook his bells.

"The Holy Man entered next and, after a time, came out. The knight reported no change. 'Holy Man,' the king said, 'you were chosen that you might bring piety and Christian brotherhood to my people. Of what did you dream?' 'Sire,' said the Holy Man, 'I could dream only of sainthood.' And the jester danced and shook his bells.

"The Philosopher entered third and, after a time, came out. The knight reported no change. 'Philosopher,' the king said, 'you were chosen that you might bring wisdom and knowledge to my people. Of what did you dream?' 'Sire,' said the Philosopher, 'I could dream only of being wiser than Solomon, Plato, and all of the ancients.' And the jester danced and shook his bells.

"Then the Judge entered and, after a time, came out. The knight reported no change. 'Judge,' the king said, 'you were chosen that you might bring order and justice to my people. Of what did you dream?' 'Sire,' said the judge, 'I could dream only of being king.' And the jester danced. 'And of women,' the Judge added. And the jester laughed and shook his bells.

"Finally, the time came for the Dead Man to enter the magic cave. The knight was poised upon his horse. The jester readied his bells. The king scratched beneath his crown. 'Tell me, Dead Man, of what do you dream?' 'Nothing,' said the Dead Man, 'for I am dead.' The jester laughed. The king tried a different path, 'What has death taught you?' he asked. The Dead Man thought. He answered thus: 'Prosperity should be spread to all. Piety and brotherhood warms men's hearts. Knowledge and wisdom keeps their heads cool. Order and justice make men kind.' 'And what of the dreams of these others?' the king asked the Dead Man. He answered thus: 'Luxury is fleeting. Sainthood is corrupt. Wise men are foolish. And kings are stupid.' The jester laughed.

"The king cleared his throat in irritation. 'Very well,' he said, 'Now you may enter the magic cave.' The Dead Man remained. 'Please, Dead Man, enter the magic cave. My kingdom and my place in history depend upon it,' the king said. The Dead Man remained. 'Get in the cave! I command you!' the king screamed. The Dead Man remained. 'I refuse,' the Dead Man said calmly. The jester laughed. 'For what reason?' the king pleaded. 'It is wrong for all to be ruled by the dreams of one,' the Dead Man said. 'Have you not learned this by being king?' The jester laughed.

"The king grew furious. He screamed. He flailed. He beat his scepter against the stones. He ordered his men to bind the Dead Man and take him away. They bound him. 'Where should we take him?' his men asked. 'Return him to his grave,' the king said bitterly. 'The jester will show you where.' And the king went out and got into his royal coach, again, in great despair. They looked inquiringly at the jester. 'To return the Dead Man to his grave, look no farther than the magic cave.' As he said this, the jester shook and danced with glee.

"The king's men shoved the Dead Man into the cave and rolled a large stone in front of its entrance. Not long after, the king, the kingdom, the countryside, the great men, and all the people faded into nothing. And the last sound was the ringing of the jester's bells as he danced his final dance."

In the dim of the night-light, Jacob walked quietly across the small room to the bed where his son lay sleeping. He pulled the covers up over his shoulders and kissed him on the cheek. "Goodnight," he whispered. The boy did not stir. He breathed in deeply as his father rose and left the room, his keys jingling against some coins in his pocket.

* * *

Abraham had gone with the priest to the diner in the morning. Grotto had finally got his appetite back, and he had come along. The little man had devoured four waffles and finished Abraham's neglected eggs and toast without asking. Then he sat quietly while they talked on until it was time to go. The funeral mass was planned for the afternoon and was to take place between the picnic pavilion and the grass volleyball court at Friends Creek. Camperman and Miss Jolly asked if they could attend even though they weren't Catholic. Abraham told them he wasn't Catholic anymore either, so he didn't think it would be an issue. The priest told Abraham that Slocum planned on coming by for it, though he would be a few minutes late, since Barbie Meadows' funeral was to be held just a couple hours earlier. The plan was then to drive the coffins in the ice-cream truck out to Croninger

Cemetery for the burial, and, with any luck, the Meadowses and their clan would be gone by that point.

Abraham sat in the pavilion with his little guitar, working at a song. Maybe it had something to do with dredging up the past for the priest, but, alongside his own recollections, he had found memories he could not place. Images from the past, but not his past. Perhaps they were pure fantasy. Perhaps his mind worked on this barren country like an empty canvas, peopled it with remote tragic figures, with stories. Or perhaps it went the other way round. They scratched their way into his dreams, into his waking hours, gouging him with their sufferings, their forlorn faces, their obscure longings. They were out of control. He could not quell them. He could not will them away. They would not wash off of his mind. He had begun to lose time to them. Maybe they just wanted out. Maybe they had been marooned in his mind like some mad army of macabre marionettes. Maybe, he thought, they could be furloughed in song. There was the man drowned in the Sangamon, twisted up in a beaver dam; the dead Indian woman by the pond; the bent figure swinging from a rope on the overpass, clutching a beer can; the man shot and strangled, a handful of nails in his mouth; so many others.

Camperman drove up in a golf cart. He steered with one hand and rested his free arm across the top of the empty vinyl seat, as if he were inviting someone to come sit next to him, but he was not. He stopped the little vehicle near where Abraham sat in the pavilion.

"Know any Dylan?" He curled his upper lip a little. "Or Elvis?"

"No," he lied.

"Whatchya playing there then?"

"I'm just passing the time."

"Sounds kind of somber. You playing something for the funeral?"

"No."

"Can I give you some advice, Abraham?" He didn't wait for a reply. "I lost some family, and I lost some real close friends in the service. Couple to suicide. Those were hard days. Real hard days. Hard ones. Now, I got some advice, and it might sound harsh."

He paused now. He took his sunglasses from his nose and wiped them on his shirt as he squinted at Abraham against the sun. He spoke more tenderly.

"You got to just take a warm bath and get over it."

There was a silence between them, filled only with a dog bark and an unseen car speeding by on the outer road.

"Okay."

"You can't change it. You can't go back in time, and tell them all the things you wish you'd said when they was here. You can't. You just can't."

He paused again, the glasses still in his hand.

"You just take a warm bath."

He put the glasses back on.

"And get over it."

"Thanks," Abraham said after a few seconds.

"Nothing else you can do. You gotta get over it." He said it like he was asking. "Got to."

"Okay."

"Alright, my friend. I will see you in just a little while. Sayonara."

Camperman hit the accelerator and took off noiselessly through the grass, just as a man from the coroner's office pulled through the gate in a white station wagon with an official county insignia emblazoned on the side. He parked in the lot near the pavilion. He got out and leaned forward, squinting into the shade of the enclosure where Abraham sat. He righted himself, hiked his trousers up over his bulging belly, smoothed his shirt down around the waste, retucked it into the trousers, and then shook one of his feet for a few seconds. The foot-shaking brought the trousers back down, and one side of the shirt tail had liberated itself in the process, though the man did not seem to notice. He walked into the pavilion.

"You Abraham?"

"Yeah."

"Can you sign here please?"

Abraham took the clipboard the man held out and looked at the document for a minute, while the man waited, crossing one hand over the other on his paunch. He signed it and handed it back.

"I thank you," the man said. "Can I leave them here?"

"Yeah."

"Will the funeral be taking place soon? Because these gentlemen need to be in the ground in the next hour. Tops. The county cannot afford to embalm wards of the state. That's why we would normally cremate in these situations."

"What's a cremation cost?"

"Normally, upwards of $500. Little cheaper if we do 'em together, like with John Does. Maybe a little less still, if they's as small as them midgets."

"God. And embalming?"

"Anywhere between two and seven."

"So, really, it's about the same, on average, either way, huh?"

"Not always." The man was annoyed.

"Seems like it."

"The county coroner's office cannot afford it!"

"The county coroner's office is run by assholes."

"I beg your pardon, sir?" The man put his hands on his hips and pointed a toe, cocking one hip out to the side.

Abraham stuck a cigarette in his mouth and went back to his guitar. Then he said as he began picking randomly at the strings, "If you'd be so kind, would you unload my dead friends onto that picnic table there, before you go fuck yourself?"

The man made a puffing sound with his lips.

Abraham lit his cigarette. "Thank you so much," he said.

The man did his job hastily. When he left, he slammed down on the gas pedal so hard that the tires of the station wagon left ruts in the gravel. Camperman was waiting for him at the gate to give him hell.

* * *

Slocum looked at the clock. His desk was a collage of grisly photographs, handwritten notes, newspaper clippings, and empty plastic blister-packs of nicotine gum. Trudy had caught on to the smoking. He held the headset of the telephone to his ear with his shoulder, his head cocked against it.

"Mmhmm. Of course she did," he said. "Well, what else can you expect?"

He snatched up a clipping with the headline "Missing Man Found in Home in Tolono" and read it over as he tried to listen.

"Trudy, I've got to go. Don't wanna be late for the Meadows girl's funeral."

He waited.

"Yes. I'll be sure to. Okay."

Another few seconds passed as the chirping continued from the phone.

"No. I'm gonna try my best not to. I got some."

More chirping.

"Alright, I love you too. Bye bye."

He looked at the clock again. He straightened the mess as best he could into a couple of piles. He grabbed the phone again, shuffled the papers for a number, and dialed. He looked at the clock again and hung up. Better to be early.

Sheriff Smalley greeted him at the bottom of the church stairs. He was a fat, bald man. He wore a powder-blue summer suit, a yellow shirt, and an orange tie. He held out a hand to Slocum. Slocum took it and went in for a brief back-pat hug. As he did, he spoke softly in Smalley's ear.

"God damn it, Rupert. You can't wear a bright blue suit to a fuckin' funeral. This is serious."

His face scrunched up. "What? Says who? None of the other ones fit no more."

"And the tie?"

Smalley's mouth opened in disbelief.

"This tie is a designer one," Smalley said in a desperate whisper. "It costed forty dollars."

"Well, just try to look somber then. With your face."

"Like this?"

He frowned deeply and drooped his eyes.

"Be serious! Damn. What's wrong with you?"

"I *am* serious." He was insistent.

"Forget it. What time you got?"

"We got a half hour for it starts. Oh! Reverend Crocket wants to see us. He said it's about the girl." He said it like an excited child.

They went up the stairs together and into the church. Mrs. Crocket was arranging flowers around the casket. It was closed.

"Dave wanted to see you two, if you have a minute."

"Yes, of course," Slocum said. "He in the office?"

"Mmhm. He's expecting you. Just go on in."

The two men entered the office at the pastor's gesture through the window.

"Hello, gentlemen," he said. "Forgive me if I skip the formalities, but there's something I need to tell you, both of you, about Barbie Meadows." He put in the white tab that served as his clerical collar.

"Okay, Crocket. Shoot," Slocum said.

"I'm not sure if it's even relevant to the case, and I may be the only one who knows." He rubbed his thinning black hair and took off his glasses.

Slocum bit his lip. "Okay."

"Well, except for my wife." He sighed. "And probably Bull.

I'm sure he knows."

Slocum relaxed a little.

"Anyway," Crocket went on, "we all know how Barbie was. She was the sweetest girl in the world, but she was indeed handicapped. Mentally, of course. I'd never heard her speak a word that made any sense to anyone. But we all, all of us, could tell how big her heart was."

"Yes, that's the truth, I was just thinkin—" Smalley started.

"Shut up," Slocum said. "Go on, Crocket."

"I don't really know how to put it other than that I think it was a miracle." His voice broke over the word "miracle," and his face drew up, as if a string had been sewn into its perimeter and pulled. He blew his nose in a hanky with a loud honk and tried to pull himself together. The lawmen waited.

"Now, she'd come and see me when Mrs. Crocket and I would come in and do the cleaning. We'd give her some candy and she'd help dust or something, but it was always, forgive me, it was almost like when you ask a toddler to do a chore. She would play at it, and then she'd give us a hug and go back to her bike and disappear with the candy. But she came for a visit a few days ago. . ." He trailed off again in tears. "She came in, just a proper young lady. Her clothes were normal. Must have been her mom's, God rest her soul. She walked normally, like her muscles had loosened up. Her arms were straight. And, she spoke to me, my hand to God, as I am speaking to you now. Now, gentlemen, I have been a pastor for twenty-five years, and I thought I'd seen miracles. You know, couples reconciling when it seemed hopeless, people's cancer going into remission: stuff that happens, if I'm honest with myself, with or without God's intervention. But I have never seen anything like this. Never."

The men stood silent. Smalley had begun to cry. Slocum pinched his lips between his thumb and fisted fingers and looked at the floor.

"And someone took her away. Took that miracle, took God's

good work, and they crushed it. Snuffed it out." Crocket's voice broke into a high falsetto over the last few words as he started to sob again.

Slocum spoke. "Now, Crocket, there's no way you's misunderstood somethin'? You absolutely sure?"

"Yes, Sheriff. Beyond a shadow of a doubt. It's renewed my faith in God."

"What's it done for your faith in humanity?"

"Evil lurks in the hearts of *men*, Sheriff." Crocket looked at him very seriously.

"Maybe so. Maybe so. You say your wife saw Barbie this way too?"

"Yes, Sheriff," he said. "Honey?" he called.

Mrs. Crocket appeared in the doorway.

"Will you tell these men about Barbie Meadows?"

She immediately started crying and attempting to speak in a tiny, high voice. It was indecipherable.

"Okay, okay," Slocum said, a little impatiently. "Just nod yes or no, okay?"

She nodded yes.

"Did Barbie speak to you just like a normal, regular person, just like I'm speakin' to you now?"

She nodded yes.

"And you never heard her speak at all before that, period?"

She shook her head no.

"And the way she carried herself, she weren't all wrenched up like before?"

She shook her head no.

"And you say it's a miracle too? Like you'd never seen before?"

She shook her head yes.

Slocum looked at his watch. "One more thing, Crocket, and then you gotta get out there, 'cause it's 'bout time. What'd you talk 'bout with her? You come outta somethin' like that, where do you start?"

Crocket leaned forward very seriously. "I remember the exact words she started with. She said, 'Reverend Crocket, I think I've had a miracle done on me by the man from the Tower of Babel.'" He started crying again. "I'll never forget it. Never. Then she said, 'My life has been a crucifixion of time and place, and that's what Jesus is too.'" Then he lost it again.

"Thank you, Crockets," Slocum said. "I'll be in touch."

Smalley lingered and watched the Crockets console each other with kisses and caresses.

"Smalley, come," Slocum said from the hall.

They found a spot in a pew in the back.

"What I want to know," Slocum whispered to Smalley, "is when did ministers of the gospel of Jesus H. Christ start quoting the Shadow?"

"What do you mean?" Smalley said.

"Never mind."

* * *

The priest chanted the mass in the old style. Miss Jolly had been stricken with a "sick headache," Camperman said, and she didn't attend. The tiny caskets lay in the sun on the ground, and except for the smell, the funeral went off without interruption. Grotto, Abraham, and Camperman stood in the short-clipped grass facing the priest, the little black boxes between them, while Petunia grazed in the distance. The volleyball net bobbed silently like a taunt rubber-band over the painted court. The priest broke a large wafer into four pieces and served himself a double portion, since Abraham made no indication of partaking. He placed a piece in Grotto's open mouth when he came forward, and then held out a piece for Camperman, who held out his hands to receive.

"All due respect, I don't like people's hands in my mouth," he said.

"It is fine. The body of Christ," the priest said, placing the sliver of wafer in his hands, but he lingered there for a moment. He stared down at the piece of wafer as if it were a tiny painting that he was working hard to figure out.

"It isn't really the Lord's flesh is it? Now, I know you're supposed to say it is, because the pope says so, but just between you and me, it is just bread, right?"

"Yes, of course," the priest said. He saw no use in belaboring the point.

Camperman ate it and went and stood with the others while the priest finished up on his own.

"I guess Sheriff Slocum will meet you for the burial. Said he was gonna try and make it when I saw him the other day," Camperman said.

Grotto wiped some tears with the back of his twisted paw. Camperman blew his nose. The priest folded his stole and pocketed it. Abraham lit a cigarette.

"Nope, I can't make it out there," Camperman went on as he stuffed his hanky into his back pocket, "but I did set up the stone this morning. It's already out there waiting on you. No charge. It's my gift. Now, my best work is done on the scroll saw, but I can engrave purty good when it needs to be done."

"Thanks," Abraham said.

"You bet. Nope, I got to get the big tractor running. Flat tire and a new set of plugs. You know the drill."

Camperman helped load the caskets into the ice-cream truck, and they parted ways. The priest took his own car.

* * *

Bull Meadows was a broken man. Slocum had watched him try his best to hold it together throughout the funeral and the handshaking afterwards, but as he sat in the car, waiting to lead the procession out to Croninger, Slocum saw Bull in the rearview mirror. He got into the passenger side of the hearse, waved to someone before pulling the door closed, and the man just fell apart. His tiny image in the mirror shook and gasped. The head went up, and then it went down. The broad shoulders quivered to the rhythm of his sobs. Slocum put his car in Drive and eased off the brake. It was time to get moving, to put a little distance between himself and the mourning man behind him. He felt guilty for having seen as much as he did.

Slocum led them, the blue lights going on his roof, Bull in the hearse behind him, and the throng who had come along, come to see the last among the county's oldest names be put into the earth. They understood that this was the end for the Meadowses. Bull had outlived his line. He would go on living, sure, but on his grand family tree, he would be the one green branch, the one out of joint with the rest, the one near the top that had not felt the saw bite into its flesh. Yes, everyone was kind. They said the things you say, but, Slocum thought, mostly they want to say that they had been there.

Bull had composed himself by the time he emerged from the hearse. He and a few men carried the shiny ivory casket to the graveside, where the undertaker and his man got it strapped into the gurney-like lowering device. Then, as Reverend Crocket read something aloud, Slocum watched Bull trace with his index finger the delicate trefoils engraved in the palest pearlescent lavender in the ivory lid of Barbie's casket. He seemed to lose himself in the labyrinth of their interlocking rings. The sun was bright, and rubies seemed to sparkle from the design. The pastor nudged Bull gently when it was time for the casket to be planted. Crocket had the congregation sing "When We All Get to Heaven" a few times through. Then they all watched Bull scoop up a handful of dirt and scatter it over his dead daughter in the box below. The dirt scattered, and some blew off in the hot wind. The song went on.

* * *

Slocum parked his car between the road and the cemetery entrance and got out, propping himself on the side of the hood, the lights still flashing. It was a safety precaution but there was no traffic. Never was much. They all filed past in their sedans and trucks, one young fool on a motorcycle, and he nodded and waved as they passed by and made their turns out onto the highway. He looked up the hill into the graveyard and saw the undertaker's man pat Bull on the shoulder. Crocket walked him back to the hearse and drove away with Mrs. Crocket in their beige Cadillac. Slocum spotted the ice-cream truck at the crossroads about a mile off.

"Christ," he said to himself.

It closed in and turned in the cemetery drive. Slocum waved to Abraham, who only glanced at him, his beard flying around in the wind from the driver-side wing, smoke curling around from his cigarette, the slack-jawed midget next to him in the passenger seat. The shiny black hearse was creeping down the gravel slope, as Slocum walked back up after the ice-cream truck. Abraham pulled the truck off in the grass to let the hearse get by. Slocum was about even with them in the grass on the other side of the hearse. The undertaker rolled the window down and motioned to Abraham. Abraham got out and leaned against his door.

"Hello there," the undertaker said with a preacher's voice.

Abraham peered in the window at the smiling undertaker but said nothing.

"Are you lost?" the undertaker said. "Maybe I can help."

"You may not," Abraham said.

The undertaker glared back but then rolled forward and away. Bull Meadows rolled down his side and spit before they pulled out onto the highway.

The priest drove in finally and led them to where Eco and No-no would rest. They took the cars as close as they could get and went the rest of the way on foot in the grass. One hole had been dug, and the earth was piled between it and the couple of small pines nearby. Camperman's stone of roughly cut deep burgundy granite was planted at the head. Its script was etched in beautiful calligraphy in four lines:

"Echo & Nono
Real Nice Little Fellers
Yours has the suffering been
The memory shall be ours"

"There ain't no dates," Slocum whined to no one in particular.

Abraham was hauling the coffins, one under each arm to the graveside. The priest and Grotto helped him lower them in the grass. The three of them stood over the hole and peered down within.

"Will they fit end to end?" the priest said.

Grotto did some measuring with his hands and transferred the lengths, with his arms outstretched, over to the grave. He shrugged, and then he nodded in the affirmative. Slocum was still staring at the stone in disbelief.

"How do we, you know, get them down there?" the priest queried.

Grotto made a kicking motion but then smiled, his tongue sticking out a little. The priest laughed.

"Let me get in and you can hand them down," Abraham said finally.

He lowered himself into the grave. Slocum saw what they were doing and shook his head as if it was beyond his comprehension. The priest and Grotto handed one down. Abraham pushed it as far as it would go against the head-side of the grave.

"Hey," Slocum called down to Abraham, stepping up near the edge of the hole, accidently kicking some dirt in, "Camperman didn't put no dates on."

Abraham looked at him, "Move back."

Slocum moved, muttering. Grotto and the priest handed the other coffin down. Abraham tried to wedge it into the other side as gently as possible, but it would not go. He moved it on top of the other one and dug out the side with his hand. He tried it again. It fit now, but the end seemed a little too high, since it was resting on the earth he'd gouged out of the side. He bounced on it a couple of times.

"Good God!" Slocum said, leaning over the spectacle in the grave.

"Shut up. Move back," Abraham said.

Slocum let it go.

The coffin was almost level. Abraham hopped a couple more times. A sharp crack came from the coffin, and the grave filled with the stench of death.

"Holy shit!" Slocum hollered.

Abraham retched a couple of times before finally scrambling out of the grave, his beard, hands, and the faded grey knees of his trousers blackened with earth. He shook the dirt off his hat and held it over his mouth and nose.

"What do we do?" The priest was panicking.

"We bury them," Abraham said.

And the three of them started moving dirt in as quickly as they could in whatever ways came to mind. Slocum walked off, leaned on a tree, and watched, nodding his head disgustedly from side to side. Abraham grabbed a shovel from near the trees. The priest edged the earth with the insides of his shoes. Grotto pointed his ass at the grave, his legs wide, bent over, and scooped it in like a dog. A wind whipped up and blew over the little slope where the graveyard was and then shook the tall green corn in a wave and then on down to the trees where the ground leveled out by the river. The smell went with it. They had worked enough of the dark earth back into the hole to staunch the flow of fetid air, and they relaxed, laughing a little.

Slocum ambled over. "This is pure desecration," he said, "and there ain't even no dates on those boys' stone."

"The memories shall be ours," Abraham said.

A small laugh forced itself from the priest like a burp or a hiccup. Grotto smiled crookedly.

"No," Slocum said, "no, I'm serious. This is serious."

And then Abraham came alive. He threw down the spade near Slocum and it stuck in the ground.

"Why the fuck are you even here? What do you want from us?"

Slocum stared.

"Have you come to watch us mourn? Well? What's your judgment? Have we mourned to your fucking standard? Or have we behaved like guilty men? Do you not approve?" His voice was harsh and hoarse. He flicked his cigarette butt at Slocum, and it threw sparks when it hit his shield.

Slocum took it, wide-eyed, but he just took it.

The wind rolled over again and played in Abraham's beard and hair. His hat went rolling across the green.

Then there was nothing. The wind was dead, and there was nothing.

Chapter 7

The East End was appropriately named. It hung like a scab on the outermost eastern edge of the little downtown district in Monticello that surrounded the courthouse, across from a chiropractor's office and an abandoned brick warehouse of some kind, and it looked and smelled like the end of something. The priest had selected the spot, mostly because of the dearth of other options. Most of the respectable bars closed early that day or weren't open at all. Since circumstances hadn't allowed for a proper wake, he figured sharing a few beers would be the next best thing. He thought it might help take the edge off. Abraham and Grotto found a little round table near the back of the bar, by the door. A sign in the window advertised an "Open Mic Night," and there was a little corner set up with a microphone in a black metal stand and a spotlight, but they were either between acts or no one had answered the call. The light shone on an empty barstool, the seat of which was gashed, and pale yellow fuzz poofed out.

A worn-out-looking, droopy-eyed girl in green sweatpants and a blank t-shirt raised her eyebrows, as if to ask what they wanted. Camperman saw someone he knew and went over for a chat.

"What do you have on tap?" the priest asked.

"Bud and Bud Lite," the girl said, just loud enough to be heard, indicating the two handles between them on her side of the bar with her finger.

"We will have four Buds then."

"It's cheaper by the pitcher."

"How much is it by the glass?"

"Two dollars."

The priest waited, expecting more. She only stared.

"And the pitcher?" he said finally.

"Seven fifty."

"And how many glasses in the pitcher?"

She sighed and stared at him some more, then she fetched a glass and filled it at the Bud tap seven times over. When the urinous fluid crested and spilled out through the spout, she kept pouring till the glass was empty.

"Almost seven."

"I will take it," the priest said, handing her a ten-dollar bill.

"Foreigners. . ." She said something else he did not hear, and a blonde woman at the bar laughed. She gave him the change. He kept it and went to the table with the pitcher.

The priest set down the pitcher of beer and said, "Gentlemen, I give you Bud." They seemed already to have settled in, but Abraham sat still, and Grotto looked longingly into the piss-colored pitcher. The priest smiled and sat down.

"Who wants the first sip?" Abraham said.

"Oh! Glasses."

The priest returned to the bar, where the girl was complaining to the blonde, who had been joined by a leather-clad, musta-chioed man with a red bandana tied over his head, about her boyfriend's fathomless sexual appetites, as she mopped up spilled beer with a rag.

She raised her eyebrows again.

"Glasses. Four of them please."

She set them on the bar in two stacks of two without saying anything.

The priest returned to the table and filled and distributed the glasses and then sat. Abraham drank half of his beer at once and set the glass on the table, wiping foam from his mustache with his sleeve. He found a cigarette and lit it and offered the priest the pack. He took one and they smoked and looked around the room. Grotto lifted his glass, sipped his beer, and then returned the glass to its liquid ring on the table a couple of times, finishing the process each time with a shudder and a grimace. Camperman finally made his way to the table as a young man with long hair and a mostly red, half-unbuttoned plaid shirt sat on the barstool under the light and started tuning a small acoustic guitar, which was plugged into the bar's PA. The bar was crowded with loud-talking, backslapping men, most of them in caps, jeans, and t-shirts, and a few women wearing the same uniform minus the caps. The youngest by a good ten years was the man with the guitar, and he looked to be in his thirties. The conversations would lull and lift with laughter and then die down again, and the pinging of the guitar strings barely penetrated the indecipherable roar of talk, until the man had finished tuning and strummed a couple of chords and began speaking into the microphone, saying "test" over and over again. Abraham was already three beers in; Grotto was still cautiously sipping at the first; Camperman had downed two; and the priest was just finishing his first. Camperman went for another pitcher.

"Watch this guy. He's real good at songs. He plays it all," he hollered to anyone who was listening.

"Alright," the man at the microphone said. "I'll play a couple more, if no one else is goin' to."

"Freebird!" Someone yelled as the rest hushed. Others laughed. Someone whistled. Someone coughed and then spit.

The man began strumming a little.

"Oh God," Abraham said over the man's whine of the first line.

The priest looked at him and laughed, "You know this one, yes?"

"I hate this fucking song." He finished off the glass and wiped his mustache on the damp spot on his sleeve.

The man sang on about his inevitable resistance to mutability, adding his own flourishes as needed: "oh no you can't" or "but I wish I could" or simply a drawn out "yeayeah."

Camperman returned with a new pitcher.

"Man, I love this song. Yeah." He nodded his head as though

he were affirming whatever he took to be the song's message and then pushed his glasses up.

"I'm on empty here, Camperman," Abraham said, lifting his glass.

Grotto laughed.

The man went on, repeating the same phrase over and over, reinforcing the stalwart constancy referred to in the lyrics, it seemed, by refusing to move on and finish the damn song.

Abraham drank half the beer in a couple gulps and set the glass down. His eyes looked wet and his gaze settled in on the man, who had worked into a guitar solo, as the bar swelled with woohoos and whistles.

Abraham had drunk another beer by the time the song was over. Everyone was cheering. Camperman stuck his index fingers into the corners of his mouth and emitted a long loud whistle, finished off with a loud "yeah!"

"Thank you, kind people," the singer said. "Thanks. I think I'm done. I can't top that."

"Yeah!" Camperman shouted again.

"Somebody else wanna play?"

The room got quiet. After a moment, Camperman called out, "Yeah, my buddy here plays." He looked at Abraham. "Get up there, Abraham!"

It took a few seconds before Abraham seemed to register what was happening, but by the time he did, the crowd was already issuing their woohoos, yeahs, and whistles. One woman moaned out in a threatening slur, "Come on! I need to hear some music!" like she really did.

"Come on up, stranger, and give us a little something," the man at the microphone said.

"Nah, I don't have my guitar," Abraham muttered.

"What'd he say, Camperman?"

"Said he don't have his guitar."

"Well, shit, he can use mine. Come on."

"Come on," a man said with angry drunken disappointment.

"Play some ZZ Top," someone hollered out from the dark by the bathrooms.

"I do not think you are getting out of this," the priest said. Abraham nodded, a little drunkenly. "Go on, play something."

"What the hell," he said finally. He stood up, pushed his hat down low, finished off his beer, and made his way to the stool.

"What's your name, stranger?" the singer asked him.

"Abraham."

"Alright, everybody, let's hear it for Abraham. He's gonna play us something."

A half-hearted cheer went up.

Abraham sat and lit a cigarette and dragged it deeply as he strummed a little. His fingers picked at a rhythm as he dragged a couple more times on the cigarette. He edged up to the microphone, scooting the stool as he did. He stopped, pulled the capo from the head, and placed it across the strings a couple frets from the top of the neck of the guitar.

"Alright," he said. The spot on his hat brim cast his eyes in shadow. He was all hat and grey beard and black besides under the light. He started picking out the rhythm again. Otherwise he was still. He began growling out a mournful song in a low grumble that cracked across the higher notes.

"Down at Hobson's Crossing, still water mirrors the sky.
Black birds move behind me and call into the night.
A yellow moon hangs, cut in two, by the shadow of the earth,
Its missing twin spilled out below, the forgotten afterbirth,
The forgotten afterbirth."

The bar had fallen quiet by this point except for a few. They all gazed at the dark scarecrow that moaned into the microphone. Someone shushed out the conversations that remained, and they listened.

"Mother won't cry for me, Father passed before.
Crows will be my angels, hell ain't got no doors.
My hand into the water, the sky is trembling and slow,
Cross myself and mouth a prayer, the only one I know,
The only one I know."

The cigarette fog held the light from the spot around him. Against the outer relative dark beyond, it looked like he was singing from within a pillar of smoke.

"Morning starts in darkness, the living from the dead,
Hate and hurt from love and words, from every word you
    said.
The moon's a stone flung in the black that poisons Hobson's
    sky.
Casts its cloyin' pallor down, an iridescent lie,
An iridescent lie."

He rode out the rhythm and ended in one slow strum of a minor chord and left it hanging, ringing into the smoke and beer. After a moment, they all cheered. The other singer came up and shook his hand.

"Man, you got one more? That was amazing. That was like some Tao Te Ching shit or something."

Camperman brought him a beer. Others clapped and whistled. Someone called out, "Damn!" A few just squinted at him like Abraham was the higher algebra. Someone coughed again, and the priest spotted a small, ancient woman as she spit whatever had come up into a corner.

Abraham nodded a couple of times. The young man went back to his seat. The room quieted again before he started strumming a folk progression that sounded like something from a bygone age. It had a rollicking rhythm, the kind that carries the prophetic dignity of a church hymn or a tragic ballad, and the priest found himself nodding his head in time. Abraham, too, rocked back and forth with it, when he finally gave in to the pattern. Then he was howling out in his broken voice.

"They found him in the Sangamon twisted among the trees.
John Byrd, an aged stableman, someone had broke his knees.
They say he kneeled to Jesus Christ at night and noon and
    morn.
And who will judge what's wrong from right out there
    among the corn?"

A dropped glass shattered somewhere near the bar.

"They found him o'er the interstate; he was danglin' from a
    bridge.
Ed Hensen was a newly-wed; Moll bore him his first kid.
They found a beer clinched in his hand, and his hair had all
    been shorn.
Who tells you how to live your life out there among the
    corn?"

"What the fuck?" someone said, almost as if the curse were a prayer, from near the bar. "Who does he think he is?" the ancient woman said before coughing and spitting again.

"They found her in her kitchen slumped in a pool of her
    own blood.
Edwina Pierce had made a meal then went to meet her God.
She gave herself the wounds of Christ, right down to the
    crown of thorns.
Who tells us when enough's enough out here among the
    corn?"

A man stood up and looked across the room at a woman who

was crying. The priest began to notice several locals shifting around, exchanging bitter glances, some slowly shaking their heads no. He looked at Camperman. The song went on.

"They found her out by Hogchute Bridge, hidden among the weeds.
Some nameless baby thrown aside and buried in the leaves.
Doc Burton said she'd starved to death, two days since she'd been born.
Who metes out justice for the dead out here among the corn?"

"He ain't got all the details down exactly, but he's sure as hell got the stories," Camperman said. Abraham was strumming out a bridge. "We may see some trouble here." He locked eyes with the priest. "Some of them are blood to folks in this room."

"What do you mean?" the priest asked.

"Them he's singing about. They're our blood, our friends. Old wounds, old embers. They ain't the kind you want to stir. Not unless you're looking for fire."

Abraham's rasp took the room again more softly, desperate, the guitar only faintly holding on.

"Someday somewhere not far from here they'll find another soul.
Me or you, your kin or mine, down in some shallow hole.
The grave's been dug. The plan's been hatched, for some night or noon or morn.
And who protects the innocent out here among the corn?
And who protects the innocent out here among the corn?"

The first bottle shattered against the mic stand and carried a loud thwop through the PA and another when the microphone hit the concrete floor. Abraham's eyes opened just as the priest shouted to watch out. Another bottle cracked against the wall behind him. A third slammed the strings on the guitar as Abraham was pulling the leather strap over his head. The other singer spun around: "That's my fuckin' guitar, motherfucker!" He grabbed the man's shirt and shook him a little. When he spun back around, Abraham was offering his guitar back to him. A skirmish had broken out on the far side of the bar, and the noise of yells and curses came up and filled the room and became one shrill voice, saying nothing.

The priest motioned towards Abraham, indicating that it was time to go. Abraham handed off the guitar, but still had the strap in his hand. He spoke to the other singer, and the man smiled and was nodding; then he waved his hand as if to say "it's nothing" or "don't worry about it." He watched the chaos grow and sweep across the bar as a few more fights broke out. An old man pushed a young man who pointed back at him. Two old ladies were pulling each other's hair; one fell to the floor, leaving a handful of gray bristles in the clutch of the one left standing. The priest looked back for Abraham and saw the long-haired singer punch a man in the mouth. A fat man tackled the singer but then was thrown down on the floor. He winced and held his back. The priest stood, panicking, but finally found Abraham as he was scanning across the room. He saw the black fedora move out of the shadows near the bathrooms and weave its way through the bodies. When he came into view, in the spotlight, near the felled mic stand and the fuzzy stool, he was smiling a little, the priest thought.

"There he is!" someone screamed. Abraham grabbed the barstool and hurled it into direction of the scream then sent two chairs to follow it. Two men hit the floor, a third clutched his ear and screamed; a woman's nose was bleeding. The priest shot a look at Grotto. Grotto shrugged and turned back towards Abraham. Camperman had disappeared. The priest found Abraham again, just as the fat man who had tackled the singer was coming at Abraham at full speed. Abraham slid a chair towards him, and the fat man yelled out and fell, tangled with the chair, into a table of women. The priest peered in and made out the thin leather strap from the singer's guitar coiled around Abraham's knuckles, his right hand fisted around it. He swung at a tall, broad man and hit him in the throat. When the man doubled over, hands to his neck, Abraham threw a few more punches. His left hand was done up the same way, but with what looked like a black leather belt. The big man went down. Two others approached. One grabbed a bottle by the neck and broke the end off on a table. "My God!" the priest said, throwing his hands to his face. But Abraham's eyes were dead. They calmed him somehow.

The man with the bottle thrust it towards Abraham, while the other man moved in. Abraham jabbed the bottle-wielding man in the middle of the face. The other got in an open-handed slap that knocked Abraham's hat off and landed on his neck, but the man was not able to pull his hand back before Abraham's leather-wrapped cudgels found their way to his mouth, his throat, his eye. The bottle-man found his feet again but not his bottle. Abraham raised a swift boot to his balls and turned a table over on top of him. The man's wailing seemed like it was never going to end. As it persisted, one more, a thick-built farmer, stepped forward and yelled at Abraham that now he was going to have to pay. The priest glanced out the window near the door at the flash of lights.

"There's nothing to pay," he heard Abraham say.

His hands were up, his black shirt half-untucked, blood smears emblazoned on the tan leather strap, more dripping from a deposit on the black belt. Broken locals were moaning all around. The farmer took a wide swing which drew him out sidelong. Abraham's two shots to the exposed ribs left red splotches on the man's white shirt before he winced and withdrew his hand. This time Abraham didn't wait. He hit the man's face until his hands went up; then he went to the ribs again. The farmer got in two head shots, once in the jaw when Abraham glanced out at the cops, and the second in the forehead, just before Abraham knocked him down with the mic stand and stomped on his groin. A minute or so later, when Slocum, Richie, and two other cops tried to pull him off, Abraham's bearded face was red-speckled but dead, bored-looking, as it hung over the farmer's. He was still swinging, impervious to the priest's pleas or the screams of the only two women left in the bar. The straps were digging in, flecking flesh away. Two red-capped teeth lay nearby. The blood smeared across the leather on his hands like wounds, like two gaping mouths, but when they had finally pulled him away, he loosened his hands, and the straps slackened and fell to the floor. His hands were smeared and sprinkled, but where the blood-hungry wound-mouths had been, there was nothing.

The priest watched them cuff Abraham. He and Grotto followed them out of the bar. Slocum shot him a look he couldn't quite decipher. Grotto gestured with his thumb towards the priest's car and nodded his head one time in the same direction.

"Yes. Yes. We should go," he replied, and they walked off.

The last thing he heard was the cop, Richie, saying, "You have the right to remain silent."

* * *

"Listen, Abraham, I need to know about the miracles."

The priest couldn't sleep. Their night at the East End had left him frazzled. It was probably near dawn, but he wasn't sure. The room at Foster's was dark, but he made out a little grey leaking out from behind the thick curtain. He sat propped against the headboard, the two feathered pillows behind him, smoking a cigarette, the headphones on. Grotto snored deeply from the extra bed on the other side of the little table. The priest had sat in the dark for a long time, working the blood-baptized image of Abraham around his head. He went over the night, searching the chaos for details, for things that mattered, but the figure of Abraham singing or the figure of him beating the hell out of someone faded into a blackness that wed itself to the dark of the room. And then out of the darkness came the light, and into the light appeared the image of Abraham's face, shadows thrown down and around his features like some spectral Francis Bacon portrait, his face maligned by that bitter smile.

There was silence in response to the request, only the sounds of distant dishes clinking, distant voices speaking, Grotto's fork against his plate.

"Do you not want to talk about them?"

"I'm just not sure what the hell you're talking about."

"Well, let us see." He heard himself flipping through his notebook. "You first attracted our attention about a year-and-a-half ago when a Jesuit schoolmaster outside New Orleans reported to a cardinal, a friend of his, that a paraplegic boy from school walked out of a church, pushing his own wheelchair, after praying with you at one of your Bible dramas. That pricked up some ears, but there is never any action taken after such isolated occurrences. But then we heard another report, from a Monsignor Eamon McNulty of All Saints Parish in Houston, that you had, let me find his words." There was a pause. "Ah, here it is, 'This prophet of God resurrected Sister Mary Margaret, who had passed due to cancer, to the bafflement of her physicians, and, I must add, of her spiritual mentor, by which I mean myself.' I have a copy of his letter right here. And I have similar letters from parishes on through Texas, from Chihuahua, from Albuquerque, and so on. Then a through-the-grapevine communication from our Orthodox brothers, a Father Konstantin from Platina, and back across the states. And that's just the Catholics, Abraham."

No response.

"My God, my friend, and what about that poor dead Meadows girl? There is word that you made her whole again! This, this is what the hell I am talking about. You know this is why I am here, why I have been sent, why I have been tracing your trail."

He sounded exasperated, too intent on getting answers, and, looking back now, he understood Abraham's reluctance.

"So it's official church business here in Shitsville that has you, a man of God, tied up in a couple of murders, repeatedly visiting a campground known as a rendezvous for gay men, watching boys perform sex acts on statuary, deep in the dark woods of the Prairie State? You're the fucking miracle, priest."

Grotto's little chuckle could be heard against the noise of the breakfast hour during the pause. Abraham's lighter flicked, and the priest heard Abraham pull the smoke in.

"You are skirting the subject. And no. This sort of thing is always *off* the record, yes? Unofficial. Almost nothing gets investigated any more, and certainly nothing in the States. It's always bullshit."

He heard himself relaxing, coming back down. He felt the turn through the headphones, and it came with the word "bullshit." Coarse language did not come naturally to him, but when it came, it always felt right.

"Now, my friend, answer as you see fit, but do please answer."

"Okay, the nun. I know about the nun. It was an awkward situation. They asked me to fill in for somebody for the vigil, recite some psalms over her, and there was a hubbub about me smoking in the cancer wing. And I remember the other stops, and I remember the blind girl in Chihuahua, but I don't hang around. When we're done we get out, and Eco and No-no were pretty good about keeping people away from me. If what you're saying is that weird shit happened in these other places, that's news to me." His voice paused for a moment. "Look, here and there, weird shit happens. It doesn't mean it's a miracle."

"It seems to me that these are no less than acts of God. Acts of God, all of them connected to you, most of which I have authenticated. For further investigation anyway. There is a process, yes?"

"No. No, you can't have it both ways."

"I do not understand. What do you mean?"

"I mean you can't have God both ways. Is God the creator, sustainer, ground of all being, the absolute, whatever the hell you want to call it, or is God the exception, sheer possibility, the God of chaos and anomaly?"

"He is God. He is both. The divine mysteries are not all given to us to understand."

"No. Both is precisely the one thing he cannot be. If it's the first, then anomalies are out of the question as God's. Either they're within the realm of what's possible in nature, like Grotto here, or like the Meadows girl or the paraplegic, all descendants of the Fall, the first fruits of a fallen world, or they reach out past the border into the unseen chaos beyond. They are literally *im*possible. The dead waking is *un*natural."

"Of course, the acts of God are beyond the rules that bind nature."

"No, anomalies beyond nature are what should make atheists out of men, not believers, because if God is all of that other shit you say he is, then the dead waking is strictly off limits. It marks the place where God is not, where the fabric of creation is fucked up, where order is lost. It marks the world as out of control."

"And if he's sheer possibility?"

"All bets are off. Then nothing that happens can be held up against anything else. Nothing is natural or unnatural. But the other side is that nothing is miraculous either. Such a world has no place for church, for sacraments, for the divine mysteries. It's all divine mystery. All bets are off."

"How do you explain the miracles then, what I am calling

miracles?"

"I don't. I told you. When we're done we get out. Look, I don't forget things. Anything. But I've learned that I don't have to remember them."

"But you do remember. You have been anyway, yes?"

"Yes. But only for you, for this place, for the dead. Call it an act of love."

Abraham laughed and called for more coffee. He lit another cigarette. The priest heard himself light one.

"Can you tell me about the first one? The first miracle?"

"Yeah. Happened when I was four years old. My grand-father—great grandfather on my mother's side. He had some kind of disease. I don't know that they knew what it was then. Alzheimer's maybe. It was well on, probably, by the time I was born. But they just thought it was age, that he was dying. Only he didn't die, not right away anyhow. He just hung on, frozen. That's what my grandmother, his daughter, always said, 'Papa is frozen.' I started reading early, and I used to crawl up in his big wooden bed and read his Bible to him. Grandma said it was good for him, help keep his mind busy. His eyes would move around in his head. He'd look at me like I was a stranger, like I was an alien life form or something that had found its way into his bed. His mouth would work against his tongue, and sometimes it would stop and his tongue would just hang out between his lips. Hell, maybe he was just trying to remember how to swallow. I don't know. Otherwise, he was like a piece of furniture that required a lot of maintenance, that they liked to rearrange. They'd feed him, bathe him, dress him, comb his hair, sit him in a chair. But the way they talked, it was like he'd been dead for years. You know, how old people are? When someone dies, anyone close to them anyhow, that person changes in their memory. Like whatever kind of asshole they'd been, whatever they'd fucked up or done wrong in life, gets burned away as their memory works across what sense to make of them being gone.

And all that gets left behind in the mind is the best possible interpretation of whatever that life was. Not who they'd been or the
sum of their actions, but whatever image of the dead is the least
repulsive for the living to go on remembering. You see what I'm
saying?"

The voice was genuine, the priest thought, and he heard
himself say "Yes."

"So by all indications, except the one that really seals the deal,
he *was* dead. He was as near dead as one can be in himself, and
he'd already been lost and mourned according to them. But there
he was still, eating, shitting and pissing, taking up space,
haunting his clothes, his bed, his room, the house, like a material
ghost. I had gotten used to him. He'd been around like that since
I could remember things. But like I said, about the time I was
four, in the summer, things changed. I was reading in the book of
Samuel, and his tongue was out, his eyes dull, but not closed. I
stopped reading and looked at him and laughed a little and
pushed his tongue back into his mouth with my finger. Like that.
And his eyes found me again, a stranger in his bed. I went back
to his Bible and read, I shit you not, these words: 'And the Lord
said to Samuel, Behold, I will do a thing in Israel, at which both
the ears of every one that heareth it shall tingle.' And my grandfather sat up. My head knocked the headboard, and he pulled me
up, spoke to me in this horrible, airy, creaking voice."

"What did he say?"

"'Get off my bed, you little shit.' And then he pushed me into
the floor, climbed down the other side, and took a piss in the
corner, soaked the carpet through. After that he cursed and
screamed about his pain. He beat my grandmother with the leg
of a chair that broke under him at dinner one night. He drove my
mother's car into the side of the neighbor's house. He always
called her 'the whore' in the third person like that, he never spoke
to her directly. And I was '*her* bastard' to him, even when my
mother wasn't around. 'Tell '*her* bastard' it's time to shape up.' Six

weeks later he was dead again, only this time we were fortunate enough to put him in the ground. And he didn't come back."

The recording fell silent, except for the noise of forks on dishes, some distant voices. The priest had been unsure of what response to give. It took as much self-control as he had not to laugh as not to cry. He had been caught off guard somewhere in-between.

"Found out later that he'd always been a prick, only no one in my house remembered it or they were unwilling to. But neighbors will talk when a kid asks, or when they hear something, you know, that makes both ears of them that heareth tingle."

"Do you remember what it felt like?"

"What what felt like?"

"Enacting the miracle, healing him."

"Oh, right." And the priest recalled this moment precisely. Abraham seemed to consider the question. He had stroked his beard, kind of gathering it together in his hand, as he peered up at the water stains on the ceiling. Then he fished for a cigarette in his breast pocket. "You know that feeling you get, not every time, but every once in a while, like a release, your head clears a little, when you sneeze violently? It felt kind of like that." The flick of his lighter sounded again, and he remembered Abraham's crooked, bitter smile, barely apparent within his beard. "Yeah, it was kind of like that. Only less satisfying. It was almost nothing. Then it was nothing. And now it is less than that. Like I said before, I get out. I keep moving."

"But now you have stopped moving."

"True enough. But this place feels safe."

"Safe? There have been three murders since you have been here, and you may very well be a suspect in all of them."

"What I mean is this place, most of it anyway, the outer blanks, are like the desert or the sea." They had sat and smoked for a minute as Abraham put his thoughts together. "You know that Bosch tryptich with Saint Anthony or Altar of the Hermits?"

"Of course, yes."

"Yeah, thirteen years he lived in the desert, Saint Anthony. That's the legend anyway, that and the Devil's bestiary in the paintings? Anthony, hell all of the ascetics, they needed the desert because it was safe. Because it was a safe place, not for spiritual warfare. They believed that, sure, but that's where I call bullshit. They needed it for a canvas where they could spill out their minds, their memories, their desires, themselves. For purification. For purgation. But their demons emerged as monstrosities, mutant figures of weird shit that was lurking in wilds. Whatever was within them joined with what was out in the desert and then came calling. But they were too blind to recognize themselves in those monsters and saw them only as demons from somewhere beyond. Because they misunderstood. Even the nothing-places are plagued with content. Just like the mind: no matter how deep the absolution, it leaves a residue, a film of guilt or desire, for you or me or the hermits themselves. But you take what you can get. This countryside is what I can get. It's as safe as it comes for me. And my monsters are all around, but they belong as much to me as to this place. Just like Anthony, only I can see they're mine." He had gazed out the window for a few seconds. "Only he who first attains madness will reach enlightenment."

"Is that from Saint Anthony's desert sayings? I am not as familiar with him as I would like."

"Nah. That's from Saint Abraham of the Plain." He laughed a little. Grotto chuckled too.

The priest heard Abraham ask for the check and then the garbled sound of the diner, Abraham's voice, and his own fingers handling the tape recorder. He had paused it accidentally instead of pressing stop, and it screeched a little on the headphones, but the garbled sounds came back in, muted by his thumb over the microphone, and then loud again as his thumb hit the volume knob. The audio cracked loudly from when he had set the device down on the table, and the noise of the place and their voices made him dizzy as he lay there between waking and sleep. Grotto, like a child, had unconsciously been spinning the recorder with his hands, the priest remembered. The sound made him feel drunk again, and he fell asleep to the chaos in his ears, as the light around the parameter of the dark curtain flared up with the full force of the sun and glowed behind the block of black.

Chapter 8

Sheriff Slocum sat in the Allerton Public Library, just off of the square, in Monticello, at a wide wooden table built for four. There were newspapers scattered around him across the plain of the table top, a stack next to him in an out-scooted chair, and another in the floor nearby. At the circulation desk by the door, two librarians whispered in thin voices that filled the space of the high room like a song from far away. In a padded chair near the magazines, a thin, bald old man stared through a plastic-handled magnifying glass into a photograph of naked tribespeople from a remote corner of some foreign land in a *National Geographic* spread across his lap. It had been some time since he'd turned a page.

Slocum sat still, his chin resting on the backs of his interlaced fingers, his wife's red-rimmed drugstore reading glasses at the end of his nose. A shadow came across the page, and Slocum felt breath on his neck.

"You're in my light," Slocum said.

"What're you doing, Sheriff?" It was Richie.

Slocum turned his head to find Richie's head perched next to his, just off his left shoulder, like a second head of his own.

"I am reading, Richie," he said slowly, as though he were speaking to a little child.

"Yeah, but why, Sheriff Slocum?"

"Why?" Slocum said it like he didn't understand the question. "To learn some things."

"That's sure a lot of papers. You just kinda take'em in all at once, so you don't have to trouble with it every morning?"

Slocum continued to stare at him. Richie went on in a library whisper that was more like a falsetto you'd use for a character in a children's story.

"You know them papers are old ones, Sheriff. They keep the

current papers on the wood sticks over there." He pointed.

Slocum backed his chair out a little. "Richie, I'm not the brightest bulb in the box, but I learned some things from them Chicago detectives a few years back. You remember when they found that Mexican feller out there on Route 10 in the Guthrie's field, back when Sawlaw's runnin' the show?"

"Yes, Sheriff. I heard he was from the cartels, my dad said. That was before I got hired on."

"Yup. Them detectives were all over the scene out there, snappin' pictures, measurin' things, plasterin' boot-prints and tire tracks, takin' soil samples. Blood. The whole nine yards. Used gadgets you and I only seen on the TV."

"Yes, sir."

"Um hm. But all for nothin'. You know they took over two hundred pictures out there in that field. They studied 'em with magnifying glasses, just like old Keith over there is studyin' the tits of those poor aborigines."

The old man in the corner looked up, shushed them, and went back to his tribespeople. Slocum went on without acknowledging him.

"They threw in the full extent of their resources and all whatnot, but what they couldn't figure on was why that boy was killed there, three hours outa Brainerd, up in Chicago. You know what they found?"

"Huh uh."

"Richie, they found that that boy had a girlfriend, a white girl from up there, who'd moved in with her sister-in-law's folks some years before to take care of 'em — she's a nurse or somethin'. She and the Mexican been on-again-off-again 'fore she tired of it and left out. Hadn't seen him in eight years or some shit, but that's why he come. Just didn't know one of his hombres was knockin' him off 'fore they headed back home. Took 'em months 'fore they finally figured it out, and it happened on accident. Just got lucky."

"I don't understand, Sheriff."

"You know what else you won't understand?"

"What!" Richie seemed excited to hear something else he wouldn't understand.

"I come up with the same info a good six weeks 'fore they did. Told 'em 'bout it afterwards, just so's I could fuck with 'em. You know how?"

"No, sir."

"Obituary. That part where it says, 'the deceased is survived by' blah blah blah. They mentioned her. I guess they grown real close, the nurse and the family, so they included her. Said she was formerly of Brainerd in Chicago. Them folks left her a real nice car too. Once I caught that, wasn't too long 'fore I had 'em connected on paper. So what's that tell us then, Richie?"

"You're smarter than them detectives?" He laughed.

"History." Slocum paused and pointed his finger. His mustache curled down with his sharp, serious frown. He looked over the glasses. "Now the details, the scene, pictures—the facts—all that shit is fine, but your biggest and best friend is history, and I'm not talkin' criminal neither. Just the past. And sometimes you gotta go lookin' for it, dig it up."

"I'm not sure what we're talking about anymore, Sheriff Slocum."

Slocum pulled his glasses off his nose and held them by one side and then stuck the end of it in the corner of his mouth. "That's what I'm doin' here, son. Why I'm here readin' old newspapers. 'Cause the kind of history we's lookin' for very well may not be in any reports, in any of the details. In the facts. I've checked and rechecked. So now I'm goin' for history and see where the rabbit trail takes me. Goin' from the trees to the forest."

"So, you follow the facts?"

Slocum sighed. "Know that old sayin' you can't see the forest for the trees?"

"Yeah. I heard that. My mom says it to me sometimes."

"The facts is the trees. They's connected, but sometimes they get in the way of findin' the truth, of seein' the whole picture, the forest, for what it is. Can't see the forest for the trees. There's wisdom in that."

"Shit!" Richie lit up. "I just remembered what I come to tell you. That Abraham woke up finally. What you want us to do with him?"

"Hold him. I ain't done with him yet," Slocum said, nonplussed, going back to the papers. He tossed on the glasses and let them slide into position.

"Clifton ain't gonna press charges. Says he shoulda known better after watching him beat the shit outta all them others. Says they was all drunk. Says he's gonna let it go. Still looks like shit though. Got more bandages on his face than the Invisible Man. Kirby ER released him little bit ago."

"Hold him," Slocum said without looking up.

"You want me to cut him loose at the twenty-four-hour mark?"

"I want you to hold him until I say otherwise." His sharp voice bounced around the hard walls, on to the high ceiling, and came back to them. The librarians were whispering again, their faces inclined towards one another, but their eyes on Slocum.

"I'll be back in a couple of hours, Richie. Get him somethin' from the Subway for dinner." He handed him some cash from his pocket. "Get yourself somethin' too."

Slocum held the paper in front of him with his arms wide and he watched Richie walk away like a beaten puppy out into the pale green light of the tiled entryway. The old man in the corner had fallen asleep in the chair, and the magazine had closed and slid between his legs at a diagonal, the corner sticking up, like a wide arrow pointing from his crotch towards his drooping head. Slocum slapped the man's knee with his right hand as one side of the paper fell slowly and folded in on itself. The old man started and the magazine drooped and fell into the floor.

"Put your tits away, Keith. Time to go home."

The old man fetched the magazine from the floor, tossed it onto the table, and walked away blubbering out a few breaths of annoyance but not saying anything. Slocum righted the newspaper and read on.

* * *

The priest woke up to a deep laugh that slowly spilled into his ears in chugs as from a large jug overturned. It took him a minute during the silence that followed to reach the conclusion that the laugh had come from the headphones he had fallen asleep wearing. He was about to remove them when he heard a voice he did not recognize ask, "Is it true that the Meadows girl came to see you?" He was still foggy with sleep, but the voice sounded demonic. It slid up and down syllables. It moaned across vowels. It lingered like a serpent on s-es. He felt around for the tape recorder. He pressed the stop button. It must have been playing, rewinding, and playing again for hours. He rubbed his eyes, backed the tape up an instant, and pressed play. He heard the end of the laughing and the question. He sat up and saw the battery light glowing. The voice he had heard was his own. As he listened on, it occurred to him that he seemed to be eaves-dropping on a telephone call from Screwtape to Wormwood.

"Yes," said a demon parody of Abraham's voice, "that's true."

"Why did you not tell Slocum?"

"I hadn't realized she was the one."

"Will you tell me what happened?"

"Yeah. She came for absolution."

"For what?"

"She didn't give specifics. Said she had kept secrets from God, that she'd done horrible things, but all of it was secret, especially from God. She said she didn't deserve to be healed. That's all she said. She cried a lot. She asked me some things. She told me some things. And asked me to forgive her."

"Did you notice her," there was a pause, "how shall I say it, changed?"

"Yes."

The priest had left space enough for more, but nothing more came.

"What did you say to her?"

"That from what I understood of God, he either already knew her secrets, just didn't care about them. Or that she simply didn't matter enough in the grand scheme of things that she needed to worry over how God felt about her. Or that God was nothing. I told her that, from what I understood, secrets were like diseases that spread around when you kept them to yourself. That you had to decide whether or not you could live with the symptoms in yourself and whoever else. She said the truth of what she'd done was ugly and evil and she'd never tell it. I said that truth is truth, what is, that it didn't need her to be what it is. She asked me to forgive her. I said I couldn't, that that wasn't how things worked. She asked me what I thought of her and her miracle, that's what she called it. I told her I hadn't thought of either. She asked me what I thought she should do. I told her that wasn't how things worked either. She told me that she hadn't hurt so bad before her miracle. She asked me why I did it. I told her if I had done it, I hadn't meant to. I told her I was sorry. And then she left."

The tape recorder was dying. The negative space between words had never struck the priest so much as they did at this moment. The speech lurched on in slurs.

"Why did you say such things?"

The device finally died after Abraham's response, the play button still depressed, the tape unwilling to move: "Because they were true."

* * *

The car crunched up the winding gravel drive that led to Bull Meadows' farm. It was a good ways back in a thicket of oaks, their long, low limbs reaching down before they crept out and touched each other or the few pines besides. Bull had an old two-story farmhouse, a couple of wooden barns near the back of the lot, which opened up to the pasture beyond, where the cattle grazed. He kept his shop and office in two rooms set off for that purpose in the big pole barn, which stood about parallel with the house, but on the other side of the driveway. The drive broadened out about a hundred yards before either building and took over the ground from there. Everything was covered in white chalkrock gravel; it went clear out to the grain bins near the barns. Slocum pulled in and parked near the office, just as Jody Barnes and his brother walked out. Slocum never could remember the younger Barnes kid's name. Jody shoved the younger Barnes at the car and pretended an escape.

"Shit, Bud! It's the cops!"

Slocum laughed as Jody turned around, smiling. Bud still looked confused.

"What're you boys into today?"

"Well, Sherriff. We gotta scoop some shit before we bring the cows in. Castratin' in the morning. You want in?"

Bud laughed.

"Hell no. I done had my share a that when I's a boy."

"Good eatin' though, Sheriff." Jody lifted his t-shirt and slapped his belly. Bud laughed again.

"Well, I'll leave it to a Barnes to be eatin' cow nuts."

"Bull's in there. We'll be seein' ya, Sheriff."

Jody and Bud climbed into their rusty red pickup and drove it back on the property. Slocum watched them out his open window as they parked at the end of the drive, near the barns, found shovels and went to work. He got out and knocked on the door to Bull's office. He entered after hearing someone holler from within.

Bull was at the desk, an old kitchen countertop set on top of two two-drawer filing cabinets. It smelled of grease and cigars. Bull motioned for Slocum to come in as he said something into the telephone he held to his head with the other hand. Slocum found a green plastic school chair and sat down. Bull rolled his eyes at Slocum and held a finger up. Slocum laughed noiselessly and looked around the office. There were invoices everywhere, a pile of green bills on the desk, a stack of feed sacks near the door that led out into the shop, tools, some engine parts, a two-year-old calendar with a red Corvette and two blondes in swimming suits with high-heeled shoes standing on either side of it. But his eyes settled behind Bull, on the side of a tall cabinet papered with crayon drawings done by Barbie. Bull hung up the phone.

"Well, what brings you out to my neck of the woods, Sheriff?" Bull's voice boomed in the little room.

"I just come to see how you're holdin' up, see if you got a few minutes to talk."

"I'm just trying to stay busy, you know? You stop for a few minutes and your mind wanders. So I'm keeping busy. There's no shortage of things to be done."

"You got a few minutes?"

"I'll do whatever I can, Sheriff."

"Hey, how're them Barnes boys workin' out? They stayin' on the straight and narrow?"

"Oh yeah. They's good kids. Long as you keep 'em busy. I try to wear 'em out so they don't cause you no more trouble." Bull laughed a couple of times.

"Let me ask you somethin', Bull. I's speakin' to Reverend Crocket the other day, and his wife too."

"Now, she's a piece of work." Bull shot his eyebrows up as he traced a circle in the air with an index finger around his right ear.

"She is that. But they seem to think Barbie had some kinda miracle, now that's their word. Said you probably knowed about it."

Bull sat for a moment and rubbed his cheeks with his hardened fingers. Then he took his hat off by the bill and tossed it onto the desk. He sighed.

"Listen," Bull said, "I know they all loved Barbie down there at the church, and they're real sweet to her. You know they still let her come to the VBS?"

"They's nice folks."

"I heard from some of the bluehairs that Barbie said something after a Bible-story play or something, but I don't know if that qualifies as a miracle. Barbie would talk sometimes, when she wasn't around a lot of folks, see."

"So she didn't seem no different to you, then, after that?"

"No, Sheriff. She was the same sweet girl she always been." He was rubbing his face again, sniffling a little.

"You know, Slocum," his voice was sour now, "Barbie was retarded. I remember the way the doctors put it. It wasn't her mind that was the trouble, it was her brain. They said they wasn't the same thing exactly. Her brain didn't grow up, the organ in her head, you see, it didn't grow up like it was supposed to. They said her brain was round about that of a two-year-old, maybe. But the rest of her grew up anyway. Without it. But her brain was stuck in the past at two, you see."

"Yes. Course, Bull. It's just, well, you know I gotta ask."

Bull put his outspread palm in the air before him and it punctuated his words with a motion like he was intermittently pushing keys on a piano. "What I'm saying is shit like that doesn't change, Sheriff. Brains, the meat in your head, doesn't get normal, doesn't grow up like it's supposed to be, just sixteen years late, because somebody prayed real hard."

"Course, Bull, of course."

"You know I heard Reverend Crocket was cracking up maybe." He was calmer now, and he said it as if it had just come to him. "Maybe he's looking a little too hard for miracles. You know what I mean? A man starts to break down, he may start to look for something to hold it together."

"Yes, I had thought of somethin' similar myself."

"He looks real hard he's bound to find himself something."

"So you're sayin' no. Absolutely no. She's the same as she ever was right up until. . ." He stopped himself. ". . . Well, Christ, 'til the last time you seen her?"

"Yes. That's what I'm saying." He said it intently, his eyes glassy.

"Okay," Slocum said, frowning. "Okay."

Slocum stood up. He bent forward and shook Bull's big hand. It was rough and hard, but his grip was gentle. "I'll be in touch, Bull. You let me know if you think of anything you ain't already told us. Or if you just need an ear."

"Thanks, Sheriff." Bull held his gaze as he held his hand and then let go of both.

Slocum pulled the door open. It squealed metal on metal.

"Sheriff?"

Slocum turned, his hand still on the knob, his eyebrows up.

"I wish that preacher was right. You know? God owed her something."

"I know, son. I wished he was too."

Slocum waved at him and shut the door behind him. He stood by his car with his keys out watching the Barnes boys shovel cow shit. His mustache broadened a little with his smile underneath when Jody flung some manure at the younger Barnes, who came back at him with a broom handle. Slocum shook his head and got into the car.

He started the engine. "I can't never think of that boy's name." He backed her up and then drove away.

* * *

Abraham opened his eyes and wasn't sure what he was looking at. The screaming had been rising and falling for some time now through the cloud of sleep, and the screams and curses had joined his dreams and then finally pulled him away from them. He took to wakefulness slowly. He smelled the rich, rotten stench of beer, blood, and cigarettes on his breath, clothes, and beard, and it reached his nose with the smell of the place, which carried its own odors of mold, men, and shit. He lay on his side with his head pillowed on his left arm. It had fallen asleep too, and it tingled as it came back to life with his slight movement. After a moment, he sat up and rubbed his eyes with the heels of his palms and looked again.

In the dim gray of the cell he saw a shirtless, bloodied wiry little man, speaking through the bars to a straight-laced-looking man with glasses, his hair parted neatly to one side, a powder-blue short-sleeved button-up, and a wide, striped tie. A kid of maybe eighteen or twenty stood with the man on the outside. The kid silently looked around with his hands in his pockets. He looked at Abraham, and Abraham looked back, nodding finally. The kid nodded back and then smiled a little and cocked his head in the direction of the wiry man and raised an eyebrow, as if to say, "This guy's nuts." That's what Abraham took it as anyway.

"I'll fuckin' do it, Ron. I don't give a shit," the wiry man hollered out as he worked up his courage to crash his head into the bars, gripping them, rearing back from his abdomen. His voice was shrill and torn.

Abraham watched, squinting. The wiry man was wearing some kind of contraption around his head. It was a metal halo that encircled his skull. At two- or three-inch internals around the circumference of the halo were little screws that tightened down against his crown, like a globe in a light fixture. The halo was framed into some more metal and thick wires and rubber and straps that fitted around the man's shoulders and buckled around his chest. Abraham concluded that it was some kind of medical device to stabilize the spine or something. It was a hell of an image to wake up to though. It reminded him of drifting off, watching TV, when he was a kid, waking up in the middle of some late-running channel's midnight broadcast of *The Man from Planet X*. He pawed around for his cigarettes, but couldn't find them. He noticed that his hat was gone too.

"Why is it that you don't give a shit?" the straight-laced man asked. He said "don't give a shit" with the practiced elocution of a TV news man or an educated minister. Abraham smiled a little. He noticed that the kid was smiling too.

"I got nothin', Ron. My mom's dead. Judy don't want nothin' to do with me. They come and took my trailer. I ain't got shit and I ain't got shit to live for no more. And now they stuck me in here. I'm just gonna fuckin' end it right now." He lowered his head, as much as possible anyway. "Fuck!" he screamed. He poised himself to smash his head, along with its accoutrements, into the bars again.

The straight-laced man didn't bat an eye.

"Why did they stick you in here, Kenny?"

"Fuck, I dunno, Ron."

"You don't have any recollection of it, or you don't think it merited incarceration?"

"What?"

"You really don't know why you're in here?"

"Yeah, Ron, I know. 'Cause me and One-Eye Jack Potter broke into the True Value. One-Eye Jack's faster'n me."

"Why did you break into the hardware store?"

"Steal shit and get some money."

"For what?"

"We's gonna get some speed."

"Drugs?"

"Yeah."

"Why? You were released from the hospital yesterday."

The wiry man spat but didn't say anything.

"I did some checking, Kenny. They said you detoxed after your car accident when you were in the critical care. So, there you are, you're healing, clean, and you go and mess everything up again. You know why?"

"'Cause I'm a fuck-up?"

"No, Kenny. You're a nice kid, you're a good boy, but you're an addict. They kicked you out of the trailer park because you're an addict. Judy left you because you're an addict. They stuck you in here because you're an addict. You need help. Can you see that?" He moved in, squatted down like a kids' baseball coach and looked up to connect eyes with the wiry man. "When you wrecked your car, were you high?"

"And real drunk," he muttered.

The straight-laced man stood and took a card out of his wallet and wrote on it and handed it to the wiry man.

"You can call me whenever you need to. That's my beeper number. Now I think you should go and see a drug counselor, but you have to make that decision for yourself. But if you ever need someone to talk to, you can call me. You've got my number. Okay?"

"Alright, Ron," the wiry man said. He had been defeated and his passion was gone.

"I want you to tell me something, Kenny."

"Yeah, Ron?"

"I want you to tell me I am not a fuck-up."

"Ron, you ain't a fuck-up. You're a good man. Best I know of." He seemed hurt that the straight-laced man thought so lowly of himself.

"No. I want you to say it of yourself."

The wiry man was quiet for a moment. He spit again. "Oh. Okay, Ron."

"Say it. I am not a fuck-up."

"I'm not a fuck-up."

"Again," the straight-laced man said as he crossed his arms.

"I am not a fuck-up."

"Again."

The wiry man was unable to say it anymore. He was sobbing too hard, kneeling, trying to hold his head steady, so as not further injure his spine. He had broken.

"Goodbye, Kenny. You're a good boy." The straight-laced man and the kid walked off into the dark, the kid waving to Abraham as they did.

Finally, still bawling, noiselessly at first through his nose, in the floor, gripping his halo, the wiry man finally bellowed out through his sobs, "I'm not a fuck-up." Abraham could only decipher the words because he figured they were coming sooner or later. They sounded like the noises Petunia made. Kind of a bleating cry. It was a desperate sound.

Abraham found his boots. The laces were gone, but he put them on anyway. The wiry man stood and turned his whole body towards the sound. He was reaching through his halo to rub tears from his eyes.

"I thought you was a dead man."

Abraham sat, slouching on the cot. "Nope."

"Thought maybe the morgue done filled up with bodies or somethin', 'cause a all the murders, you know?" He was still rubbing his eyes with his fingers. "You know the law ain't too bright 'round here. Never know what kinda shit they's gonna pull."

"Yeah."

"So you ain't a dead man?"

"Not yet."

The wiry man was still working on one of his eyes. He laughed hard but then immediately drew back sharply. "Fuck!" He squatted, his hands hovering around his halo, unsure where to go, but drawn to the pain it seemed. He was whimpering now like a beaten dog but trying not to show it.

"It's real hard to be happy in this fuckin' thing," he said.

Abraham wasn't sure how to respond, so for a moment he did not. He just sat, frowning.

"It's real hard to be happy outside of that fucking thing too," he said finally.

The wiry man kneeled and turned his whole body towards him. "That's truer n' poetry right there." He sat that way on his knees for a few minutes, rubbing his eye again, and then just blanking out, staring in the only direction he could.

"Mister?" His torn voice sounded weakly in the hard room. "I know we ain't friends, but I don't think I can get up. I ain't slept in a few days. Would you help me up?"

Abraham rose from the cot. He was there in two steps, and even in that distance lost one of his laceless boots. He noticed his pants sagging and remembered his ruined belt and a broken button from the night before. He took the man's out-reaching hand. The wiry man strained, quaking as he did, and made it halfway up before dropping again, crying out and puffing like a woman in labor.

"I think you've got a fever. You're burning up," Abraham said. He placed a palm on the man's forearm, then the inside of his elbow.

The man reached out to Abraham with his other hand but only caught the leg of his trousers. Abraham reached through the halo and touched the wiry man's forehead. His torso bent weakly back, giving in to the faint pressure of Abraham's hand. Up close the wiry man looked much older, his face lined and contorted.

"I know we ain't friends," the man said again weakly, but his voice trailed off as his eyes closed. Then the wiry man contracted, over and over, pulsing in slow convulsions back and forth, tugging at Abraham's pant-leg, pulling his trousers part-way down.

Richie walked in from the dark hall, peering into the cell, sucking the straw protruding from an obtusely large Styrofoam cup, the priest following him.

"Fuckin' queers!" he yelled.

He dropped the bag of sandwiches and the cup and frantically searched for the key, ranting.

"Kenny, you can suck dick at the truck stop in Macon County and peddle your ass in any other in the great state of Illinois."

He pulled his nightstick from his side as he opened the door and cracked Abraham in the arm with it to back him off. Then he went after the wiry man.

"But you cannot..."

He hit him.

"Suck..."

He hit him.

"Dick...

He hit him.

"In my jailhouse."

He hit him again, and the wiry man fell over.

"And you, motherfucker!" He pointed the stick at Abraham. "I knew you's queer the moment I set eyes on you."

The priest's eyes were wide, his hands pointlessly out in front of him.

"Please, officer. Stop. Please stop," he said, frenzied.

"What is it, Father? You don't want me to ugly up your girlfriend?" Richie slammed the cell door. He eyed the priest. "You got ten minutes." He looked at Abraham. "And no more!" He pointed the stick at Abraham through the bars. "No more, no more, queer stuff." He said it like he had been betrayed.

Abraham pursed his lips and made some smooching sounds.

"God damn it!" Richie fumbled with his keys again.

"Richie!" someone yelled from farther up the hall. A light flicked on.

"Yessir?"

"Clean this shit up. Why do you leave a mess wherever you go?"

"I will, sir." He pointed at Abraham with the nightstick again and backed out.

The wiry man stirred against the concrete floor. He moaned a little.

The priest was lost somewhere, gazing into the gray concrete of the wall, rubbing his beard.

Abraham lay down on his back on the cot, his arm folded behind his head.

"El Greco. . ." the priest whispered to himself as though he had just remembered something.

"Did you say cigarette?" Abraham said. "Hell, yes." He got up.

The priest handed him the pack and a lighter, and Abraham lit up and smoked, leaning against the bars, while the wiry man stood, loosened the screws of his halo, unfastened straps, untwisted ties, and finally pulled himself free of it, tossing the thing on the floor, and then, finding an already filthy rag, and laughing giddily, he stripped naked and washed himself from the sink by the commode.

"Time's up, queers!" Richie's voice sounded from down the hall.

"Mind if I hold on to these?" Abraham said, holding up the pack of smokes.

"Not at all. . ." the priest said absently.

"I'll give you a call when they let me out."

"Yes. Yes. Okay."

The priest walked out, the piss-colored light illuminating his way, around Richie and his mop. Abraham inhaled deeply and blew out a plume of smoke towards the ceiling. It coiled and spun magnificently as it clouded the yellow light. He stubbed the butt out on the bars and flicked it out into the hall, near where Richie was mopping up his drink.

"God damn it!"

Abraham found the cot again and fell asleep to the sounds of the wiry man's endless, laughing bath, to the gentle sounds of his unwrung rag dripping water on the floor. It sounded like rain.

Chapter 9

The priest found an open seat next to Grotto at the counter at Sadie's, a little coffee shop on the west side of the Square, a few doors down from where they had parted ways on the sidewalk earlier, in front of the florist's. Grotto was perched on the stool like a gargoyle, his lazy jaws wide, his hands folded in his lap, his eyes squinting against the late-afternoon sun. He did not seem to notice his friend. The priest ordered a cup of coffee and a piece of apple pie, topped with a thin slice of sharp cheddar, peppered with diced black olives, and warmed with butter in skillet. The waitress grimaced.

"That sounds nasty. Are you sure you wouldn't rather have it a la mode?"

"Quite sure. Thank you."

"Okay," she said, as if she were giving one last warning to a reckless child. She wrote in her order pad, ripped off the page, and walked off to explain the pie to the cook. The cook asked her to repeat the order twice more; the third time through, he listened as peered through the pick-up window at the priest with the surprise and reverence reserved for the most exotic birds at the zoo.

Grotto nodded a greeting finally and patted the priest on the arm. The priest smiled at him. He had become quite fond of the little old man. There was something quietly noble and gentlemanly about his manner that reminded him of a Europe now gone. The waitress brought the pie, though she tried not to look at it, and slid a coffee in for the priest. She refilled Grotto's cup, dropped off a couple of creamers, and picked up his spotless dishes. He nodded and smiled a humble little smile. She winked at him. The exchange brought a chuckle from the priest. He forked in some pie, savoring it as he chewed, while Grotto looked on bemused.

Someone took the seat next to Grotto, on the other side. The waitress went over.

"Well, hello, sweet Anne. How are you this fine afternoon?"

Grotto gave the priest a crooked half-smile and pointed him towards the man with a thumb. The priest sighed and sipped his coffee.

"What'll it be, Sheriff?"

"Coffee and a piece of that apple pie a la—what the hell is that?" He was gaping at the priest's cheese and olive-covered pie. "If that ain't against the law, it should be," he said loudly. A few patrons laughed. So did the waitress.

"I tried to tell him, Sheriff, but he said he was quite sure he wanted it that way," she said, attempting to mimic the priest's accent when she said "quite sure." They laughed again.

"Oh, it is very tasty," the priest said, forcing a smile. "A flavor combination, yes?"

"No! Hell, no!" Slocum said.

"Oh, come now, Mr. Slocum, it is not all that rare."

"Now, Anne, that is a fact. My granddaddy used to eat cheese on his fruit pies, come to think of it, not olives now. He said back in the East End, that's shit town slums in London, sweetie, you ate whatever your mum served up. 'Course he also ate fried cow brains and whatnot. How's that for a flavor combination, eh priest?"

The waitress moaned her disgust, and they all laughed again. The priest tapped his fingers on the counter, waiting for the moment to pass, but Slocum glared on at him.

"Well?"

"Well what?" the priest said politely.

"You ever tried fried cow brains or, um, what? Blood omelets?" They laughed again. "Shit-ka-bobs? They eat that in your native land, priest? They eat shit-ka-bobs?"

The priest did not respond. He sipped the coffee again, waiting for the moment to pass, but, again, Slocum seemed intent on embarrassing him, teaching him a lesson.

"Where is it you said you's from anyway, priest? I can't quite place the funny way you say things."

The priest only sipped coffee, figuring he would try to remove himself from the café conversation.

"Now, I been in the service and they flew me here and there, but nowhere's where they speak English quite like you do."

The priest gave up. "I am from all over."

"All over, huh? A man of the world?"

The priest nodded. It seemed that the chatter in the room had started up again. The waitress had gone to retrieve Slocum's pie. She returned with it, slid a mug in front of him, and filled it with coffee. Slocum took a bite.

"You know," he began, still chewing. He swallowed. "I even been to Vatican City." He gulped some coffee. "Yes, sir, there's a lot of money locked up there in Vatican City. Beautiful place though."

"Yes," the priest said.

"They got a lot of, what you call 'em. . .street vendors! They got a lot of them street vendors there, sellin' food out of carts and cookin' in little booths along the sidewalks. It's like the whole god damn town's a big carnival. Men parading around in dresses and funny little hats, buyin' sausages all day long out there in the street. Big times there in Vatican City."

"Lovely city," the priest said.

Slocum wasn't eating anymore. He had swiveled his stool a quarter turn and was facing the priest, looking at him over Grotto, who had slowly turned back towards the door behind them and was staring vacantly outside, not seeming to notice that the slow swivel had spun him halfway around. The priest was facing the counter, his coffee cup in his hand, his elbows on the corner of the surface, under his hunching shoulders. He did not look at Slocum.

"You know the funny thing about a carnival, priest?"

No answer.

"Nah, I guess you don't, seein' how's you live in it." Then loud enough for all to hear, "Shit, you're wearin' a dress right now!" He laughed exaggeratedly. A few old men at the tables laughed with him.

The priest gave him nothing more.

"The funny thing is there ain't no rules in a carnival. No place for the law. Shit, half the fun is 'cause it's anonymous. The inside is out. The upside is down."

People were listening. Some seemed to be taking interest in Slocum's words.

"Now, sure, there's freedom in that. But that kinda freedom, it ain't natural. It ain't real freedom. You know what comes of a place or a people when it's all just a big carnival? When they's allowed to be anonymous? They don't give a damn 'bout their rules no more. They get to thinkin' they's above the law. Like it's got no connection to 'em." Slocum sipped his coffee dramatically.

"That's why we see so many of your class, priest, takin' things ain't theirs to take. Usin' people, hell, even children, in ways that ain't natural." He looked around the room. "In ways that just ain't right." He set the cup down and put his hands on his knees. "But in your Vatican City, it's just like the carnival. Ya'll got your costumes on, so it's all out in the open, and no one gives a damn." He laughed again, looking at the glazed faces at the tables on the floor. "You're an odd lot, padre." He laughed, though his eyes were set, serious. Some at the tables muttered a little. A few laughs went up. A woman sneezed.

"Miss? May I have the check please?" the priest said politely.

"No, no," Slocum said. "I'm just cuttin' up, padre. You don't hafta leave on my account."

"I am quite finished," the priest said, still without looking at him.

"Nah, not yet, you ain't even ate your cheesy shit pie yet." He had given up the jokey tone now.

The priest looked at Slocum now, and the coffee shop went silent. An old farmer blew his nose into a red bandanna, but no one took notice. Their eyes were on the men at the counter. "I am done, Mr. Slocum," he said over Grotto. "I would like to pay now, yes?" He turned to the waitress. She looked to Slocum.

"No," he said. "No, I ain't done with you. Annie," he went on sweetly, still staring at the priest, "why don't you give me his check. I'll make sure he don't skip out without payin'."

She set the paper down in front of Slocum. The priest laid a twenty on the counter, and headed for the door. Grotto carefully climbed down from the stool and started after him. Slocum cut him off and stood between them, fencing the little man from making his exit, his arm out behind him, his fingers fanned.

"No. I said I ain't done with you, priest," Slocum spat.

The priest turned. "What!" he yelled. "What do you want from me?"

"I want you to be honest with me," Slocum said, quietly now. "You said you's on my side but your actions prove otherwise."

"I am not on a side." He tried to calm himself. "I am on the side of the truth, of God. That is all. I look at the facts, just as you do."

"Just as I do, huh? And what have you found? What're the facts? D'you press him about the Meadows girl?"

"He said she came to talk. That is all."

"And you believe him, do ya?"

"Yes."

"You know she couldn't hardly carry on a conversation with a good-natured dog?"

"She had been changed. Healed."

"By your friend Abraham? A miracle, huh?"

"So it seems."

"So it seems," he said disgustedly. Then his voice rose. "Well, I'd say it'd be a damn miracle if that Abraham and his midgets ain't a covey of strange birds. Fuckin' perverts. Fact is, I heard he's caught with his pants down in the jailhouse with a known man whore, a sex offender hisself, this very afternoon." The herd in the café stared on. They were not even eating anymore.

"A misunderstanding," the priest said softly. He noticed their faces. He looked at the floor.

"Misunderstanding," Slocum spat back mockingly. "You know, I'm startin' to think them two little shits out at Friends Creek maybe got their comeuppance. I think this thing's 'bout to crack the fuck open." He got his cuffs out. "You go on about your business now, priest," he said, roughly grabbing Grotto's shoulder and pulling him through the door. "Think I'll hold on to this one for a while though."

He tugged sharply at Grotto. He fell down on the pavement behind Slocum.

"Sheriff, please," the priest said, walking towards them.

He drew his pistol and held it on the priest.

"Walk! God damn it." He clicked the safety off. His eyes flared. "Get out of my sight."

They stared back at one another through the open doorway in silence. It was a stand-off.

Then Slocum screamed out in a feral howl, sharp reports blowing from his gun into the air. The priest ducked down in confusion. By the time he got to his feet, Grotto had already scampered off down an alley near the florist's shop, blood trailing from both sides of his mouth and down his chin and shirt collar. He glanced back at Slocum, who was shouting curses into the sky. He lay in a fetal pose in the doorway to Sadie's, gripping his ankle with two bloodied hands. The priest hurried around the block to the car. Grotto was lying face down in the floorboard of the back seat, wheezing in short, frantic breaths. The priest looked in the rearview, waiting, catching his breath. No one appeared. He put the car in gear and drove away.

* * *

The canoe was motionless under the bridge, the river still, and everything was quiet. A sliver of silver shone out in the sky, a celestial nail-clipping frozen in its fall. It cast enough light to see only gradations of blackness. Abraham realized he was holding his breath, but he was afraid to let it go, afraid of disturbing the balance. It was cool, but no wind moved the foliage. The long grass along the banks was still. Nothing moved. He felt his fingers burning. He looked at his hand and found a cigarette, the cherry burning into the filter, and his fingers besides, the smoke trailing over the side of the canoe and down across the water. He wrung his hand, flinging the butt into the dull black wash of the sky, where it stuck high above, its smoke winding a path down to the water. He finally exhaled a cloud. He felt dizzy as he watched it swirl into the night. It joined itself to the curl of moon and took its light, and the moon was full. Abraham gazed at it from the boat. It flared up, leaving an incandescent halo of pale light behind, but the sphere itself contracted within the haze, then darkened to mercurial black, and leaked a sloping string of liquid black metal down towards the water, but haphazardly, like a piece of yarn in a gentle wind. All else was still. Abraham watched it trail slowly down and dip into the water, and the oily blackness filled the river. In its stillness it threw back the image in the sky in reflection.

Abraham found an oar and eased it into the water. It parted and rippled out in circles. He withdrew the oar and watched as the ripples radiated, distorting the grim picture from above. He glanced back at the sky and found it unchanged, the black balloon holding its eclipse, the flicked cigarette red as a drop of blood. The image in the water warbled in tremulous shivers that eased with time, the light flashing across the face of the black ball. Abraham waited for it to stop, watching as the tremors faded off and the water stilled again.

He frowned and drew his browline together. The black water was slick with stillness. He looked back at the sky. It was the same as before. The image that had settled in the water, though, had locked in its distortion, the mirror-effect corrupted. He squinted at it, his head turning to right the image in his mind. The black ball in the river seemed to be revolving slowly around. He checked the sky again. It was untouched. He peered back into the river. The black ball, now marbled with white and red, turned over and over, the colors merging and pulling away, a thick monochrome tide poisoned with blood. Its revolutions slowed and finally halted. Abraham waited as his mind made sense of the image it found. He reached out and touched the water with his fingers. It was cool and as hard as glass. He beat the water with his fist to shake the image loose, but it was as if he were beating a stone. Finally, he raised the oar above his head and struck the surface of the river. As wood met rock, the water flowed and everything went dark. The boat was gone. The moon was gone. The sky was gone. It had all been washed into nothing, and Abraham was caught in the current. He gasped and flailed but could not find a shore. So he gave in and let himself be washed away.

* * *

He awoke on the floor of the cell, his skin burning. Richie and another cop were shouting and hooting as they shot him with a sprayer on a hose affixed to the spigot on the water heater. He writhed in the corner against the wall and finally crawled under the cot and curled himself up like an infant in a crib. They sprayed on, laughing. Abraham closed his eyes again, but opened them after only a moment, for when he held them tight he could only see the grinning clown shining out in smears of light from the black balloon from the dream.

Richie quit with the hose.

"Time to wake up, asshole. Sheriff Slocum's gonna take you for a ride."

They laughed again but went off down the hall. Abraham looked around. The wiry man was nowhere to be found. The cell door was open. Abraham rose and stood in the water pooling on the concrete. He watched it swirl into the dark of the drain near the center. Then he walked across the water towards the open door.

* * *

The priest studied the atlas spread out across the passenger seat and scribbled with a stubby pencil in a small notepad. Grotto watched him through the space between the seats. He figured him as a man capable of much. Grotto worried about the priest though. He was driven. That much was obvious. But Grotto had searched the man for signs of failure, of having been broken somehow, and he found nothing of the sort. Whatever disappointments his life had brought, whatever shortcomings he may have suffered, Grotto took him as the kind of man who drove through them like a mule tilling hard earth. The priest was a will-driven man. He liked the priest very much. He reminded him not a little of his own son, though the priest was a kind man. But, he thought, as he watched him grind the pencil into the paper, as he watched the priest's eyes flick mechanically from the map to the notepad and back, his hand moving again, a will-driven man can be a dangerous man. And that made him worried for Abraham.

Grotto wasn't sure where they had stopped, but soon the priest was driving again, and it wasn't long before the high buildings and the stop-again-start-again were gone, and the wide signs and long trucks zoomed past the window and were left somewhere behind. He could feel the priest speed through the gears and settle into the hum that whipped the wire poles by. He had become used to the sequence from his travels with Abraham, though often the gentle shimmy of fast travel in the ice-cream truck, together with the warm drone of the engine, put him to sleep. Abraham rarely hurried though, so it was the same process, just faster. Grotto listened to the priest speak a few times, and he even entertained his bad stabs with his rough Italian, but he was tired. He slouched himself into the corner of the seat, behind where the priest was driving, out of the sightline of any adjustment on the rearview mirror. He thought he should save his sleeping for the plane, but he did not feel like talking or listening. So he watched the sky.

It was bright blue and clear, except for the mountains of clouds that floated in billowing clumps. They gathered together and broke apart, all of it at a pace appropriate for farming country. The sun was not visible from where he was looking, but its light saturated everything. It was the brightness in the blue of the sky. It was the whiteness in the perfect ruffles of the clouds. He kept watching. He smiled a little when he thought that even in a car moving so fast, he could watch the slow play of the heavens, not losing sight of a cloud's dance before the blue curtain behind for what seemed like a long time. This fact made his life seem lucky somehow. Even though everything was changing, even though his brothers were gone, and even though this next change, which was probably his last, would take him far away from the man he had come to love more than the sky, the man who would occupy his prayers at Monte Casino. At least the sky would be the same. And he would share it with Abraham. And that was lucky indeed.

Like the world itself, Grotto thought, he had come from nothing, and his life, perhaps, had stayed closer to that origin than most, but he was an old man and would soon be dead, returned to the dust. But he looked across his life as he looked across the sky. Its collisions had seemed a chaos at times, and the moment he lived was but a speck of cloud in the sky, pulling others to it, and being pulled into others, all lit up by the sun, all given their truth by God. His life had moved him towards

Abraham. God had given him the gift of a part to play, and He had given him his brothers to play it with him. And the others had seen it too. It had not taken them long to see it. But Abraham was a hard man. A harder one to follow. How do you serve a man who wants nothing? They asked this among themselves. It was Emilio who said it: we do as he asks. So they did, and it had changed them, even Nino.

As they drove on, the sky dimmed. Grotto let his head slide over on the seat and rested it on the back. He let his eyes close. After a few moments, the rearview mirror caught the setting sun behind them. The priest pushed it away with his hand. Grotto felt the light the mirror cast over his closed eyes. It felt warm, even so diminished, removed from its source. His open mouth curled into a great smile. He said a silent prayer for Abraham.

"La luce," he whispered. Then he fell asleep.

* * *

Slocum knocked on the screen door. Then he rang the doorbell. Then he pulled the screen door open and knocked on the wooden door within, while pushing the doorbell over and over. The little light in the button went off when he pushed it and came on when he let it out, and he had the thing blinking at a pretty good clip. Finally, he gave up on the entrance and hobbled back to the cruiser; the engine was still running. He pulled it up into the front yard, to the second set of windows, and turned on the spot on the mirror, shining the light into the house through the screen. He clicked on the PA horn.

"Sheriff Smalley," his voice popped and fuzzed over the horn, "get your ass out of bed and answer the front door." He said it like it was a public service announcement.

A dark shape within, not unlike a potbellied silverback, waddled, half bent over at about forty-five degrees, through the window, then back in the opposite direction, then fell from sight, and then emerged from below the sill, and returned to its original direction. A light went on in the living room, and the shape moved behind the curtain. The porch light went on, and the front door opened, and there was Smalley. Slocum turned the spot on him. Smalley blinked against it, waving his pistol back in its direction.

"Hold your fire!" Slocum shouted. He bleeped the siren and had the lights going now. Neighbors were emerging from their front doors, some peering from behind curtains in windows. Smalley panted and bent over with his hands on his knees, still holding the pistol, the mound of his belly eclipsing the tight red underwear he had on. He stood, shielding his eyes from the light.

"Damn you, Slocum!" he huffed. "It's three o'clock in the AM."

Slocum bleeped the siren again before his voice fuzzed loudly into the night. "Do beware that the white rhinoceros can respond with violence when provoked." Laughter rose from the darkness. Someone gave a cat call. "Get your pants on. We gotta go somewheres," Slocum's voice sounded again. "That's it, folks. Show's over. See you next week."

A few minutes later, Smalley got in the passenger side.

"How do you expect my people to respect my authority at all if you keep doing shit like that?"

"I don't, Smalley, but I don't think I'm hurtin' your reputation none neither."

"Now that's just unkind, Slocum. I thought we was friends." Smalley crossed his arms and stuck his lip out and looked out the window.

Slocum drove out of the yard to the road.

"What're we doing anyway?" Smalley said finally.

"Brainstormin'."

"And it couldn't wait 'til tomorrow? My God, Slocum."

"Listen, I think we been goin' bout this case all wrong. You remember that old Fred MacMurray movie?"

"You mean the one with the genie, where he can't get into the army 'cause of a 4F?"

"No. That's *Where Do We Go from Here*. What? No! What the hell's wrong with you?"

"I don't know. I thought that one was real good."

"*Double Indemnity*'s one I'm talkin' bout."

"That the one with Barbara Stanwyck and Edward Robinson?"

"Yeah. You know that claims man, Keyes, the Robinson character? He's always goin' on about his little man."

"I don't remember no midgets in that film, Slocum. You sure you're not thinking of *Smart Money*? Jimmy Cagney played second fiddle in that one. Now, Cagney's built real small but he wasn't no midget."

Slocum sighed. "No. It's like a metaphor. His little man. Like a feelin' inside. Won't let him sleep at night, gives him heartburn, and whatnot?"

"Oh." Smalley closed his eyes. "A metaphone, huh?"

"Meta*phor*. Somethin' that *really* means somethin' else."

"Little man. Yes." Smalley opened his eyes. "Yes, I do recall that," Smalley said after staring out the windshield for a minute. "Kinda like a gut hunch about something, huh?"

"I got that sorta feelin' bout this case since that night it all blew up. Somethin' bugged me bout that Abraham feller. Still do. But I ain't had nothin' to go on. Thought maybe somebody killed them midgets for spite or fun."

"Plausible. But what about Barbie? Thought you said they was connected?"

"That's it. If they's not, then it's plausible. But my little man tells me otherwise. 'Cause if they are, then we got ourselves a whole other can of worms."

"How you figure on that? That another metaphone, by the way, can of worms?"

"Yes," Slocum growled. "A killin' like that, that hard, don't it look more like revenge?"

"You mean the passion in it?"

"Yes I do. Whoever did it went well beyond killin' them little misfits."

"I see that. What you make of it then?"

"Who wasn't there that shoulda been?"

"Us?"

"No. Who might whoever done it might've expected to be there, you think?"

"That Abraham."

"Bingo."

Smalley laughed. "Damn! But why they after him?"

"You read them notes I dropped off?"

"Not yet. I been installing the new commode."

"Well, if you had, you'd see that little Barbie Meadows was spotted out there with Abraham and his midgets day or so before them three wind up dead. Camperman seen her steppin' outa that nasty ice-cream truck of his. Where's your mind go with that info?"

"Perverts?"

"Think about it. Some simple girl like Barbie ain't nothin' to some deviant outsiders, is she? They take what they want from her and send her on her way, thinkin' she ain't got smarts enough to tell. Only her daddy told me that sometimes, just sometimes, she could talk. Not much, mind you, but what if it's enough?"

"What if what's enough?"

"What if someways she conveyed that them freaks fooled with her in that ice-cream truck?"

"You mean told her daddy?"

"That's exactly what I mean. Or told somebody and he found out anyways. And what if them freaks thought of that too, but not soon enough?"

"I don't copy."

They neared town, and the streetlamps were making slow

pulses of orange light that painted over them through the windshield. Slocum pulled into the drive of the carwash and put her in park.

"How you figure is the best way to shut someone up so they don't tell nothin'?"

"Probably duct tape, but now I ain't tried that sort—"

Slocum was looking at him. "No. Kill 'em."

"Shit, Slocum. Your little man's been working overtime."

"And you ever seen Bull Meadows angry? I mean really pissed?"

"That bad?"

"That's how Jack Potter got hisself a nick name."

"No. One-Eye Jack?"

"That's why I set them boys up to work for Bull, ones I think can work worth a damn anyways. 'Cause he's gentle as the Jolly Green fuckin' Giant, 'less you do him wrong. And most of 'em go pretty straight. But Jack Potter's busted sellin' meth durin' the harvest from one of Bull's trucks. Had a regular circuit built up."

"He do time?"

"Potter? Nah. I told Bull Meadows though. Now he's One-Eye Jack Potter."

"How'd he get away with that? Bull Meadows, that is."

"Well, Potter come cryin' when he got outta the ER. I told him, in the eyes of the law, man he most wronged was Bull Meadows." Slocum pulled out and headed towards the jail. "Said he could press charges if wanted to, but if he did, I had a airtight case on him for the meth. If he took his punishment like a man, and kept his fuckin' mouth shut, I'd lose track of that folder."

"Shit, Slocum. That's Leviticus-type shit right there. I thought we'd moved on past that."

"For most we have," Slocum rubbed his chin, "but others, some others anyways, only understand the law," he paused for a moment, "when you put it directly to 'em." He looked at

Smalley. "Plus, if he showed Bull he could take it like a man, he'd have a chance that Bull would take him back on."

"Why the hell would he want that? I'd figure a man with any sense for getting about as far in the opposite direction as possible."

"That's what I'm sayin', Smalley. These boys ain't got no sense. Now, Bull Meadows is a harsh man, but like I say, only if you cross him. Otherwise, he's 'bout as close to a father as most of them boys got. Kindest daddy in the world still gotta discipline his children, don't he?"

"I suppose you're right on that count." Smalley rolled the window down and spat, and then rolled it back up again. "How you figure on getting that Abraham to confess?"

"I don't rightly know. He's a queer one."

"He's a queer?"

"Kinda shoots our theory if he is, don't it? Richie thinks so, but he thinks just about everybody is. I mean queer in the old sense. Oddball."

"You should've put a tail on him."

"My men are not capable of subtlety, Smalley. You imagine Richie on that detail? What would that prove for a done deed anyhow?" He pulled into the lot at the jailhouse.

"I seen this show on the TV—"

"Oh God."

"No, really! The detectives follow this fella they think done some murders or something, but they can't pin him for it. So they follow him around, and you know what he does?"

"What?" He was covering his eyes, rubbing his temples.

Smalley delivered it as if it were the golden key to everything: "He returns to the scene of the crime."

Slocum was still rubbing his head.

Smalley went on, after giving his TV wisdom a moment to suffuse the air. "Hey, I thought that Abraham did some kind of miracle on Barbie, Reverend Crocket said."

"Nah, Bull Meadows says he's imaginin' things. Crocket all but cracked up few weeks ago. We picked him up out in the street naked, drunk as hell. He's full of tears, carryin' on 'bout how his soul's dark night would never end. The silence, the silence, he keeps screaming. Man that needs a miracle that bad, far as I'm concerned, probably is lookin' too hard for one."

"Well maybe you and me should have a stake-out."

"What're you talkin' bout now?"

"That Abraham. See if he returns to the scene of the crime?"

They got out of the car.

"He won't."

"Why not? They *do* do that sometimes."

"'Cause I got him locked up in here goin' on two days now. I do like your idea from the TV though."

Smalley stopped outside the door.

"Really? Maybe we should let him out and follow him back," and here he put his index finger up and said the following phrase with special emphasis, "to the scene of the crime."

"How bout we pull out ol' Occam's razor and just stick him in the car and take him out to Hog Chute, see what happens?"

"You's about the smartest god damn person I know. I just don't understand all the things you say."

Slocum held the door for Smalley and limped in after him.

"Where's Richie?" Slocum asked a cop at the desk.

"He's scrubbing up the floors in the back."

"Richie!" Slocum yelled.

He appeared from the hall door.

"You usin' fresh water this time?"

"Yes, Sheriff Slocum. Soap, spray, scrub, mop, just like you said." He said it as if he were doing it for a commercial.

"Alright. Prisoner awake?"

"Sleeping, sir."

"Get him up and put him in my car. Me and Smalley's gonna take him for a ride."

"Yes, sir."

"Any word on that big-headed midget?"

"Afraid not, Sheriff."

Slocum nodded wordlessly, looking out the front window. "Alright. We'll be out there. Bring him on out once you get him up."

"You got it, sir."

"Richie?"

"Yes, Sheriff Slocum?"

"Not too gentle, you hear? This ain't a fuckin' motel. Cuff him. Treat him like a prisoner."

He tried not to, but Richie smiled. Then he went off through the door.

* * *

The priest was slurping noodles in a little Chinese place he had spied on his way out of the city. Even though it was late, the place was crowded and smelled rich and salty. He had missed being in a real city. He watched the steady rhythm of people walking by the window under the colored lights of the signs outside as he finished the noodles and sucked the broth from the bowl. He set it down and pushed the bowl away. A Chinese kid in a white button-up came and silently placed it on a round tray without looking at him and disappeared with it. He got the atlas from the chair next to him and pulled his notepad and pencil from his breast pocket. His plan for the return trip was to stay off the interstate. The route would be less direct, but he wanted to feel the city longer and get some idea of the towns between Chicago and Piatt County. He moved his finger along the jagged lines.

He scanned his hasty scribbles from the day before: phone numbers for contacts in Rome, flights, times, and prices, and the rest. Grotto had taken it all so calmly. They had smiled their farewells and shaken hands. The priest had even been given special permission to escort him onto the plane. Grotto left this country with almost nothing, only a child's backpack with some toiletries and a pair of "husky" boy's jeans, a few t-shirts, whatever they could grab from the K-Mart they found along the way. His contact had been given Grotto's arrival time and instructions for transporting him to Monte Casino. The priest had tried to explain everything. Grotto had nodded uninterestedly, his mouth open, his eyes squinting. The priest was pleased that it had all gone off so smoothly. He drew a single line through the middle of those pages. He turned another, read something, and put his hand up.

"The rest of your meal will be up in just a moment, sir." The kid with the tray smiled.

"Yes, of course. Can I call long distance somewhere close by?"

The kid spoke and gestured. The priest left the atlas open on the table. The kid refilled his coffee and closed the atlas and slid it to the far corner. A minute or two later, he brought a plate piled with sizzling meat on rice, flecks of red peppers visible in the greasy brown sauce. The priest passed by the window before he came through the door. He smiled and nodded at the kid, and the kid half-bowed. The priest sat, dropping the white napkin across his lap, took a bit with the chopsticks, and scribbled on two lines in the notebook:

Prescott: dead, cancer, two weeks ago.

Mother: dead, heart attack, today.

He dated the top corner of the page, shaking his head as if he were gently refusing someone. He pocketed the notebook and pencil, ate quickly, and was gone.

* * *

Richie made him strip at gunpoint in the front office of the jailhouse, and the gaggle of deputies, or whatever the hell their official distinction was, cops, scrutinized him as he did, giving little honks of laughter, making cat calls and hoots. And then they just watched, dumb, dull-eyed. He had refused initially, but Richie hit him a couple of times with his little nightstick and then slugged him in the face, while a fat one chewing gum held a rifle on him. It hadn't affected him much, but then he'd figured, what the hell, at least the orange suit will be dry. When he got down to his shorts, though, he stopped again.

"I said strip, motherfucker," Richie said.

"Sorry, boys," Abraham said, his mouth and nose running blood. "Any more will cost fifty extra."

Richie hit him again, and he drew back a couple steps into the corner by the radiator.

"You're up to a hundred now, sweetheart."

Some of the cops laughed.

Richie grabbed the rifle from the fat, gum-chewing man and popped Abraham in the gut with the butt end. Abraham doubled over. Someone threw the jailhouse clothes at him, and they fell in the floor. He got them on finally. He slipped on his boots, Richie cuffed him, and they took him out. When they passed through the patch of grass between the sidewalk and the lot, Abraham saw an insignia stenciled in red spray-paint on the back of the Piatt County Jail sign. He couldn't quite make it out. Richie shoved him on to the car.

Slocum hadn't said a word. He and Smalley waited in the car for the door to close, then he eased out of the drive, and on out of town. He gnawed a toothpick as he drove. Then they were out on some country road between Monticello and Cisco. There was a faint moon somewhere, but what light they had was from the car. Outside, the headlights shot out unevenly into the dark, pitching and swaying with the dips and lumps in the road. Inside, the green glow from the dash caught Slocum's profile, or as much of it as Abraham could make out from behind the cage, where he sat on Smalley's side. They hadn't said where they were taking him, but it didn't seem to be back to the campground. Abraham figured sunrise wasn't too far off.

Slocum squinted back towards Abraham a couple of times, snapping his head around at him as he drove. After a while, he pulled off in the grass and let the car idle there. He turned on the dome light and got a good look at him.

"What the hell happened, Mr. Abraham?"

Abraham didn't say anything, but he didn't look away either.

"Richie do this to you?"

Nothing.

"Guess he don't want to talk," Smalley said.

"The guilty rarely do. They know they got it comin', I suppose. Now, I'm not sayin' that in this case necessarily. Just my experience is all. Mr. Abraham?" He peered back at him again. "On behalf of the Piatt County Sheriff's Office, I do apologize for any mistreatment you have suffered while incarcerated, and I'm sorry we done held you so long without bringin' formal charges. But we'll be done with you real soon and send you on your way. Okay?" His voice was saccharine, but it didn't match his eyes.

Nothing.

Then they got out.

Abraham was left in the car with the green glow and the hum of the engine. The police radio crackled a few times but no one spoke. A few minutes passed before the driver-side rear door opened, and Slocum motioned him out with an impatient hand. They walked into the night, away from the car. Slocum's flashlight bounced a yellow beam around ahead of them, leading the way. Abraham looked over his shoulder at the car. Its taillights looked like eyes glowing red in the blackness, some beast lying in wait. Smalley took his right arm, Slocum the left, and they marched on in the gravel beside the road. The crunch of their six feet overtook everything. Slocum seemed to be limping.

The yellow light found a bridge ahead. When they reached the guardrails leading up to it, Slocum shoved him roughly onward into the grass, telling him to keep walking, cursing. He kept on. Underfoot the ground was rough with rocks and clods that fell away, and the grasses brushed his arms. Abraham stumbled a couple times, once rolling headlong down the embankment before a shrub held him up. They had not uncuffed him. They waited while he got to his feet. He looked around for his missing boot.

"Go on," Slocum said, his voice coarse but quiet. "On down to the bottom."

Something nearby bolted off into the dark of the trees. Coyotes bawled out yips and yelps. Abraham went on, one foot bare, farther down towards water's edge. The noise of the river swelled as he drew closer, but from where he stood, it was a flat dark plain, a void hollowed out of the ruffles of night trees, somewhere out in the middle distance. It threw light around, but it looked hard. Slocum clicked off the flashlight, and there was almost nothing. Abraham waited for his eyes to settle in to it, but they wouldn't, so he stopped again and waited. He looked up and found the specter of the bridge and traced it down to where it walled in concrete down to the ground. He made his way there in small, careful steps and inched his way down the hill until he found where the slab levelled out under the bridge, before it pitched hard downward to the water.

"Is this far enough?" he whispered.

No one spoke back.

He could hear them approaching, but they were lost to him somewhere behind. He turned back to the river and found it lapping up onto where the concrete cut down into the water. It was black and featureless against the blank grey of the pavement, the line it made there stuttering without pattern. He sat across the angle in the concrete squinting around at the underside of the bridge, at where the river cut through, at the banks and tree shapes beyond, and the place took shape in his eyes. Either the moon found its way through the gloom or his eyes finally took to it, but he could see a little, and what he found he met with the vague dread of recognition.

"Someone tell you to sit?" Slocum spat.

Abraham ignored him.

"Well?" Slocum's palms were turned up.

"Well, what?"

Slocum came closer and took a knee, cursing as his wounded leg hit the pavement. Smalley hung back. Abraham heard a snap click and saw him draw his weapon slowly out.

"I can tell by lookin' at you. You know this place, don't you?"

"What do you want me to say?"

"Yes or no?"

"It's familiar. Yes."

"God damn it, I knew it." Slocum sighed.

"Why have you brought me here?"

"Cause this is where they found her."

"Who?"

Slocum stood. "Don't fuck with me, you fuckin' pervert. Who!" Slocum kicked a clump of grass, and hobbled back over. "You've got some balls, I'll give you that. Who? Barbie Meadows, that's who, you piece of shit." He was almost shouting. He leaned his face into Abraham's. "I've had it up to here with you." He demonstrated where with his fingers; it was near the shoulder. "You ain't foolin' nobody no more."

Abraham was smirking somewhat when Slocum put the light on him.

"You laughin' at me?"

"My mother used to say, 'I've had it up to here with you'. I guess my wife did too."

"And your father? What'd he say?" Slocum mocked him.

"Nothing. He was dead."

"You'll be there soon enough."

"Won't we all. Listen." He didn't leave a beat for the banter to continue. "I don't know anything about anything. This place is familiar. That's all I have to say. Are we done?"

"Get up." Slocum was annoyed.

Abraham stood.

"Just take a good look out there. She was tangled in against that fall-down tree there, twined up with a beaver trap, where them branches come out. Face in the water. One of her eyes was gone, chewed out by somethin'. One shoe missin', summer shorts, t-shirt. Floatin' dead as a fuckin' fish. Can you see it?"

He waited, but Abraham was mute. Smalley was crying behind them.

"Can you see it?" he repeated quietly.

He pointed out, his hand on Abraham's shoulder, like a father. He spoke more slowly now, in brief phrases, almost whispering in Abraham's ear.

"There she was. The current spun her into the V of the tree. And there she stayed, bobbin' and swayin', dancin' with the river, the ripple in the water, hair all fanned out in tangles with the grass, them Jesus bugs skimmin' all around her. Lungs full of water. Skin like pickled ginger. Can you see it?"

Nothing.

"Can you see it?" he asked softly.

He waited.

"Okay, son," he whispered. "You're released."

Then Slocum shoved him down the pitch.

His face hit the river, then the pavement, underwater, where he slid deeper down, before plunging into the mud. The current was already taking him, as he lurched, like a netted fish in the air, to find up and down, his hands still cuffed behind. Everything had gone black. The current held him under, but he couldn't place the river bottom. He kicked against the moving water and found the air for just long enough to catch a breath, the current dragging the dead weight of his top half back down into the black swirl of the river. His head knocked a branch. His feet found mud and worked in it to take hold of something underwater. He steadied enough to pull his arms around his bare feet, and when he thrust his hands up over the tree and got himself anchored in, he spotted Slocum under the bridge. He still hadn't moved.

"Can you see it now?" Slocum hollered, laughing.

Abraham got his bearings and found himself in the V of the fallen tree.

Slocum called out between his hands, "Weatherman says heat wave's comin', motherfucker. The sun's comin' out. Gonna bleach everything. You got no place to hide."

And they left him there in the dark water where the girl's life had run out.

Chapter 9

"Most philosophy is just lying, only it's the lies you forgot were fictions. Or it's dreaming shit up because it makes a certain kind of sense, you know? It seems to answer some questions you had, almost like in mythology. You need to explain some shit that's real hard to figure out, that spurns your attempts to even think about it, but you do it anyway, and you begin to think you've cracked something open, that you, Johnny Q. Dipshit, have figured out a novel explanation for why things are here instead of not. And you close the book feeling real good about yourself. And maybe you share it with someone, and they read it, and you're expecting them to have the same epiphany. But it doesn't happen that way. It doesn't happen that way because what you thought up seems crazy. Now, even to you, it seems crazy. Lunatic ravings scratched into the wall of the shitter stall in a mental institution. That's philosophy. The good stuff anyway. But what I'm interested in are those moments when it works, when you've convinced yourself, or maybe even when you've read something, and it's got you, or you it, or both. Those moments can be rapturous, even if you're convinced that the world is shit. For just that little interval, all the shit in the world makes sense. But then life goes on, as it will, and undermines your enlightenment. And you lock that thought away. You file it under 'bullshit'. You give it up. But what if you don't? What if you leave it open? What if you take the pages you've written or read, and you toss them up and let them fall where they will in your mind, because, if even for an instant, they helped you. For one fucking second the whole cesspool contracted around an idea, like you glimpsed into the boiler room of the universe, before the door swung to, and you got it. If you refuse that impulse to cast them aside, and if you've got some luck, and the memory for it, maybe they'll help you again. That's how I got into fighting anyway."

The tape clicked off. The priest was almost out of gas, so he drove on into another anonymous town between Chicago and Monticello and turned into a filling station. He went in, got a coffee, dropped his twenty dollars with the clerk, and came back to pump the gas. A bent old man was sitting on his tailgate with two tall cans of beer, on the other side of the pumps. He seemed to have no intention of pumping anything but the beer. He snapped one can open and took a long draft. The priest watched the knob in his throat, nested in some wrinkles between his chin and his collarbone, as it danced up and down. He looked back at the numbers spinning on the pump. They had just passed twelve. He glanced back at the man but, instead, found him standing next to him, a can in each hand.

"What d'ya say?" the man said. He emptied the first can, squeezed it, crinkling the sides, tossed it in the garbage can by the pump, and snapped the second one open. He took a slurp of the beer.

"Good evening," the priest replied with an informal, nodding bow.

The man's hips and shoulders eschewed the usual parallel. His neck was nowhere to be found, as if he had taken a bad fall from a high place and landed exactly upside down. One arm hung, useless, and bent at the elbow, as if it were in a sling, but it was not. He wore a red tank-top with grease stains on the front, denim shorts that had had a previous life, and a red and white hat that said "mixed nuts" on the front.

"Mind if I ask what the deal is with them clothes you got on?"

"Not at all. What would you like to know?"

"What the deal is with them clothes you got on." He sounded irritated. "You a priest? Or from California or something?"

"Yes, I am a priest."

"From California?"

"I am afraid not."

The bent man seemed relieved.

The pump clicked off. The man held out his open palm, up and near his face, as if to stop him from something. The bent man pulled the nozzle from the gas tank and returned it to the pump. He screwed the cap back on, closed the little door, and eased back onto the side of the car.

"Thank you. You are very kind."

"You Catholic?"

"Yes."

"My mama always said the Catholic Church was a cult. Taking millions to Hell. I believed that for a long stretch myself." He sipped.

"That is a popular opinion I am afraid."

"You know, I still ain't sure it ain't true."

"Well—"

"I ain't sure it is, neither." He sipped again. "But I figure if Catholics is a cult taking millions to Hell, then the rest of 'em probably are too, churches—hell, religions—I mean. What's good for the goose, you know."

"I suppose it is a difficult call."

The man turned towards the priest, his good elbow on the top of the car, his fist against his cheek, the beer next to the elbow. He asked, kind of sweetly, "So why're you a priest then if you don't think you know what's what?"

"I fell into it. There are worse things to be, I suppose."

"Shit. You said a lot there. Seems like the only things worth being are the ones you fall for or into, don't it?"

"I suppose so."

"Welp," the man said as a punctuation mark, crushing the can, and pitching it into the garbage, "it's been a pleasure. Name's Jerry. Pray for me if you think about it, 'cause sometimes I just ain't right."

The bent man held out his good hand. The priest took it. The man smiled with his mouth closed, pumping the priest's hand a couple of times, and then he headed between the pumps towards

his truck. The priest opened the car door but then turned.

"Jerry?"

"Yeah, buddy?"

"Would you like me to bless you?"

He rubbed his face, his head turned ever so slightly to one side, and he took his hat off.

"I guess I don't know how," he said, his mouth wrenched to one side.

The priest smiled. "You do nothing but receive it. Just stand there."

"Yeah, I sure as hell ain't gonna turn down a blessing. Who knows what'll happen?"

The bent man held his hat to his belly, with his good hand over the other one, which was there already anyway. His thin hair played in the breeze. He seemed afraid to look up at the priest. His eyes squeezed tight, his head bowed, as much as possible, towards an oil stain in the pavement.

"Jerry, I bless you in the name of the Father, the Son, and the Holy Spirit." He made the sign of the cross in the air between them. Then he waited.

The bent man remained frozen.

"That is it, Jerry. Short and sweet."

He smiled before his eyes opened.

"I'm savoring it," he said.

The priest smiled too.

The bent man struggled into his truck and drove off. The priest watched until the taillights disappeared around a curve. He got in the car, found the next tape in the sequence, and loaded it. He drove out of the town and back onto the roads and their hard, square angles, through the countryside. He found the play button in the dark and pressed it and listened in again.

". . . the connection. Could you explain?"

It was his own voice, but he had missed half of the question.

"It's the ghost in the machine. Classic, huh?" There was a

sound on the tape, perhaps a car? A machine anyway, but the priest couldn't place it. It had garbled something Abraham had said. He'd missed it, but he went on listening.

Abraham's voice was saying, ". . . the object of pure mathematics as, for example, colors, sounds, tastes, and the like, although with less distinctness. And inasmuch as I perceive these objects much better by the senses, through the medium of which and of memory, they seem to have reached the imagination . . ." The noise went again. ". . . I should at the same time examine what sense perception is and inquire whether those ideas that are apprehended . . ." The noise went again.

The priest stopped the tape. He blinked at the windshield a few times. "The milkshakes," he said to no one with a glint of recollection. Then he turned it back on.

"I was fighting a little at the time. Working in a carnival as a geek. The years after I'd left Irene."

"Was this during the Jacob Abrams era?"

"Nah. I gave that name up with the life I'd used it for. I went by whatever. Jack, Jake, John, Albert, Tom, Sam. Nobody cares what your last name is in that world. Carnivals don't cut checks. Most of them then didn't even pay taxes. Cash in cash out. I was nobody. I was the only geek you've ever seen with a weak stomach."

"I don't know this position, geek."

"You've gotta look for them now, but any shitty carnival with a freak show twenty, even ten years ago, had them. The shittier the better."

"What is it?"

"Gaff freak, an act, but it can be a sublime one. There's a range, I guess. On the low end, the hacks, you've got a guy who acts crazy, or oftener is crazy, which is why the geek spot has such high turnover. Sometimes they're addicts, like I was, and they get paid mostly in pills or booze or something in a needle. These are desperate men, pathetic, desperate men. The bad ones don't even know they're doing an act. They rant and rave and tear shit up. There was a guy from Russia, the guy I replaced, who just destroyed furniture. That was it. He screamed, smacked his head into it, tore it apart with his hands, pissed on it, anything. Sometimes he set it on fire, shit in his hands, rub it all over himself, screaming, watching it burn."

"My God!"

"I'd been a roughy, working set-ups mostly. I'd always watch him. Vlad the Impaler, that's what they called him. One night, he's ripping drawers out of a dresser, and he starts in on the body of the thing, but he can't get anywhere with it. It won't break. How, I don't know. He's kicking and raving around, and then he just collapses, bawling, bowing before it, completely naked. His handler sticks him with a cattle prod, and he goes nuts again for a few minutes, shits in his hand and claps it with the other one. Punching the dresser frame, bleeding everywhere, smashing his face on the sides. And then he just starts scooting it around, like he's rearranging his apartment or something. His eyes go dull and wide, he's gaping at the audience. He pushes it over on its side, climbs up on top, and pulls his balls off."

"His testicles? Off? Is that even possible?"

"Only once."

"God!"

"So that's how I got to be the geek? Middle range is the eater geek. Now, philosophically, I like the eater geek very much, for its consummate, carnal humanity. You eat. Anything and every-thing. Live animals, mostly small ones, unless you're doing something really special, light bulbs, books, shit, money, bowl full of cigarette butts, whatever. Anyone can do it. It's a matter of will. You consume the world around you and you turn it to shit, like everyone else. I, literally, couldn't stomach it. Everything came back up. But people love to watch other people fail. So it worked. Then I'd eat it again, lose it again, and just keep on with it until they couldn't watch anymore, until they started puking in the stands. Try, try again."

"I cannot believe this sort of thing takes place."

"It was my life for a time."

"I cannot even imagine a third tier to this geek."

"I'm getting there. But back to Descartes. So I'm the geek for the shows. After that I fight. The carnies would set them up with the locals during the day, and there was money involved, of course. For a while, I was getting the shit beat out of me every night, using, waking up, geeking, then fighting again. After a time, the beatings replaced the drugs, but it's just as addicting."

"Fighting?"

"Mostly just the getting beaten. That's the high. Like that movie, *Raging Bull*, came out a few years ago?"

"I do not keep current with film."

"Shame. Anyway, same thing there, and it's the same thing with the eater geek. How much shit can you take? How much of the world? Plus, there can be euphoria to a beating. Have you ever been hit in the face?"

"No." The priest heard himself laugh incredulously.

"Not even as a boy?"

"No. There are few bullies in libraries."

"It's unlike anything else, but only if you take it. It's that evolutionary response to retaliate or run that kills it, wastes it, that burns it off. And there's my point. The money's better if you win a fight."

"Of course."

"So after a while they tell me it's time to start winning. People are getting suspicious because a lot of the carnies have been betting against me, their fighter. I say okay. And I try. I would get hit and get that adrenaline rush, that high, and use it. I'd go nuts. And sometimes it was enough, with a dumbass, but never with a fighter, somebody who knows what he's doing. That's when Descartes came back to me. Do you know who's speaking in that passage: I am accustomed to imagine many other objects besides that corporeal nature which is the object of pure mathematics yada yada yada?"

"Descartes himself, I suppose."

"No. It's the thinking thing. The cogito. That's the sixth meditation, the last one. He's already divided everything off."

"I do not understand, though, what—"

"I became the thinking thing, the cogito cut off from all extension. Well, not cut off, but there's a degree of independence. I became the ghost, the ghost in the machine."

"But surely you do not take Descartes that seriously?"

"No, of course not. But, then, maybe more so. But it wasn't a matter of finding it intellectually compelling. That shit gets taught as already debunked. It was a matter of finding it useful as a strategy. For an instant, it all made sense. I had a peek into the boiler room and no one else had, no fighter anyway. It's almost like with sex. If your mind is going, if you're thinking, doubting, affirming, denying, and the rest, the body fails, the two seem separate things. You close off desire. The same is true with fighting. You get hit, you get the instinctual, animal response, along with the charge that deadens the pain. You want blood. Both acts emerge from desire, open, animal desire. But that's the machine. The ghost within wants pure mathematics. Sensation, pain, taste, and so on, all of that is secondary. It comes with the addition of memory to imagination. That's what it says anyway."

"So you forget yourself and give in to desire, uncage the animal? But somehow through the cogito, yes?"

"No. You break the animal. You train it, like the dog it is. You, the thinking thing, you work in math. When you get hit, you don't lose your mind, you recalculate. If you give in to the high, to the rush, you've already lost. Fighting is about presence of mind. You force memory into the machine with training. The thinking thing, within, abstracts to its proper objects: shapes, angles, strategy. It becomes the I think. Present tense. It knows no pain. It refuses the body. It refuses desire. That's how it came back to me anyway, how it helped me."

"And you began to win, yes?"

"After I got it down, I didn't lose. Not a fair fight anyway."

"And your repulsive job as geek? Did you quit?"

"Yeah, no one stays a geek. Maybe the mad ones, but if they're that crazy, they don't live too long. The fights took over after a while, and I left the carny circuit altogether."

"And the third tier? Did you make it there?"

"The sublime geek."

"An oxymoron, no?"

"No. The sublime geek is total presence. It's an absolute, human, religious experience, a transcendent one, a horrifying one, but it's pure bliss. There's no audience, there's no God, there's no you. Only life, raw life."

"The cogito?"

"No, it's shadow. It's pure desire. The machine rebels. The animal awakens. You get out of the way."

"What happens?"

"It's hard to say. You begin to lose yourself, to lose time. That's when you know you've arrived. Getting to that point takes a while, has its own kind of training, its own philosophy. The manager had seen it before, so he saw it coming. And he'd been betting on fights, so he knew what could happen. He started putting me in a cage for the show, like the ones the big cats are in. Then, the last one, he put one of them in with me."

"And the outcome?"

The priest shut it off. He didn't want to hear it again. He found a cigarette, lit it, and sucked it down in four drags.

* * *

Camperman turned off of Hobson's Crossing, one of the many dirt-path short-cuts he had learned over the years, onto County

Road 320. He eased the truck to a stop and pulled it off into the grass on the other side of Hog Chute Bridge. It had already been a hell of a day, and his hands were blistered from the shovel. It was early yet, and the sun was bright. The grass was still wet, but things were heating up. He walked into the road and made his way down the middle, weaving in and out of the dividing line, the way a child does on a bicycle. He stopped at the bridge, inspecting some markings done in red spray-paint. The picture spanned both lanes in a broad circle.

"Shit," he breathed. He squatted there, touched the paint with his fingers, pulled his hat off, rubbed his head, replaced the hat, stood, and walked slowly to the wall on one side. He peered out, over the river, into the thick grass, off into the trees, and then back near the base of the bridge. He returned to the truck for his binoculars and went back to the spot and surveyed the same material. Then he made his way to the other side. He checked downriver with the binoculars, bringing them slowly back from the distant reaches towards the bridge. He walked, on the same side, down the road a hundred yards or so, repeated the same movements, finally letting the binoculars hang around his neck, against his belly. He went forward a few paces, pressed himself against the rail above the concrete bridge-wall, and leaned out, holding the binoculars to his eyes again, scanning the river, the banks where he fished sometimes. He locked on to something. "What in the hell?" he said. He moved towards the center a few paces and returned the binoculars to his eyes yet again. He leaned over the side as far as he could, squatting a little, bracing his hips in against the wall so he wouldn't slip over the edge. And he stayed like that, peering out into the shadow the bridge cast onto the banks. He turned the knob at center to focus in. "Well, I'll be damned."

It was Abraham alright. He looked like the sun, but deflated, shrunken like a leaky balloon, fallen out of the sky, thrown in the mud. He was lying on his side, his knees hugged up by his chest, his head down. The orange jumpsuit glowed out dully, a dim bulb in the shadow. The image cut an orange circle in the mud, a slice of it cut out, the space between his thighs and chest: but nestled there, in that void, cuddled up with the man, between his arms, its tiny head pillowed in his beard, was a little fawn, its constellation of speckles like white gravel scattered out in the dirt, like stars in the sky. Sleeping there together, or, hell, maybe even dead, they made a ragged little circle. Dead or alive, he thought, it was beautiful.

Camperman put down the binoculars and walked down the road, off the bridge, stepped over the guardrail and found the path through the grass alongside of the concrete wall. But then he halted. He dropped slowly into the tall grass, straight down, pulling his second eyes up again, holding them to the originals with one hand, fingering the focusing knob expertly. Further in, under the bridge, maybe a foot or two from where Abraham lay with the fawn, he spotted the coyotes. It looked like four, maybe five. They slept in a pile, so it was hard to tell. He moved in a little closer. One of them spotted him as he closed in. She growled, bared her teeth, gave the yip that woke the others. They didn't bolt though. A couple got up. One even closed some distance between them, snarling. In the pile, now diminished by two, Camperman spied a doe. She craned her neck in his direction, her ears pricked, but she didn't get up. She dismissed him after a moment and lay her head back down on one of the coyotes' rumps. Another one pawed her side gently and nuzzled in against it like a pup. Camperman backed off from the snarling dogs. It occurred to him that, even from a short distance, he couldn't make out where the doe stopped and the dogs began, their pelts blended browns and grays without seam. One became the other in rolls and folds of merging fur.

He called out to Abraham. First he tried his name, but found it difficult from his remove to give voice to three syllables sharply enough to wake him without upsetting the beasts. So he cawed out between his hands like a crow. It proved effective, and he enjoyed it. "Win-win," he whispered, smiling to himself.

Abraham's head came up slowly. The fawn woke with him. And they both peered around. Camperman gave him a wave. He nodded back and sat up. The little fawn stood and stretched its spindly limbs. The mother roused, and the pack of pelts rose and separated. Abraham went to the water's edge, kneeled, and splashed some on his face and hair. The animals followed him in for a drink. Camperman lingered where he was, afraid they knew, somehow, of his history hunting both brands of beast. Abraham rose and made his way towards his friend. He still wore the cuffs.

"Now, I've been around, and I've seen some things, but never have I seen nothing like that."

"They must have crept up on me after I drifted off."

The animals cocked their heads around, the doe's ears pointed towards the voices. The men watched them drink again, before the deer walked gently away, the coyotes scuttling off in the opposite direction.

"Can you help me with these?" Abraham lifted his hands between them.

"I've got keys to just about everything."

They made the trudge back up the hill to the truck. Camperman opened the toolbox that lay across the breadth of the bed behind the cab and found a giant ring of keys. After a couple of tries, he had him free.

"They really fucked you up, didn't they?"

"It's not as bad as it looks."

After the water, his face was bleeding again. One eye was raccooned, and a big knot protruded from the top of his forehead. The cuffs had cut into his wrists. He blotted them on the jailhouse clothes.

"That's good, 'cause it looks real bad."

They got into the truck.

"How'd you know where to find me?"

Camperman squinted off down the road, into the sun. He hadn't started the engine yet.

"I come out here sometimes. Used to be for fishing, but not since I found her out there."

"The Meadows girl?"

"Yeah, I found her too. I'm talking about the other one though. The baby. The one from the song."

"How long ago?"

"Hell, it's been over a year, maybe two now. You'd think I could move past it."

They were quiet for a moment.

"She'd been born all wrong, I guess. Her little legs were all tangled around, her mouth amiss, cut up into her nose, you know? Cleft, I think they call it. But she was a baby, for Christ's sakes, wasn't stillborn or nothing like that, the coroner said. Just dumped. Died in the grass, there under the bridge, where I found you. Then Barbie Meadows a few days back. And Grow-toe's unicorn this morning out at the park even 'fore the sun come up. And you here now. Shit, buddy. I thought you was dead for a minute."

"Petunia? What happened to Petunia? Is Grotto okay?"

Camperman started the engine. He looked over at Abraham, at the lump in his forehead, then back at his eyes.

"You're the only man I ever met with a resurrected unicorn. Lonnie'd done shot that damn thing 'cause he thought it give him bad luck. A travesty, he called it. Or was it an abomination? Something like that. He tried to get me to help him bury it, but I got a job, you know. And he never pays anyways. He still ain't recovered from seeing you bring her back." Camperman laughed. "Shit." He said it across two syllables. "But she's gone again. Kids maybe. Hell, so much shit's been happening the last few days I can't keep up with it. Slocum said he don't give a damn about it. But someone crucifies a unicorn, even an ugly one, at my campground, splays it open and spills guts and mess every-where, and sets the whole god damn abomination, or travesty, afire in the middle of the night? I don't care who they are. I will crawl up their ass and fight my way out."

"Camperman. Grotto. Is he okay?"

"Little guy has disappeared. Word is he damn near chewed off Slocum's foot in town yesterday. No one's seen him. He ain't been back at the Creek."

Camperman drove down the road a stretch, made a wide U-turn where it Y-ed, and headed back for the bridge.

"What's that symbol painted across the bridge up here? I saw one just like it, a stencil, smaller, of course, on the back of the sign at the jail."

Camperman was quiet, his face serious.

"Yeah, they're all over town now. At the lodge, on the court-house, the post office, the churches, the school. Everywhere. Showed up overnight."

"Do you know what it is?"

He stopped the truck again. They were almost exactly where they were before but pointed in the opposite direction.

"Listen, I'll tell you, 'cause I think you need to know, 'cause I think it may concern you, and 'cause, maybe, you'll wanna get the fuck outta Dodge."

"So, did Slocum tell you then?"

"What? That he thinks you killed Barbie Meadows? Maybe raped her too? He didn't have to. It's in the air, my friend. That's what I'm talking about. That's why that emblem's appearing everywhere."

"I don't get it. What're you talking about?"

"The Calithumpians. That's their sign. The cross there, behind, the head of the donkey, the body of a man, the halo around it all." He traced the lines with his finger in the air behind the windshield as he spoke.

"Alexamenos worships his god," Abraham muttered blankly.

He blotted blood from his face with his sleeve.

Camperman thought he was cursing in some sophisticated variety he didn't understand.

"A stubborn pursuit of the will of God in the world of man. I guess that's the short version."

"It looks like the donkey-man is crucified."

"Hell, maybe he is. It's an old symbol. The Calithumpians rose up when they started civilizing the place, back when this was the Wild West, you know? Before there was much law official. Lynched some. Tarred and feathered others. Rail-pullings."

"Mob justice?"

"With a righteous flare. The higher court, they call themselves, the left hand of God."

"And they persist, even now?"

"Not too much. It ain't like it was then. Back then, a man with gumption and guns could come in and take what wasn't his, and if you got less balls and lighter artillery, you're shit out of luck. You know how it is, the law comes, and most of that falls off. Things settle down, and you've got a civilized county. Order. But the same folks live in a place for a time, they get to thinking it's theirs and they belong to it. The streets are named for families that still drive around on them. Hell, the Piatts still live here, the Meadowses, well, now Bull anyways, and the rest of them. They become like the heart of the place, you know? They're given a kind of reverence. They're untouchable in a way. The Calithumpians only ride again when the law fails those folks or don't go far enough in punishing wrongs against them."

"Like with the Meadows girl."

"You got it, buddy."

"And the law? What's their role?"

"Hard to say. Failure is their role in the whole process, but sometimes they fail winking, you understand. They only go so far 'cause they know they can't go far enough, not far enough to quench the call for blood."

"And when they fail, or fail winking, they've already found the man."

"It's delicate. And it don't happen much, like I said. Last time was maybe eight or ten years ago with the Dover boy. This is why electing a sheriff is such a shit storm. He's gotta be vetted. He's gotta understand his role. And he's gotta make it invisible. You ain't supposed to be able to tell nothing. That's the whole point."

"So who are they? The Calithumpians, that is."

"Nobody knows. That's the thing. It's blind. Anonymous. They say they're the left hand of God, the will of the people, and whatnot. Whoever reads the signs and answers the call. Could be a handful, could be dozens. What is it they say? Whoever loves justice, seeks the right, and desires in his heart the will of God. I think that's it. Closer than not anyway."

"So you've been yourself?"

"I was young once."

"And I'm the man, right now, this time. I'm the man, right?"

"I'm afraid so."

"Is that what's happening now? Are you taking me to them?"

"I ain't so young anymore." He put the truck in gear, and they rode over the sign of the Calithumpians, leaving Hog Chute behind. "I do my own thinking these days. My property's aimed at a different tradition. Come one, come all. No Jew, no Greek, no male, nor female. Judge not lest ye be judged. All that will of the people, God's wiping hand shit? Fuck 'em. Besides, I ain't so scary, huh? If you come across the Calithumpians, you'll know it. They wanna put the fear of God in you before they turn you over. But if you want out, I can get you out."

"Wait. What do you mean turn you over?"

"That's all they do these days, since way back, when the law come in."

"They turn you over to the law? What's the point?"

"Not the law. They give you to the one they think you owe. Short-circuit the law. Sidestep it. It's direct justice from the injured party."

"So they're restoring the natural right to punish?"

"I call it vengeance. That about what you mean?"

"Yeah."

"So you want me to get you out? If the signs have gone up it won't be long."

Abraham was staring out the window, and he stayed that way, the wind whipping his hair. Then he closed his eyes.

"I don't know," he said. "I need some clothes."

"Alright."

"But first, could you buy me some smokes?"

"Not a problem."

After driving for a bit, Camperman said, "You're thinking of staying aren't you?"

Abraham caught his eye. "Do you think I killed that girl, Camperman? You think I raped her?"

"If I thought that, buddy, I'd've killed you myself, fed you to them coyotes back there. Once I got them riled up anyways."

Abraham nodded.

"Couldn't have you giving the Creek a bad name."

Abraham smiled.

"So you're staying."

"I see no just cause not to. Why should I go? Like you said, fuck 'em."

"Brother," Camperman said, "you are an American original. Ain't you afraid of nothing?"

"I'm afraid of everything. That's why it doesn't matter."

"Don't take this the wrong way, but I could kiss you right now," Camperman said, laughing.

"I love you too, Camperman," Abraham said, and he leaned his face out into the wind.

Chapter 10

Slocum looked like hell. He felt worse. He stood naked in the bathroom, shaving. His wife had steered clear of him, which was probably just as well for both of them, and was gone, running errands. He'd gotten maybe four hours in the bed before he got the call about Kenny Percy. A couple of third-graders had found his body in the little alleyway on the back side of the square, sitting upright against the back door to the State Farm offices, not even a day since his release. He wasn't sure what the fuck was going on, but it was damn well time he put a stop to it. He let the others handle the scene, and he called Smalley in to supervise, since that was about all he was good for. He was going to see Bull Meadows, plainclothes, to get to the bottom of it. He finished up with the ivory-handled cutthroat razor that had been his grandfather's, and he leaned in and looked at himself in the mirror, frowning. He toweled the cream from his mustache and rubbed on some alcohol. Slocum bandaged up his ankle with some white gauze and medical tape and pulled a sock over it. He dressed, grabbed his folder of meagre research findings, and headed out.

As he drove through town, he spotted the medallion every-where you'd expect to find it: the library, on the pedestal under the bronze cast of the horse's head out front; the back side of the jailhouse sign; City Hall; the courthouse. Time was up. And that was fine. That's how it was. He knew it when he signed on. But if his hunch was right, if Bull Meadows was mixed up in this other shit—the midgets, Kenny, the fucking goat-donkey, or whatever the hell it was out there that had met the same fate as Jesus, Judas, and Joan of Arc all at once—if he was calling those shots, he was jumping the gun, taking more than he was entitled to. And making a mess of civil order on Slocum's watch. And that smarted some.

When he got to the Meadows farm, it was about lunchtime. The Barnes boys were out in the yard with One-Eye Jack Potter and another kid he had seen before. They were throwing a football around. Slocum rolled down the passenger-side window. Jody Barnes ran over.

"Bull in?"

"Yeah, Sheriff. In the office. Something wrong? Don't usually see you twice in a week. Not here for a while anyway."

"Just business. Go play. You boys stay out 'til I leave, ya hear?"

"Yessir."

"Alright."

He drove on up and parked by the Barnes' shitty red truck. He got out, looked around a little, checked the back of the truck: bean-walking hooks, a can of white paint and a brush, a couple of lunch boxes. He gazed out at the biggest oak that marked the center of the farm, its gnarled branches reaching around in tangles, jutting here and there, like something out of an old horror film. The sun, at its highpoint, only tolerated sparse shadow, and it hung on everything like a little black crescent on the earth. The oak seemed reprieved from this though. The sun saturated it from all sides somehow, and it cast no shadow at all. In the old days, he had heard, this oak had been the center of the county, like its navel, and before they had thought to elect a sheriff to enforce the law, this oak had been the lynching tree. It was as old as anything around. It seemed as old as God himself.

He went and beat on the door of the office in the pole barn and entered without waiting for an invitation. Bull was standing at the desk, counting out a stack of cash into separate piles, his lips moving as he did. Slocum had forgotten what a big son of a bitch he was. Bull stopped.

"Hold on, Slocum."

Slocum sat and let his eye scan the place. He threw his folder up on the front of the desk. He saw Barbie's pictures, the calendar, the tools, the engine parts, a greasy shop rag, but back behind the telephone he spotted most of a human skull, worn down with time, cracked and brown, the jawbone gone. Once he locked onto it, he couldn't let it go.

Bull quit with the money. He looked up at Slocum as he stuffed the cash into separate envelopes.

"You bored, Sheriff? What can I help you with today?"

"Shit. I'm sure you've heard some things. You know I ain't got time to be bored. What in the hell is that?" He pointed at the skull.

"This?" He fetched it with one hand, tossing it up and catching it, as if it were a baseball. "I can't believe you haven't heard this one. This is Buck's Bride."

"You mean your granddaddy Buck?"

"No. Well, he's the one that passed it on to me. But no. You know Buck's Pond, out there by Lodge Park?"

"Yeah."

"This is his bride, what's left of her anyway. Been in Meadows hands since before there was a Piatt County. Hiram Meadows found it when he was a boy, squirrel-hunting. You know the old Indian legend of Buck's pond?"

"I guess I missed out on that one."

"I forget a lot of them old stories. I ain't good at telling stories anyway. I get them all mixed up. Granddaddy could hold you with a story though. He could make you feel like you was right there."

"Old Buck was a good one."

"There was this Delaware Indian chief, Chief Buck. He lived out near where Lodge Park is now, with his tribe, had a woman and whatnot. He steps out with this fine lady, here," he held up the skull, "and she has a baby, a papoose, my granddaddy called it. I think the kid's name was Caleb, no Calish, that's it. Traded some with the first Piatts, Meadows, and the rest. The mother of Calish, though, was Kickapoo or Pottawatomie, one of them: point is she's an outsider. But Buck puts his foot down with the tribe, you see. He lays down the law. No. She's my woman. She stays. And they give in. After all, he's the chief. What he says goes, right? He brings her and Calish in to live with him and his other wife. He tells his first wife, she's your kin now too, find something for her to do. Make her a part of the tribe, you know. So, the queens give her nanny duty. And they run her ragged. Days, nights. They just run her down. One day she's out with the kids by the pond, Buck's pond. One of them kids gets in too deep. But the nanny's sleeping, been up all night with babies. Another of them kids goes after the first, and they both drown. Drown on her watch. Tribe council meets. Sorry, Chief. She's banished. Can't have lazy baby-killers around. He sacrifices it all and goes with her, and they, and little Calish with them, they're nomads. One day, though, she disappears. Buck finds her back at the same god damn pond she let them babies drown in, and she's dead. Killed herself. He buries her right there, where Hiram found her thirty years later. Well, the tribe takes pity on Buck the nomad and lets him come back as a slave, but Calish will be considered full-blooded. At some point old Buck learns that some of them queens were watching when them babies drowned, that that was the whole point. One watched her own baby drown. Just for spite."

Slocum was transfixed by the story. It calmed him somehow, and he pondered it for a moment, as Bull Meadows rubbed his palms unconsciously around the skull, as if he were polishing it. He looked on at Slocum.

"How'd I do?" Bull said.

"Fine, fine. That's like Greek tragedy."

"Deep shit, huh?"

"Yeah, I feel like I been to church or somethin'."

Bull tossed the skull back to its spot by the phone, and it rolled a quarter-turn and came to a rest on an eye socket.

"Sorry, Sheriff. Here I am jawing on about old Indian stories, and you come for a reason. What's up?"

He started easy, "Listen. It's not Sheriff, not right now

anyways. That's why I come in plainclothes."

"Okay. Shoot."

"You know I know how things work, and I been abidin' by what I'm 'spose to. I don't go stickin' my nose in what's outa my business. I only get involved when your men get sloppy. I take what comes up. I don't go lookin'.'"

"You done right by my family, far as I'm concerned, Slocum."

"Damn right I have. But here lately, you, I think it's you, or down the line it comes back to you, *you* ain't holdin' up your end. I can't have the streets and parks littered with dead junkies, pulverized midgets, and animal corpses, Bull. When you gotta grind your ax, it's your business, but you can't do it out in the open and leave it like roadkill all over my county."

"What's that you got in your folder there?"

"In a minute, damn it." He breathed to calm himself. "First, I wanna know what's yours. Tell me I'm not right about all of it."

"What happens if I can't?"

"Kenny can be explained. He was a fuck-up. No one cares 'bout them midget perverts and their pet. Long as it don't become a pattern."

"Well, I don't see how it could, Slocum. I only had Barbie, and she's in the ground."

"So's that a yes on the midgets?"

Bull turned around and nodded once in the affirmative, his back to Slocum.

"Why didn't you take the prophet, that Abraham?"

"Couldn't find him. All I had to go on was a man with some midgets out at Friends Creek. Then, when I could, he was with that priest or you had him locked up, and I couldn't get to him. But now that the call's gone up. You seen the signs. I guess it won't be long now. Except, now, I won't have to sneak around none."

"And Kenny Percy?"

"He was a fuck-up, plain and simple. If he ain't out by

Argenta getting busted with truckers, he's fucking something else up out here."

"Yeah, but you done him pretty good this last time. He's tellin' all the nurses at the ER he'd been in a car crash."

"I don't have no clue how he come back from that the way he did. But he come in here, fit as a fucking fiddle, told me he's done with me. Told me he's gonna have to turn me in to the authorities. Thought he should come to me like a man and let me know. Took balls, I grant that."

"So he forced your hand."

"What could I do?"

"I can deal with 'em long as they's afraid of somethin', whether it's you or goin' to prison. But that shit could put you away, Bull Meadows. I know about how careful you are out here. If it gets passed up from me, there's nothin' I can do no more. And when I'm gone, I'm afraid the world'll be too big to keep this shit up any longer. It's comin' to a close, Bull. "

Bull bristled at this and faced him. "You think you're my fairy godmother, Slocum? I got on just fine before you come up, and I'll do the same when you're gone," he spat.

"I'm just sayin' be careful. And for Christ's sakes, dump 'em somewhere else. Out of my county. And not in Macon neither. Smalley's not equipped to deal with it."

"Kenny had to be local. That's just the way it is. Them other boys had to see what happens to a squeaky wheel."

"Well, not no more." He was firm.

Bull put his hands up in surrender.

"Okay." Slocum opened his manila folder. "You tell me about these?" He handed him the clippings.

"Missing Man Found in Home in Tolono," Bull Meadows read aloud. "Missing Piatt County man, Oliver Bronson, was found in the residence of Barton Culver of Tolono in Champaign County. . ." He scanned the article. "You okay, Slocum? This paper's from a couple years ago. You ain't got enough on your plate? Cookin' up old cases from other counties?"

"Just look at 'em."

Bull Meadows thumbed through the headlines of the two others. He whipped them off into the air, and they floated free of one another and landed in the floor after a brief drift.

"Well?"

"Well what, Slocum?" He was agitated. Slocum eyed him.

"Any of 'em yours?"

"You gonna ask me that?"

"Just did. How 'bout it?"

"Ollie Bronson was like a brother to me. Twenty-five years. He come up with me in school, you know. He was about as close to blood as I had."

"I worked that scene. They brung me in, since he's from Piatt. He sure must've pissed somebody off. Looked like they'd choked him first. Boot scuffs all over the kitchen linoleum. Slid him around the countertops, knocked shit every which way. Six shots in the chest from an old Colt .45—kinda like that one your daddy had? Stuffed nails, roofing nails, into his mouth, probably a whole box of them damn things. It was a sight."

Bull Meadows didn't say anything. He was breathing hard. Slocum could tell he had maybe gone too far. *But, what the hell,* he thought, *let's see where it goes.*

"Looked to me like your style."

"Why are you giving me shit?" He was leaning on the counter-desk between them.

"Cause you're the common thread. You knew Ollie Bronson."

"And this one?" Bull Meadows pulled a paper from the floor and read, "Fire at Marquiss Farm, Police Suspect Arson?"

"That's about the time of that run-in you had with William Marquiss, ain't it?"

Bull stared. He plucked up the last one, "Deformed Baby Found Dead at Hog Chute Bridge?"

Slocum second-guessed himself for a moment. Then he said it

anyway: "Wasn't your baby found out there not too long ago?"

"Get out, Slocum," he whispered.

"Listen, it ain't personal. Maybe I'm way off, but I'm the sheriff. I'm the law. It's my job. You is what they all got in common, same as these here lately." He was sincere.

Bull sat behind the desk in the rolling office chair. He put on a big smile and clapped his hands together, then rubbed them. He snatched the skull from the left side of the desk, by the phone. He rubbed it again, just as he had before, spinning it between his hands like a kid with a ball. He laughed.

"You know that story I was telling you, Slocum, about Bull's Bride?"

Slocum had expected him to throw the desk at him or at least rip his filing cabinets down. The calm was something else. Bull Meadows tossed him the skull. He caught it, and he peered into the blank sockets.

"Yeah. What about it?"

"What you figure the moral of that story is, Sheriff?"

Slocum had wondered this himself at the telling.

"Maybe something about self-control, I'd hazard that as a guess, I suppose."

"That's not the way I see it." He laced his fingers behind his head and leaned back. The springs in the chair popped a little with the pressure. "This is the moral I see. Nobody gives a fuck about the chief. Don't you see that? In the end, when he comes back, and they make him a fucking slave? He's basically just getting his old job back, only now he's in on the joke, because he's finally learned his place."

Slocum locked eyes with him.

"That's your problem, Slocum. You still haven't learned your place yet."

Slocum stood and made the steps to the door.

"The joke's on you, and you don't even see it."

Slocum could still hear him laughing when he drove away.

* * *

The priest was panicking.

"I thought this sort of thing only happened in the Deep South with, what is the word? Hill people and red-backs."

"This sort of thing," Camperman said, "it happens anywhere the same blood's been around so long it's started in to spoil. And, just an FYI, it's hillbillies and rednecks."

Abraham laughed.

"How can you laugh? If they take you, that man will kill you. What plan have you made?"

Abraham shrugged, his face serious now. "I have no plan. I have nothing. I'm not holding out on you. That's it. I can do nothing more. I'm done with doing, so I'm doing nothing."

"He said he was afraid of everything, and that's why it doesn't matter. Like how two no's make a yes. Two negative numbers make a positive. That's some deep shit, man. Like it's from the Bible or something," Camperman said.

"It sounds to me like you are giving up. Is this what it all leads to, all that your life has been, all that you have done in the world, the people you have touched, the earth you have tread? You are throwing it away. You could be so much, Abraham. Will you have it come to nothing? Will you sacrifice it to a lie? All of it for nothing?"

"I'm not sacrificing anything. It's not mine to sacrifice. It's already nothing. Don't you see that? You're looking back across it, what you think you know, and you're drawing out what fits your purpose, writing it on to me. But it isn't real. It only seems so because you've forced it into a story that suits you."

"So you think it is all a fucking dream!" The priest discovered the curse, and that he was screaming, with a shock.

"God damn," Camperman said, "I've never heard a priest say nothing like that before."

The priest ignored him, his eyes on Abraham, whose gaze was

down-turned. It occurred to him that, for the first time, Abraham looked peaceful. He looked almost angelic, gentler somehow, dressed, as for a funeral, in an ill-fitting black thrift-store suit. *But he looks the same too,* the priest thought. It was an inner difference perhaps.

Abraham was still looking away, scooting the toe of his new black boot in the pea gravel of the drive. He seemed to ponder the lines he had made before he smoothed them over. Then he said, "The eye of man hath not heard, the ear of man hath not seen; man's hand is not able to taste, his tongue to conceive, not his heart to report what my dream was."

The priest cast his head downward in a sigh, but he couldn't reply. He didn't know how.

"I told you." Camperman tapped the priest's arm. "Did you hear that? He can say shit like that all day long if he wants to."

Abraham laughed again.

"If you are set on this path, how about a compromise then, yes?" The priest had calmed himself. "You have already made more than an adequate confession. I have documented it. And you have done so to me, to a priest. Will you not at least let me absolve you? Will you not ask forgiveness, engage the sacrament? Will you not take a penance? Before you let yourself be killed."

"Is the future cast and dry so soon? You want my deathbed confession? Don't you see how that's the same thing? Fitting it all to a plot that I choose. Such an expression of faith would be a feint, a fake, a fiction, all of my own design? And maybe a little of yours too. No. Hell no. I haven't the pride left for that kind of forgiveness."

The three of them were quiet. The priest stared at Abraham, his brow raised, wrinkling his forehead, thinking, trying to come up with something.

"What if what they say is true?" Abraham said, staring into the gravel. "What if I did kill that child? Would your offer stand? Open for compromise for a rapist? Would you still be offering absolution?"

The priest opened his mouth but could not find words to say with it, only a strangled voice. Just voice, empty, meaningless.

"If the answer is no then there's no point in any of it. Can't you see that?"

"Okay, okay," Camperman said, waving his hands between them like a teacher on the playground breaking up a fight between boys. "Alright. What *do* you want to do?"

They both looked at Abraham.

"I want you to take me to a place where I can get fried catfish, fish and chips. My treat. Then we get some beers and drink them by the Centaur."

"You got it," Camperman said.

Abraham walked off to get his box of money from the ice-cream truck. He stopped on the way back, lighting a cigarette, as he inspected the blackened trees and spattered earth that had been blighted with Petunia when she'd been crucified, gutted, and immolated in the wee hours of the morning. The grass was covered with birds, mostly crows, taking nourishment from her suffering.

The priest was already smoking.

"What's with the box?" Camperman asked the priest, nudging him with an elbow.

"I do not know." His frustration raw, he was still thinking.

Camperman was smiling. His front teeth barely peeked out from behind his lips. Together, they watched Abraham, out in the distance between the ice-cream truck and the scorched trees, trying not to disturb the birds, which covered the grass in a twittering, twitching black stain. He had bought a hat at the thrift shop, a faded black felt Stetson pork pie hat. It was in his hand, the box wedged in against his breast by the same arm. He smoked with the other one.

Camperman slapped the priest on the shoulder and laughed.

"What are you so happy about?" He was asking seriously.

"Oh nothing." Then after a sigh, "I don't know about you, but I never been invited to a last supper before. And Allerton after? The Lord himself couldn't've asked for a better garden. Think about it, father. That's just too much." Camperman laughed again.

He hadn't seen it. Was this Abraham's concession? Was it a joke? Had he even thought about it at all? A vague sense of disgust crept in to his mind. He pushed it away. He thought of the miracles, the mysteries.

They watched Abraham, now trying to play with the crows, waving his hat at them. Finally, he popped the hat on and started toward his friends. A crow fluttered up before him and clumsily landed on the hat and perched there for a moment before flying away.

When he got closer, the priest caught the glimmer of a foot-mark on the front of Abraham's hat, a blood-mark that threw back the dying light of the sun. Its composition was simple: three lines, conjoined at the bottom, spreading out as they went up, like three branches growing from a common root towards independence, like three paths tending towards the same end, like an arrow pointing down, down into the abysmal black of the hat. He could not settle on one answer.

"Hey, buddy," Camperman said to Abraham, "that damn crow left a bloody footprint on your hat. It looks like a red arrow pointing right at you."

* * *

The nurse came back, finally, cradling the tiny thing in her arms, speaking in coos and giggles to it. Jacob was in the rocker by the window. The mother slept, at peace, in the bed nearby. The labor had been hard; the baby had turned the wrong way in both directions, just like his father, and had been born by caesarian section, the hard birth of kings. The room was dark, but for the dim lamp that Jacob read by. He set the book aside, and received the gift into his arms. He stared down at it awkwardly. He wished the nurse would go away, but she did not.

"What'll you name him?"

"I don't know."

She lingered for a few minutes, busying herself with checking things. She clicked off the light. And then she was gone. The mother was gone in sleep. The doctors were gone. They were all gone. Only Jacob and the baby remained. He stirred little. He just stared out at the man who held him, who was staring back. And they stayed like that for a long time. There was no cooing. There was no giggling. There was no speaking or whispering. But they shared a gaze that looked deep within, that reflected each back to the other, and back again. Inside became out became inside again. There was nothing between them. There was nothing behind them. And nothing ahead. For an instant, everything was open. There were no words to eclipse them. There was no noise to interpret. There was only that eternal moment between them. It was too much for happiness. It outwore understanding. It reached beyond what either one could know. Maybe it was love, maybe, but they did not know it if it was. They did not even feel it. It was a pure moment. Jacob was not Jacob, but he was not Abraham either. The infant was not a son. The man was not a father. For that moment he was as anonymous as the infant in his arms. And, there in the dark, in that anonymous room, two nameless creatures shared a moment when nothing was, where nothing was, in a world that was not, in a world without end. And it is alive—somewhere, it is alive, even now.

Chapter 11

It was too dark for shadows, or so dark that everything became one. The moon was nowhere in the sky, and the stars were a dim glitter in the black. A factory haze glowed miles off in the distance from one of the bigger towns, and a few lights in the campground threw their shine around. Owls endlessly questioned or answered one another with the same word above the cricket drone. Camperman had gone off to Miss Jolly. The priest had driven off into the night. And Abraham sat alone against a tree, off his campsite about a hundred yards, where the kept grounds met the tall grasses and the wildflowers of the prairie. He could smell them when the wind picked up and blew the hot air across. Somehow it had only gotten hotter since the sun went down. Perhaps thirty degrees he thought. And he thought of the girl, her secrets, her sadness, her wounds. The wind or the ground or the girl took him away with hot air's perfume or drove him down like a stake into the earth or pierced him like a spectral blade from the grave, maybe all. It made no difference which. He took what the earth gave, what the wind drew in, what pictures grew from the darkness. Time had forgotten him, or he time. Had it been hours? He was too worn to have slept, and what sleep would he find in this black heat? What did it matter? He felt the hard strings under his fingers on the neck of the guitar and strummed gently.

His voice finally found words, the words a cadence. He sang them back into the night, the trees, the grass, the corn beyond. He sang them back into the wind, the earth, the dead. He didn't know what else to do.

"More than scared, he just looked lonesome,
His open eyes frozen for someone."

He strummed on, searching. Then sang, finally,

"They said his name was Ollie Bronson. . ."

And the wind took the words and whipped them off into the black night with the hot perfume of wildflowers.

* * *

The Square was quiet and empty. The streetlights brightened the walks and storefronts in a pale, pointless glimmer. The priest made his way around and parked in front of the Sheriff's Office. The clock on the courthouse tolled once. A dog called back from somewhere. The priest knocked on the door. He gave a little wave when Richie appeared in the window, his elbows angled out, his thumbs tucked into his shiny black belt, his chest roostered.

"We're closed," he said through the glass of the window. "Well, kind of, anyway."

"It is an urgent matter," the priest said, trying to make himself heard through the glass. "I must speak to Sheriff Slocum immediately."

Richie held up his index finger, which the priest interpreted to mean that he needed to wait for a minute. He did. His hand found a cigarette, the other lit it in his mouth, and he paced, smoking. Richie returned and opened the door, holding it wide.

"Well, come on."

The priest went to stub out the cigarette.

"No, bring it. Slocum's started in again hisself."

He walked past Richie into the dispatch area. A few men in uniforms stared at him from their card game. A woman at a desk with a headset was talking into the microphone at the end of a length of wire that stretched from one of the earpieces. The priest stood, his cigarette in his hand before him, trying to avoid their eyes.

"He's in the office." Richie pointed.

The priest nodded. He started off in the direction indicated. Richie followed, knocked out a special rhythm on the door, four beats, then two, like it was the secret knock to a boy scouts' clubhouse, and then he opened it, let him in, and let himself in behind. The office was dark, but for a green glass-shaded desk-lamp. Slocum was back against the wall in his chair. He was painted in the dim, green light. It made him look sick.

"Richie. Out." Slocum was firm, his voice hoarse. He pointed towards the door. He repeated it, as if he were scolding a bad dog. Richie, his eyebrows pitched downward from the center-point between them and his mouth open, obeyed with a wordless whine, and the door swung to.

"You're too late, priest. Or too early. Extreme unction? Ain't that what you call it?"

"Will you do nothing, Mr. Slocum?"

"It's out of my hands now. You know the story already, else you wouldn't be here."

"And if I go to the State Police this very night? What will happen then?"

Slocum lit a cigarette and pushed an ashtray across his desk, towards the priest. He took a long drag.

"You think that's a new idea?" He blew out the smoke with noiseless laughter. "One of two things. A: you get a city boy, and you tell him about it, and he calls the men in white coats and they stick you in Adolf Meyer for observation. That shit has happened. 2: you get a boy from the country who knows what time it is, knows you're talkin' out of turn, and, if you're lucky, he pretends to give a damn 'til you go away. If you're not, you wind up in Adolf Meyer again. So you go on if you want to."

The priest drummed his fingers on the desk between them. He was sweating even inside. Then he lit up again. Slocum leaned forward in his chair. The brighter light found his face and threw shadows into his wrinkles, lit the sweat on his forehead so it shined like so many tiny diamonds.

"There ain't nothin' more to do, priest. Nothin' but wait for sunrise."

"What then?"

"They, and you know who I mean, they ride just after dawn. That's the code. Everything by the light of day. They circle the courthouse, and then go to where they's goin'. The meanin's clear enough."

"Yes." The priest dragged on the cigarette a couple of times. "And this man, Meadows, can he be reasoned with?"

"Hell." Slocum spat it before the priest was even done speaking. "You gonna try and reason with a man who's been through what he's been through? I ain't much one for church, but I never thought you's stupid 'til now. Or blind as a god damn bat."

"Even if Abraham is innocent?"

"If you believe that, you're alone in it," Slocum said, pointing his finger in the air, cigarette in his hand.

And there they sat, the silence, heat, and light between them. They said nothing for a time.

"I would like to speak with him just the same," the priest said.

"Yeah? What for? I done told you."

"Just to plead mercy."

"You think Jesus didn't plead for mercy when he's nailed to the cross? When his belly's split open?"

The priest was silent.

"Righteousness ain't all about mercy, priest. Some days it looks like punishment. Some days like vengeance. If it was me? That Abraham couldn't die slow enough. There ain't no measure of sufferin' you can put on a man to punish what he done. There just ain't enough. There ain't no justice left, not righteous no how. Vengeance is 'bout all that's left. But Bull Meadows does vengeance purty good. Now, mercy's a word he's not familiar with. That's a dream you best forget about."

"Even so, Please. Will you tell me where to find him?"

* * *

The priest drove away from the town, his headlights alone in the outer gloom. He got lost in the country, and by the time he found his way, the sun's first beams were breaking up the horizon. They struck his eyes like knives.

Chapter 12

By the time the sun ripped into the line between earth and sky, Abraham had already sweated through his clothes. The heat was beating his pulse in his ears. In the night it had beaten him away from himself. Sleep had never come, but that had done little to keep the dreams away. Birdsong had wrested him back when it was still grey-dark, and he stood to watch the sun come up. It was more than he could abide. Even its early beams burned into him, and he sought the cover of the pavilion. It only got hotter.

He heard them coming. Their engines riled the dogs and livestock along the stretches of roads that cut the country miles. The neighs and howls seemed to follow the progression of the thwop and hum of dozens of motorcycle engines, and pick-ups behind, and Abraham knew he was their destination. He was standing in the pavilion, near the drive, still in his black suit and hat, leaning against a wide beam, when the Left Hand of God made a right-hand turn into Friends Creek. He was waiting for them. He was alone.

They cut quite an image, all Halloween and horror show, in their drab brown masks, holes cut for the eyes, slits for the mouth, twine around the necks, the bikers in their leather, the others in denim and black. They were an army of scarecrows. He readied himself as they drew near. But they drove on by, some of them even waving, some throttling their engines to loud pops and wheezes. Their masks were haloed in red bands, and their sign was emblazoned on their backs. Abraham counted them as they rode past. The Calithumpians numbered forty-seven, fourteen of them in trucks, all but one of the rest on motorcycles. The last was an ebony hearse.

They curled around the gravel circle where the campers parked. A few dismounted and made their way to the ice-cream truck and beat on it with their fists. Abraham turned and watched them from the pavilion. The others seemed to be struggling to keep the sweat from their eyes, wiping inside the cutholes with colored bandannas and white hankies.

"Just open it!" one of them yelled.

"It's locked. I tried it."

"D'you try the back door?"

"Try the back door, dumbass!"

He tried the back door.

"He ain't here! He's gone!" The man called it out like it was Easter morning.

"Hey!" One of them was yelling. He pointed towards Abraham. "Hey, Mister!"

Abraham nodded.

"You know where the guy is that's staying in this truck?"

"Yeah," Abraham hollered weakly, mopping his face and hairline with his sleeve.

"Hey, I think that's the guy," another one said in what he probably thought was a low voice or a whisper.

The message spread around. It was like watching children.

Abraham's interlocutor yelled again, "Hey! Are you the guy?"

Abraham nodded yes.

They remounted and, after not a little confusion about how to merge back into single file, they rode towards the pavilion. Two of the Calithumpians on bikes collided and spilled in the grass, one wedging his leg between the bike and the ground, the other, falling against him, pinning himself between the two bikes. Three others stopped to assist their fallen brethren. The Calithumpians numbered forty-two.

Abraham stepped out into the sunlight and towards the drive. His hair was dripping with sweat and he could taste it in his moustache. It trickled down in itches through his beard. He felt dizzy in the light and fell to a knee. Then he fainted. When he awoke, masked men encircled him. His head beat again with the heat. The rocks were lava beneath him. He closed his eyes. He rubbed them and opened them again.

"Pussy," one of them said.

Someone kicked Abraham in the side.

"Stand him up like a man so he can hear the charge."

They pulled him upright and steadied him in the gravel. He looked out towards the sun. The far-off corn seemed to sizzle in its gaze. He thought he could see a vapor rising from the field. His knees buckled and he dropped again.

"Damn it!" one of the Calithumpians called.

"Get him up," another one said.

They stood him up again, this time, back in the shade, against the beam he had been leaning on when they had first arrived. One of them fetched his hat and fanned Abraham's face with it.

"You okay?" the man said. His voice was almost gentle.

"He awake?" another called.

Abraham came to. One of the Calithumpians hit him in the face with his fist, and Abraham went down again.

"God damn it! What you do that for? We just got him up," the man with the hat said.

The other shrugged.

"Can we get this show on the road? It's fuckin' hot as hell out here."

They propped Abraham up yet again. His nose was bleeding. He looked out at the throng of monsters before him.

"Alright, hurry up and give him the charge," one of them said.

One of the scarecrows stepped forward and hollered out above the din of idling engines, "We are the will of the people, the left hand of God. In the full light of day, before God and man, we, the Calithumpians, seize you for the sins you have perpetrated against one of our own. His will shall be his right and you will bear it justly. This is the higher law."

Then they all erupted in ejaculations, most of them meaningless, the others curses.

The door of the hearse was already open, a rough wooden coffin waiting within. The Calithumpians were on him, their grasping hands everywhere, some punching as they went. Abraham saw only the scarecrow masks, the fists and spit coming at him. He felt only the angry hands, the heat, the sun. He was tossed into the box, a lid was affixed, and by the time they rode away, the prairie flowers had wilted.

Chapter 13

The line of mounted scarecrows snaked up the Meadows property behind the hearse, the trucks bringing up the rear of the train. They had lost a few more to the onslaught of the sun, two to another minor accident, and one to an urgent case of diarrhea. The Calithumpians numbered thirty-five. They parked haphazardly around the lot between the livestock barns, where the boys were spraying down some cattle with a hose, and the big pole barn, where Bull Meadows stood, his arms crossed, his face heavy, his eyes squinting. An unlit cigar stump peeked out of the corner of his mouth. He watched the masked men try to get their kickstands to grab in the gravel. Finally, Jody Barnes passed some scrap wood around, and most of the Left Hand made their way to the hearse, though a few took cover in the barn on the other side to seek the shower the cows were getting.

They crashed the box at the boots of Bull Meadows. One of the Calithumpians pried it open and threw the lid off. The bloodied ashen figure within looked like a befuddled old man or a lost child. He gazed about dumbly as they pulled him from the coffin to hand him over. He did not resist.

"Your will shall be your right and he will bear it justly," one of the red-haloed men said.

"I surely do thank you, gentlemen," Bull Meadows said. "Now, Jody, be sure to get these boys some cold drinks and cool 'em down before they go."

"Okay, Bull."

While the Will of the People headed off to seek refreshment, Bull Meadows shoved Abraham into the side of the pole barn.

"And you, motherfucker. You're coming with me."

A few of the Calithumpians hooted cheers for blood. Bull Meadows led Abraham away through the door to the office. It closed behind them.

"Sit down," Bull Meadows said, pointing at a chair in front of the desk.

Abraham sat.

Bull Meadows fetched a thermos of water from a table and gave it to him, and he drank.

"When a man is gonna die," Bull Meadows said from behind him, "a man like you," he paused. "When a man is gonna die, I think he deserves a chance for some real straight talk. There ain't no time for truth like when your time is up. You believe that, Mr. Abraham?" He slapped him on the back.

Abraham was silent, but he looked at Bull Meadows as he crossed the floor and sat behind the desk.

"You afraid of dying? Shit, everybody's afraid of dying. Never mind. You afraid of what's gonna happen to you before? 'Cause you should be. I've got plans for you, Mr. Abraham, after what you done to me."

Abraham gave him nothing. He even looked a little bored.

"Listen. Here's your only chance for anything," Bull Meadows went on. "I'm gonna let you confess, get it all out in the open. Now, if you're a good boy, and you tell the truth, then you won't suffer too much. We'll keep it quick. If you don't? Then we've got a different game on our hands. You understand?"

Nothing.

"Alright." Bull knocked on the door that led to the shop. "Get in here if you're coming."

The door opened and the priest stepped into the office.

"And if you confess, you can do it right, confess it to the priest, to God. What did you call it, priest? Reconciliation?"

"Abraham, please," the priest said. His eyes were weary, drenched in sweat or tears or both. Bull Meadows held up his hand, and the priest said no more.

Abraham looked from one to the other and back again. He laughed almost noiselessly. The heat and beatings had left him glazed in delirium. His gaze traced the small room and landed on a familiar box on top of one of the filing cabinets. The priest looked too. Bull Meadows watched them. Abraham turned back to the priest, who faced him again.

"I am so sorry, Abraham." His hands turned up, open, empty.

"Time's up, priest. You're done," Bull Meadows said, pointing towards the door.

The priest left, slouching out of the room and away, with nothing else, broken.

"That man is not your friend, let me tell you that, Mr. Abraham. But he ain't lacking in vision." He waited. "Not talking ain't gonna help your cause none. You know that, don't you?" Then, after pausing again: "We ain't so different, me and you. What we know binds us together. You know that? That's why both of us can't go on from here."

Abraham looked from Bull Meadows to the skull by the phone and back again.

"Then what would you say my cause is?" Abraham muttered.

"See? Now, there you go. What? You think how a man dies don't make a difference?" He waited, perhaps for a reply. "How a man dies stamps whatever he thought he was. Puts a certain kind of meaning on it. Now, that priest was willing to give me that box full of cash money, and you know what for? 'Cause he wants you to die in a particular fashion, 'cause he knew you weren't one to be reconciled. Better part of thirty-thousand dollars in that box." Then after a moment, "And a finger in a bottle. You know anything about that?"

Abraham held up his middle finger. Bull Meadows ignored it.

"Priest seems to think you're something akin to Jesus Christ, like you've got magic in your hands or something. You got anything to say to that?"

The upturned finger remained, as did the glowering visage above it.

"Well, I want to talk about that. I don't know if you're closer to God or the Devil himself, but I know you've got the magic.

You're flesh and blood, and you stink of the human stain, but there's something spiritual in you. That's clear as day. And I want to thank you for that. Now, I am going to kill you, but I owe you thanks just the same."

Bull Meadows held out his hand to Abraham. He didn't take it. Bull Meadows pocketed his hands and paced around near his desk.

"Why did you do it anyway? Why my Barbie? Why did you make her whole?" He had abandoned the officious country gentleman's tone now altogether.

"She was whole already," Abraham said. "But if I had anything to do with it, with the change, I'm sorry. But she was whole already."

Bull Meadows was nodding his head at the floor. "She was a good girl," he said, his voice soft and low.

If there was tenderness in it, he cut it off cold. He looked up at Abraham. "And what did she tell you?"

Abraham fell quiet again. Sweat dripped and pooled around him in the floor. He drank again from the thermos.

"God damn it!" Bull Meadows spat, snatching the water away, flinging it into the wall. "I know you know. What did she tell you?"

Nothing. The same vacant stare.

"You can't just take what you want from me and have it your way!"

"I didn't kill your daughter," Abraham said calmly. "I didn't kill her."

Bull Meadows beat his fists into the counter-top desk over and over like a giant toddler. The thing splintered and then split in two and fell between the cabinets, pitching paperwork and knick-knacks down into the Y-shape it made against the floor.

"What did she tell you!" He clutched Abraham's beard in his hand, wrenching it upward.

"Secrets," Abraham said. "She had secrets. She was suffering with them. She asked me to forgive them."

"And did you?" he panted.

"No," he said. "And you didn't either?"

"No," Bull Meadows said, looking off, releasing him. "No, I did not."

"And who is this Ollie Bronson?" Abraham said, pulling the name from his heat-dream song.

"My brother, almost." Bull Meadows scoffed. He kicked something. It pinged against the table on the other side of the room. "He's the one she told you about. One of her secrets. Or she was one of his."

Abraham said nothing.

Bull Meadows threw his cap into the mess of the desk in the floor and rubbed his eyes with both hands, and then his hair. The din of engines blared through the walls and then faded. The window unit blew in hot air from outside. Abraham watched Bull Meadows.

"That was hard. What, and then that god damn baby comes a few months later. If you can even call it that." His eyes fixed on a blank spot in the wall. "I hadn't even noticed. . ."

He pulled an old bolt-action rifle down from a rack.

"Thought it was done with. Over."

He swung it into Abraham's face, knocking him out of the chair.

"'Bout the size of my hand. Like a tangled-up fist with a head, with a smiling little demon face."

Abraham spat blood into his sweat where he sprawled on the floor.

"And it just wouldn't die. I took it from her. And it cried and cried. And there was no getting away from that pathetic little lamb noise it made."

He kicked Abraham over. He tightened his hands around the barrel and swung the stock like and ax against his ribs.

"Twisted it up in a dish towel, stuck it in a bowl in the

pasture. Could hear it from the house."

Bull Meadows loaded the rifle at the table by the door to the barn. He checked the sights. Abraham struggled back into the chair. Dog snarls and bays clamored outside.

"Couldn't take it no more. Shit. Ollie'd died with less fuss. Threw it in the river. Still heard it whimpering when I drove off. Hear it still, sometimes."

Bull Meadows found his hat. He pulled Abraham up and shoved him forward, into the door, and held him there, the rifle at his back.

"Same spot I dumped Barbie. My granddaddy always said a river's ever-changing, but she's consistent even so. Ain't she?"

Bull Meadows yanked Abraham back by his hair.

"Why don't you put that in a fucking song, Mr. Abraham?"

He shoved Abraham into the corner, keeping the gun on him.

"You know? Last time I felt something, something like conviction, for the right, for some kind of higher order, was when I shoved nails in the mouth of poor Ollie Bronson."

He jabbed Abraham in the mouth with the rifle-butt, clutched his shirt, and dragged him back towards the door.

"I don't feel nothing with you. You ain't nothing to me. You ain't a saint. You ain't nothing at all."

He swung the door wide, and kicked him out into the heat.

The Calithumpians were gone. The priest was gone. Only Jody Barnes and One-Eye Jack Potter remained, slumped against some hay bales on the ground. Two dogs, a Pitt and a Mastiff, panted from the bed of a red truck. One-Eye Jack was rubbing a hunting knife on a whetstone. They watched Abraham try to stand, but he only got to his hands and knees. He was shaking. One eye was swollen shut already, and blood covered his face and ran down in smears in his beard.

"He fess up to it?" Jody Barnes said.

"Yeah, took a little convincing. He ain't got much left anyways."

"What you wanna do, Bull?"

"Think we can get him in the bin?"

"Yessir. He ain't too big. We can get rope on him if he can't climb."

"Well, get some rope. He can drown in the fucking corn for all I care. We'll fetch him out and finish it when it cools off."

* * *

Abraham braced himself against the thin pipe railing on the catwalk that led to the peak opening on top of the grain bin. He wiped blood from his eye. He saw Bull Meadows on the ground. He seemed so small. He raised his head against the heat, dragging his gaze across the never-ending plain that smoldered for miles below. The last thing he found was a red blinking eye across the sky, parallel with his place in the heavens, not far from the blur of trees and houses where he had played Babel in Cisco.

One-Eye Jack Potter stuck him with the knife in the side.

"See you in hell, asshole," the other boy said. And they thrust him down onto the mounded grain within. Soon, the circle of light was filled, and everything was black.

And there he laid, the invisible corn beneath him, blood leaking like secrets into the silent grain. His eye took to the darkness, or maybe the heat had him dreaming, but he thought he could make out the faintest traces of light in a circle above, like the shadow moon when it is new in a clear sky. His free hand found his cigarettes. He nosed open the box and pinched one between his teeth. He found the lighter and flicked it with his thumb. The flame was blinding. A few faltering drags had him coughing smoke into the dry darkness. The blood spurted between his fingers with each spasm. He flicked away the cigarette, and it sprayed like a comet before hitting the dome and fixing itself in the blackness above. A point of red light in the void.

Time passed, or it didn't. It didn't matter. He heard a sound like something scratching, like something pouring out. Forgetting the blindness of the place, he looked around. Then he watched the light again.

The first movement was so faint that he mistook it for his own. He watched the waning light from the cherry of stuck cigarette above. And then he watched as the rushing corn obscured it when something gave, something deep down, and he was pulled into the suck, washed away, down deeper within. Despite his thrashing, he had been swallowed whole, locked inside a mountain of hard black corn.

He awoke to the pain in his side, to inside finding out, to the labor pains of oblivion. He tried not to gasp. He had swallowed so much already, and his mouth was full of corn.

Chapter 13

There wasn't any music, just the voices, together, together from a tent somewhere, somewhere off from where we were. Dusk was coming on. The woods, the woods that crept up along the boundary of the park, where the playground was, it wasn't there, but then it was so vast and tangled and dark and cool, and the wind caught there, in the trees, and the dead leaves shivered and fell like a strange snow, with all the dust in the air from the combines and the trucks and the elevator. It was harvest, and the carnival was going, the air cool, the weather dry. I didn't catch all of it. "The seed by him provided is sown o'er hill and plain," the voices sang, "and with the gentle showers doth bless the springing grain." We chased each other, Melinda and me. Her last name I never knew. Must've been a C. She stood behind Jakob Bjornsen in the lunch line, in front of Billy Crowe, so it must have been a C, but it could have been a B too. It doesn't matter. Names have never meant anything. Dusk was coming on, and the woods was dark already, behind the swing-set, by the big oak, where the tire swing was. She said get in, so I did, I always did what she said, what did I care? She swung the big black tire back and forth, as high as she could. She told me to close my eyes, and, of course, I did it. And I swayed, above the earth, not yet in the sky, still under the tree, and I heard the voices, or maybe they had finished, and I just brought them back, I don't know. "With good he crownest, the earth his mercy fills." And the dead leaves were crashing into me as they fell, but I wasn't falling. "The wilderness is fruitful, and joyful are the hills." Higher, I said, higher, but I could have been flying, it's just what you said. Maybe I fell asleep, I don't know. "With corn the vales are covered, the flocks in pastures graze." The wind was deep in the trees, in the woods, behind, and all was calm and dark, beneath the skin of my eyelids, and the leaves crashing, and the voices. "All nature joins in singing." Another voice came in, against the song, maybe it had been there all along. The song went on, the voices still going, the other voice harsh, its words were numbers, meaningless to me, lilting over syllables, amplified somehow, from the other side, sheer rhythm, rhythm and numbers. "A joyful song of praise." "Sold!" And for a moment there was quiet, almost quiet, only the wind, the leaves. I opened my eyes, and it was dark already, and she was gone. The black tractor tire turned a little. I'd sunk back inside. I'd started in the middle, but I'd sunk within the circumference, within it. I was looking at the empty middle, and there was nothing there, and I was gone, receded. I hadn't been big enough for it anyway. Then the lights were on, on the other side, and I was going towards them. I was alone. I gave a man a quarter and went in. The corn was so high and dead and dry. It sounded like ancient paper, like a scroll winding or unwinding, when the wind came up. Night was full on, but they had the floods, and there was music somewhere, away, somewhere else, the cakewalk maybe. The way kept dead-ending, and there were other boys, I heard them laughing anyway. One path led to another and over and over again, and I kept moving through the corn maze, and the voices fell away. The music, maybe from the cootch dance, going farther off, away, a plug-in organ, vamping. The lights went off. I didn't care, my pace was steady, I didn't care, it's what I was waiting for, for the darkness, to be forgotten. Up above, on the far side of where the carnival was, in the park, the trees were like dark giants dancing, titans dream-drunk, smoldering, in the cave of night, the Hecatoncheires, in tremors, shivering in the pit.

Abandon the path, go into the corn.

And I did.

It was dark, only the light from the night shows, the sound of the organ. The boundary with the blacker woods a few paces ahead. Something rustled the undergrowth there, and the wind was there. Was it man or beast? Was it Melinda? Was it my grave-gone father? Was it my stillborn brother? I thought that, I don't know why. Maybe it was me, stillborn just the same, shivering in the pit, smoldering, in the cave of night, in the grave, man but beast. There wasn't any music. Was there ever? The voices hummed or groaned, I can't say which, but there were voices, or maybe it was the dead, or the banished, their moaning, in the wind, in the night, in the blacker night of the trees ahead, but it was music just the same. It was nothing, just through the corn, in the black beyond, the lights dead behind, the past dead behind, the dark of nothing ahead, the corn between us, no light, no point of light, and it was cool. I could feel it coming at me, the leaves were falling, with corn the vales are covered, and without stopping, to consider, my pace steady, the corn was gone.

I lurched in, to find nothing certain, to find nothing, myself within it, to be, to be done, to become, to come undone, not the righteous, back to dust, unfinished, unforsaken, unforgiven, sunken back within, in dark and calm and cool.

My eyes are open.

Chapter 14

The crucifixion was an afterthought, and it was carried out without passion, in the evening, in the heat. The sun was setting, but it was hotter yet. And it was not a crucifixion, proper, though afterwards it had all the signs. They spilled him out with the corn, plucked up the corpse from the dust, and nailed him to the lynching tree, hands above his hanging head, feet below, his middle sagging, slack, between. One-Eye Jack Potter bled him and carved something in his chest, laughing, as he rubbed some syrupy used motor oil into the wound. Bull Meadows said to gut him, and they did as they were told. They stuffed the cavity with spilled corn and gravel and gave it a rough stitch with fishing line. They wrapped the body in a grey tarpaulin, threw it in the bed of the truck, and covered it with sacks of feed, while Bull Meadows pulled the auger out. By the time they had binned the corn again, it was night, and it was hotter than hell. Jody Barnes and One-Eye Jack Potter were charged with driving the dead man to DeWitt County to dump in the lake, near the power plant. The dogs were loosed to devour the mess the crows had started on at the foot of the lynching tree. The turkey vultures were already rocking back and forth as they made their patient circles high above. Bull Meadows went to bed early that night.

It was getting late when the boys got back to town, but they got to the square in time to get ice-cream cones. They sat sweating on the tailgate licking them, watching the girls in tube-tops across the street.

"I never gutted a man before," Jody Barnes said after a while, mopping his forehead with his hand.

One-Eye Jack Potter crunched into the top of the cone and chewed, grinning. "Just like a deer or that god damn donkey-goat, I figure. Only it ain't got no horns to show for it."

One of the girls waved.

* * *

The heat wave worsened over the next few days, setting record highs, driving some mad, and killing others. The day the crucified man was pulled from the water and slouched off, heading east, was the worst to date.

He disappeared into the countryside, and those on the beach were afraid to follow. The next day was hotter still, and the day after that, and the day after that, as the sun flared brighter and brighter and burned hotter and hotter and scorched into the earth.

And then it burned out.

At Roundfire we publish great stories. We lean towards the spiritual and thought-provoking. But whether it's literary or popular, a gentle tale or a pulsating thriller, the connecting theme in all Roundfire fiction titles is that once you pick them up you won't want to put them down.